The Dress

SOPHIE NICHOLLS

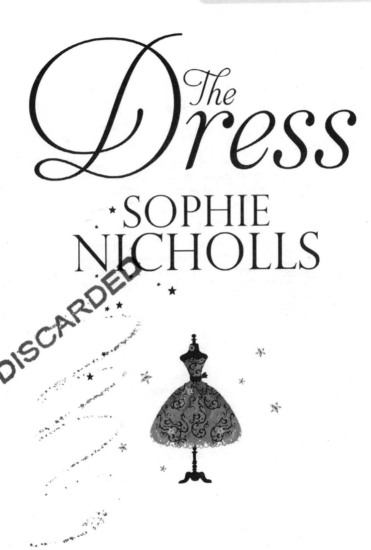

twenty7

First published in Great Britain in 2011

This paperback edition published in 2016 by

Twenty7 Books
80–81 Wimpole St, London W1G 9RE
www.twenty7books.com

A CIP catalogue record for this book is available from the British Library.

Paperback ISBN: 978-1-78577-040-1
Ebook ISBN: 978-1-78577-039-5

1 3 5 7 9 10 8 6 4 2

Printed and bound by Clays Ltd, St Ives Plc

Twenty7 Books is an imprint of Bonnier Zaffre,
a Bonnier Publishing company
www.bonnierzaffre.co.uk

For Violetta

Prologue

It all began with a dress.

'As so many things do, *tesora*,' I can hear Mamma saying now in her rich, slow voice, stirring sugar into her cup. 'As so many things do . . .'

It was a simple dress, a slip of oyster-coloured silk, made to fall over the body like a sigh of pleasure. On the morning that it appeared in the window of our shop on Grape Lane, I stood in my bedroom window, watching the women stopping to admire it in the street outside, some of them setting down their bags of groceries, folding their arms over their bosoms, cocking their heads to one side, imagining themselves into the swish of its silk, which Mamma had accessorised with a single strand of pearls, looped over the mannequin's fingers.

The story that I'm about to tell you is not so simple. It has complicated seams and concealed fastenings. It has deep pockets and interfacings that won't sit quite true. I'll shape it for you here, as Mamma taught me to do, teasing the stray threads with the lightest touch I can manage.

You'll have to forgive me if, at times, I'm a little clumsy. Mamma didn't believe in following a pattern. She taught me to trust the fabric itself, letting the texture and colour of it find its own form on the cutting table. If I asked her what to do next, she'd smile and tell me to close my eyes, while she brushed the edge of a half-made sleeve or the fold of a skirt across my cheek.

'What do you feel, *carina*?' she'd say. 'What do you feel, deep inside you? What does this fabric know? What does it want to be?'

1

I wish I had the family gift, the gift of Mamma and Madaar-Bozorg and their mothers and grandmothers before them. Back in The Old Country, they used to say that the Jobrani women could divine a dress from the fragrance of the wind, or the memory of the sun on the sea.

Mamma lives in America now, her America, the New Country of possibility that she always longed for. Without her, I'm learning to make my own story. I'll piece this together for you as best I can from everything that I remember, the things I've guessed at and the things that, no doubt, I've made up myself as I've told and retold this story.

Some of it's difficult to work with. It slips through my fingers like fine jersey or rucks up under my needle like brocade. But some of it, when I smooth it on my lap, is as light and easy as gingham, with straight lines that my thread can follow as I attach one story to another, one word to the next.

Now that I'm older and a mother myself, I can see that what I'm making here – my story, the story of Mamma and me – is a story that belongs to all of us, if it belongs to anyone.

You only need to stop for a moment, lift your arms over your head – there, that's right, just like that – and allow the rustle of it, the soft gatherings of it, to settle over your body, just so.

And now it's your story, yours to make and remake again, in your way, until it's perfect.

1

Men's black overcoat. Marks & Spencer. 2007.

The man was tall and badly dressed. Ella always noticed other people's clothes and this man wore a shapeless black overcoat, too short for his frame, so that it flapped loosely around his calves as he moved. He held his hat in his hand, kneading its rim between his fingers. From where she stood in the courtyard with Billy, she could see the dark shape of this man as he moved behind the glass. She could not take her eyes off him.

'He's a pain in the backside,' Billy said, nodding towards the shop, his brow furrowing. 'Trouble. The worst kind. Your mum had best watch herself . . .'

'Who is he?'

'Councillor Pike.' Billy's lip curled in dislike. He tilted his head from side to side, as if he were trying to shake something free, one of those thoughts that buzzes round your head like a fly.

They waited in the courtyard. Ella tried not to look, but she couldn't help sneaking sideways glances through the shop window. She didn't want to go inside.

She could see Mamma smiling, nodding, and the back of the man's head, his dark hair and his white neck against the black of his collar.

In the places they'd lived before, there was always a man, sniffing around. But Mamma knew what to do.

'*Tsk*. They are like *dogs*, these people,' Ella had once heard her say, making that clicking noise with her tongue. 'They can smell fear. Look them in the eye. Smile. Don't let them get a sniff of it.'

She thought of this now as she watched Mamma's hands parting the air in pretty gestures, her hair bobbing above her shoulders, her lipsticked smile.

And here she was, walking straight towards them, one hand reaching for the door handle, the other taking the Councillor's hand and shaking it firmly, looking him straight in the eye.

'Thank you,' she was saying, 'Thank you for your welcome. And please excuse the mess. I'm hoping to open next Saturday but, as you can see, there's still so much to do.' The shop bell jangled as she swung it wide. 'Ah. Mr Pike, may I introduce my daughter, Ella ... And Billy, of course. Hello, Billy. He's been such a great help to us with all the unpacking. I don't know what we'd have done without him ...'

Ella caught the false, bright tinkle in her voice, like the sound of teaspoons against china cups. Mamma's arm crept around her waist, drawing her in close. She could feel Mamma's heart pumping under the sprigged silk of her dress.

Ella's cheeks flushed with heat as she tried to force them into a smile. *Don't let them see it. Don't let them smell your fear.* Would the man notice? She pressed her fingernails into her palms. Her throat had closed up and she found that she couldn't make a sound.

'A pleasure,' the man was purring, 'and such a lovely little thing, just like her mother.'

She watched his eyes moving up and down, greedy eyes, taking in all of her. She imagined him licking his lips, as if anticipating a delicious meal.

Then he turned, nodding at Billy who was kicking a pebble from one foot to the other.

'Billy,' he said. 'Don't be making a nuisance of yourself now, will you?' and he walked purposefully out of the courtyard, his black overcoat swirling behind him.

Billy scowled and dug the toe of his trainer into the cobbles. Some of them were loose and bits of moss and grit sprayed up over his socks, but Mamma didn't say anything.

Instead, she waited until the last flick of overcoat disappeared from the courtyard, then she drew a deep breath, pulling her shoulders back, brushing her palms briskly against each other as if she were wiping off something unpleasant.

'You know this man, Billy?' she said quietly.

Billy pulled a face. 'Yeah, worse luck.'

Mamma smiled at him but Ella could see that she was already thinking about something else.

'OK,' she said, clapping her hands together, 'Now, who wants hot chocolate?'

Billy was the only friend that Ella had made in the weeks since they'd moved to this new city, York. None of the girls in her class at St Olave's seemed to like her. In the places where they'd lived before, it had been the same.

She was too dark, too quiet. She didn't speak in the same way as them. Something about her seemed to make them nervous. When she came near, they'd stand on one leg, push their hands in their pockets, fiddle with their hair, look at her with long sideways glances.

'Give it time, *tesora*,' Mamma said. 'Two weeks. *Tsk*. No time at all.'

But Ella knew how these things worked. She could see already that it wasn't going to be much different here, despite everything that Mamma had promised.

There was one good thing – Billy Vickers liked her. Whenever she thought about this, Ella felt a kind of certainty about it, a feeling that spread through her insides like the beginning of one of those highly inconvenient but unstoppable laughs.

'Who'll show our new classmate, Ella, how we do things around here?' Miss Cookson, the form teacher, had asked of the room of bored-looking faces on her first day there, and Billy had sprung straight up from his seat in that funny way of his, his skinny legs unfolding as if on coiled springs, and he'd taken her elbow, grinning at her all the while, steering her, firmly but gently, to the rows of lockers ranged along the back of the classroom.

She'd heard the sniggers, of course, the barely stifled whispers, and the fake wolf-whistle that had made Miss Cookson roll her eyes. But in that moment, Billy had claimed her, like a library book or a lost umbrella. His hand cupped her elbow. His smile showed a row of shiny, white teeth. She felt that ticklish sensation in the bottom of her stomach. Billy was the most interesting boy she'd ever met.

She liked his eyes, which were blue-green-grey and looked right into her without blinking. She liked the way that there was always a half-smile hiding at the corners of his mouth. She liked his mop of curly black hair that sprang out all over his head, and his skinny wrists that stuck out from the cuffs of his school shirt. He was everywhere, all at once. It was as if his long, thin body wasn't big enough to contain him.

OK, she'd said to herself, watching the crackle of blue and yellow around Billy's head as he turned to flash her one of his grins. If you like me, I could like you back. Neither of them had said anything about it, of course. Not out loud. That wasn't what you were supposed to do, was it? But it had been decided.

Now they were perched together on the fold-out stools behind the counter in the shop, cradling their mugs of hot chocolate, sipping and blowing steam off the top.

To the rest of the world passing by the window, Ella thought, they would look exactly the same as they'd done since they arrived here: that Mrs Moreno, there in that fancy new shop of hers – they say that it's going to be open any day now – with her daughter and that funny Vickers boy, Billy.

But if she tuned in, pressing herself up against the outside of her body, letting a part of herself float upwards, feeling with her mind for those squiggly lines of blue and red and sometimes electric green, she could hear what Mamma was saying to herself, furiously, over and over, inside her mind.

It made her nervous. Which was why she didn't do the tuning in thing very often.

Mamma saw her watching and smiled one of her tight, bright Whatever's-The-Matter-Ella-Everything's-Perfectly-Fine smiles, launched herself off her stool and began folding a newly unpacked tangle of silk scarves. Her hands fluttered above the fuchsia pinks and swirls of blue, tweaking them into new shapes like the petals of origami flowers.

With her back towards them, so that Ella couldn't see her expression, her voice came out too high, too Couldn't-Care-Less. 'So, Billy . . . How do you know this man, this Councillor Pike?'

'Everyone knows Pike, Mrs Moreno,' Billy said, his lip curling up again at the corner. He was looking at Mamma carefully now. He seemed to be deciding how much he could say. 'Piece of work, so my dad says. I call him Trouble. With a capital "T". Whenever that man turns up, things get nasty.'

'And what does this mean, this expression – this, how do you say it – *piece of work*?' Mamma asked.

Billy wrinkled his forehead. 'A right piece of work,' he said, 'means, you know, like someone put together all wrong, someone who's just not quite right.' He paused, searching around the shop for inspiration. 'You see, it's a bit like one of your dresses, Mrs Moreno. You know, someone might want you to take up the hem or shorten the sleeve. And then, when you get down to it, when you look up close, you realise that the dress might look nice on the outside but, really, it's not very good at all . . . The lining's a bit squint and the pockets are all cock-eyed, so you have to unpick the entire thing and sew it back together.'

Ella thought of Councillor Pike's baggy black overcoat, the way it hung off his shoulders and flapped around his legs and the sense she'd had as she looked at him that he was hiding something under his smile.

'*Squint*,' Mamma repeated softly to herself, savouring the sound of the words. '*Cock-eyed* . . .'

Then her mouth began to twitch at the corners, the dimple appeared in her right cheek and her shoulders started to shake. Laughter burst from her lips and nose and went bouncing and echoing over the floor of the shop and soon Ella and Billy were joining in, slapping their thighs like pantomime dames, their cheeks wet with tears.

'Stop now,' Mamma blurted, between explosions of laughter. 'Stop now, you two. It's cruel. We should *not* laugh at this poor man,' and then she caught Billy's eye and started to laugh all over again.

Ella felt that warm feeling spreading up through her insides. It was so good to hear Mamma laugh. Because, these days, it didn't seem to happen all that often.

Mamma. Fabia Moreno. Fabia, which Ella knew meant 'flame'. She spoke Italian, French and a little Spanish and, of course, the Old Language, the one Ella wasn't allowed to learn, the language of her mother's grandmother, Madaar-Bozorg, back in Iran, the Old Country.

No matter how much Ella pleaded, Mamma would never teach her the Old Language.

'It will only ever bring you bad luck, *tesora*,' was what she said. 'If you want to learn languages, start with your father's. Italian: language of music, of art, of food. Language of love. Very beautiful language. Make you happy. Always.'

Sometimes, Ella would catch Mamma singing to herself in the kitchen, the soft upper notes that seemed to shimmer in the air and the harder sounds that came from somewhere deep in her throat in a way that Ella couldn't imitate, no matter how much she practised in front of the mirror. Fat, blurred words, and long words with drawn out sounds that mingled with the steam from the saucepans. When Ella swallowed Mamma's thick stew, the one with beans and garlic, she liked to imagine she was eating the stories of her ancestors.

When Mamma was angry, it was the old words, dark with jagged edges, that would force themselves between her lips.

These words fascinated Ella most of all. They sounded a bit like spitting.

That first week at St Olave's, Billy walked her home every day. He was waiting for her at the school gates and fell in alongside her.

'I'm going your way, I think,' he'd said. 'You're in that shop just off Grape Lane, aren't you? The one that's been boarded up?'

Ella nodded. What was wrong with her? Why couldn't she say anything? She fiddled with the strap of her schoolbag, try-ing to hide the blush that she could already feel crawling over her face.

When she looked up again, Billy was grinning. 'It's great that someone's taking that on. It's a nice old place. Bet there's loads to do, though.'

He talked non-stop, all the way across the bridge and along the river, pointing out landmarks, asking her more about where she was from. He didn't seem to notice that she didn't say very much. He just grinned that lopsided grin and kept walking and chattering.

'Looking good,' he said, when they reached the courtyard, surveying the newly painted lettering, the polished windows. Then he lifted his hand in a half wave. 'Well, I'll see you tomor-row, then.'

'Who was that?' Mamma was already at the shop door. 'Didn't you want to invite him in?'

'Just someone from school,' Ella said, heading straight for the stairs. Why did Mamma always have to know *everything*? But all that evening, she hugged the idea of Billy to her.

At the end of the week, Mamma was waiting for them at the shop door.

'Come in, come in,' she called. 'It's Friday, after all. And I've made hot chocolate.'

Ella's heart sank. Her cheeks flushed again.

'Sorry,' she muttered.

'What for?' Billy's face split in that wide grin. 'She's just looking after you. That's what mums do. And it's OK, isn't it? If I come in for a bit?'

They stepped over the boxes on the floor to where Mamma was waiting with two steaming mugs. She flashed Billy one of her lipsticked smiles.

'I want you to know that you are very welcome here. Any time you want,' she said. 'Any friend of Ella's is very welcome here.'

'Mum.' Ella didn't bother to keep the annoyance out of her voice. There was something cold and leaden at the bottom of her stomach. Why did Mamma always have to ruin everything?

'Thank you very much, Mrs Moreno,' said Billy, taking the mug. 'Wow. This looks good.'

He grinned again. The air fizzed blue and yellow and silver and Ella had to make herself look down at her shoes.

But that was how Billy started coming round every evening after school.

'You're such a help, you two,' Mamma said, glancing up from the unpacking, wiping her forehead with the back of her hand.

Gradually, the shop was taking shape around them. The wooden counter was polished to a soft gleam, the walls were freshly painted and the mannequins stood waiting patiently for their first outfits. But there were boxes and boxes still to be opened, skirts and dresses and jackets to be shaken from their layers of tissue, primped and smoothed and hung on the rails.

'What's this?' Billy would say, examining a wrap belt in turquoise velvet. Or 'Wow, where did you get this from?' as he admired a pair of sandals with precipitous perspex heels.

Mamma had a story for everything. Stories of famous actresses fallen on hard times and old ladies with musty attics full of treasures, the jewels discovered in coat pockets or hidden away in the backs of sock drawers. Ella was pretty sure that most of the stories were made up.

'Tell us about this, then, Mrs Moreno,' Billy would say, waving a red silk devore scarf.

Mamma would smile. 'Well, all right then,' she'd say. 'Let's see . . .'

And then she'd begin.

As well as the stories that began with a scarf or a dress or a necklace, there were others too. Tales of woods and deep rivers, of nights filled with owls' cries and stars. The story of twelve princesses who, while they were sleeping, would take the shape of wild geese and fly from their bedroom window on silent, white wings. The story of the old woman with many faces who travels from town to town, arriving with the autumn wind, leaving again with the spring. The story of the man who steals the precious pelt of the selkie, the seal woman. And then Ella's favourite of all Mamma's stories, the story of the red shoes.

For the first time ever, for some reason that she couldn't really explain, it didn't bother Ella that Mamma told her stories so freely to someone they didn't know. Billy listened, sipped from his mug and grinned.

'It is nice that you are interested in my stories,' Mamma said, reaching out and tweaking one of Billy's curls. 'You are a nice boy, no, Billy Vickers?'

This time, Billy's cheeks burned red. 'Now don't go telling that to anyone, Mrs Moreno,' he said. 'I've got my reputation to think of.'

But it was true, Ella thought. He did seem nice. And actually, despite what he said, he didn't seem to care what anyone thought about him. Sometimes, he'd even prance around the shop while Mamma told her stories, acting out the different parts, making her howl with laughter. He'd be the princess simpering under a pink hat with a beaded veil at one moment, the merchant striding haughtily in a jewelled Venetian mask at another.

'Go on, then. Do the witch,' Ella would say and he'd lean on a silver-tipped cane with an opera shawl draped over his head and shoulders, rolling his eyes, cackling spells, his face contorted in a way that made tears stream down her face.

'Of course, it's not my stories that he comes for,' Mamma said, shooting Ella one of her I-Wasn't-Born-Yesterday looks. 'But he's a good boy, Billy. A clever boy. It is good that you have made this new friend. Yes, I think that you can trust him. He sees everything, understands everything. We are safe with him, *carissima*.'

Safe. Ella didn't know exactly what that meant. What exactly was there for them to be afraid of? Some days, she could feel this unnamed fear shimmering between them, like the synthetic veil on one of Mamma's hats.

2

Pair of leopard-print shoes, platform heels. Late 1950s. Size 37.

Mamma said that city life would fit them better. Less *chiacchiere*, Ella, less interfering.

'In a bigger place, no one is interested in other people's business,' she said. 'You'll see. A new start. So much better for us.'

There was a contact, someone Dad had once known, someone who knew someone else. There was a shop that no one seemed to want – such a very low rent, it had been empty for so long. Yes, a shop in a good location with a flat above it.

Mamma took the big *Atlas of Great Britain* from the drawer and flipped through the pages, her fingernail with its scarlet polish tracing the journey they would take, up from the bottom of the page, along the yellow spine of the country to a large splotch of greeny-brown, right here.

'York,' she said, stabbing at a small red spot. 'Very nice, so people tell me. Four rooms upstairs: sitting room, kitchen, bedroom, bathroom. We'll have to share. Then the shop on the ground floor, of course. I think it's *good* place for us, Ella-*issima*. A clean place with no trouble. The kind of place where we can start again, sell beautiful dresses to nice people. Everything much better.'

They arrived at the beginning of a new year. A cold blast of wind caught at the hem of Ella's coat and blew her from the train steps and across the platform.

She hurried, her bag banging against her bare legs, following the splash of crimson that was Mamma as she expertly steered the trolley, piled high with their cases and boxes, through the crowd.

The wind blew through the station portico, whipping up scraps of paper and petals from the flower stall, sending them skittering over the stones.

A man with a briefcase tipped his hat at them and smiled.

'Welcome to Yorkshire,' he said and the sound of his voice was surprising, flat and wide, with a kind of hum to it, like what happens when you pinch your nose and try to sing at the same time.

Ella watched him following Mamma with his eyes. Mamma was wearing the red suit, '40s style, with the fitted skirt and nipped-in waist, a wide belt of patent leather, a red hat with a little black half-veil, and her very high leopard-print shoes.

Ella wished, not for the first time, that Mamma could be more like other mums, her hair less done, her lipstick less red, that she'd dress in normal clothes, jeans and sweatshirts, draw less attention to herself. Who, Ella thought, glancing around her, wore red with leopard-print? Who wore a hat and gloves anymore?

But Mamma had already reached the front of the station where another man waited for them, leaning against the wall, a cigarette drooping from the side of his mouth. His hands gripped a piece of cardboard scrawled with Mamma's name, bracing it like a shield against the cold wind.

He looked Mamma up and down, an eyebrow half-raised. He's laughing at her, Ella thought. The black misspelled letters – '*Mrs F. Murreno*' – flapped and shuddered in his hands.

'Good afternoon,' Mamma said to the man, with careful precision. 'I'm Mrs Moreno.' She pronounced the name crisply, rolling the 'r' a little more than usual. 'Thank you so much for meeting us.' She extended a gloved hand.

The man took a final drag of his cigarette and then ground it under his heel. He didn't take Mamma's hand. Instead, he fished a phone from his pocket and shouted into it.

'Yeah, mate. That pick-up for Jack. I'm gonna need the van.'

Mamma's hand hovered in the air, then came to rest on the strap of her handbag, which she pushed higher up her arm. Ella saw that she was nervous. A single bead of sweat was trembling on her top lip and she was surreptitiously checking that the clasp of her bag was firmly closed.

Half an hour later, a rusty van pulled up outside the main entrance, the doors tied shut with bits of rope and the bumpers hanging half-off.

Mamma's lips tightened as the man and the van driver began to toss all their carefully packed boxes into the back, one on top of the other. She saw the men smirk at one another as Mamma negotiated the van step in her tightly fitted skirt and high heels, flicking her glove over the grimy back seat before gesturing for Ella to climb up beside her.

The van jolted and wheezed over a wide bridge, the river flowing fast and brown below. Through the spattered window, Ella caught glimpses of high stone walls, brooding clouds, a throng of afternoon shoppers shouldering their way towards the station, their heads angled against the wind. She pulled her parka closer around her.

The van bumped down a cobbled side street and sputtered to a stop. Mamma sat up straighter in her seat, craning her neck impatiently over the backs of the men's heads.

What she saw made her gasp out loud, her hand flying up to her mouth to stifle the sound.

'But it's perfect,' she said, her eyes welling with tears of relief.

And although, Ella thought with new irritation, this response was just a touch on the dramatic side, she saw that it was true.

Their new home stood in its own secluded courtyard. To enter the yard, you had to walk under a low archway of old wooden beams. The noise of the street faded away and you could feel the buildings draw closer around you, as if cradling you in their arms.

There were no other shops facing into the courtyard, only a café with a few chairs and tables outside and three or four customers staring into their cups.

They looked back at Ella with glazed expressions. One of them fed flakes of croissant from his fingers to a little dog that he'd tethered to the back of his chair by its lead. No one seemed the least bit interested in the van or their arrival.

Ella let her mind soften into a small, still point, then imagined herself floating upwards and outwards, flying across the courtyard and into Mamma's head. From here, she could see the shop as Fabia Moreno was seeing it right now, windows polished to a bright gleam, a smart sign in gilt lettering, a mannequin in the window in a red crepe dress, and scrolls of silk and velvet spilling over the counter.

'Where do you want these, then, love?' one of the men shouted, throwing a box in the air and catching it with a fake flourish. Ella snapped back into herself.

She watched as the men stacked their boxes in a clumsy pyramid on the shop floor.

'Please, no need . . . No, *really*.' Mamma's lips tightened again.

But the men were fast, deft, efficient. The van moved off in a cloud of exhaust fumes and Ella watched as Mamma removed her hat, twisting it in both hands.

She picked her way between the puddles, poking at the shop's splintering shutters, testing the footboards with the toe of her shoe, then stepped inside, peeling off her glove and running her hand over the surfaces.

'So much dust. It must have been empty a very long time.' She wrinkled her nose. 'And a bit musty.' She hugged her arms around her. 'But we will be OK here, *tesora. No?*'

Ella saw only how the white plaster seemed to glow in the half-light. She looked up at the graceful arches of the window-panes and the wrought ironwork above the shop door where the face of a woman smiled down at her. The woman's hair, unravelling over the lintel, was so realistic that Ella could almost imagine her winking.

Licking the tip of her finger, she wrote on the dirty window, 'Fabia Moreno', and beneath that 'Ella Moreno', making the 'b' and 'l's as loopy and extravagant as she could. And beneath that, she drew the shape of a heart.

3

Baby's blanket. White merino wool. Hand-knitted.

Ella had always been different from other children. Fabia knew this from the moment she took the newborn bundle in her arms, gathering the soft bird-bones of her, feeling the tiny heart beating fast and strong against her own.

The baby was strangely quiet and calm and looked at her with wide eyes that were not-quite-green and not-quite-blue, but perfectly focused in a way that made Fabia wonder what she was thinking.

She was born just before midnight on the night that people in England call All Hallows' Eve. Halloween. Samhain.

The Day of the Dead is what Madaar-Bozorg would have said, the Thin Time, when the worlds of the living and the ancestors overlap for a while.

A lozenge of moonlight fell through the window of the third-floor hospital room and spread itself across the sheets. The baby seemed to reach for it, her little rosebud fists opening and closing as if trying to hold the light in her hands.

Her name came easily. Fabia saw the shape of it very clearly in her mind – or was it that she heard it, blown in on the autumn wind, like an eddy of leaves or the smoke from the first fires? Isabella, for Isis, Brilliant One, Great Lady of the Moon and Magic, protector of the dead, queen of beginnings in all the old stories.

But she would always call her Ella, in honour of that first night, years ago already now, when she'd first met Enzo. The smell of jasmine and honeysuckle, the chink of glasses, the sounds drifting on the heavy air to the balcony where he stood waiting for her.

'Do you like, jazz, *bellissima*? Billie Holliday? Nina Simone? Listen, this is my favourite. Ella Fitzgerald. *Magnifica*. What a goddess . . .'

He'd put his hand on the small of her back, his hips swinging gently to the rhythms snaking around them and between them.

'Don't you love how you feel it all through you, like . . . like . . .' He'd lifted his hand as if to pluck the right word out of the air. 'Like *e-lec-tricity*?'

The high notes tangled with his words, breaking against her in shivers of green, red, gold.

That night, the night of Ella's birth, she let herself remember all of that, testing herself, fingering the still-fresh wound of it all.

The nurse wrestled with the window latch, slamming it shut against the wind. But the baby, Ella, lay perfectly quiet, seeming to take in everything with her calm, clear gaze.

'This one's been here before,' said the nurse, stroking Ella's cheek, letting her tiny fist close fast over her finger. 'She's not going to let go.'

Yes, Fabia thought, turning the words over in her mind, this was true. She'd been thinking about nothing else but this moment for months now, wondering what it would feel like, to go through it all alone. She'd expected to feel so small, not up to the task, so afraid. Because Enzo wasn't here with her, to stroke her hair or play her compilations of his all-time favourite jazz tracks or distract her by laughing at his own terrible jokes.

But when the moment had arrived, she hadn't felt any of those things.

Now, she flexed her feet under the white sheets, wiggled her toes. Exhausted, yes. Every muscle in her body ached and throbbed. But as she looked down at this baby in her arms, *her* baby, hers and Enzo's, something inside her seemed to soften. She didn't really know how to put it into words. Except that it had a colour, this feeling, the softest blue, spreading through her stomach, reaching up towards her heart, turning purplish at the edges and opening into a velvety pink, like the petals of the orchids that grew in Madaar-Bozorg's garden.

For a moment, the colours filled the black gap that had opened up in her since Enzo's death. They shone through all the dark spaces.

The baby kicked her feet and made a small mewing sound. Her eyes searched Fabia's face. I wonder what I look like to her, right now, Fabia thought. An enormous moon-face, blurry, all out-of-focus.

'You're safe,' she whispered. 'We don't need to worry about anything anymore.'

But she knew it was herself she was trying to convince.

In fact, Ella had never been a moment's trouble. Whenever Fabia thought about those first difficult years, which she tried hard not to do, she saw herself as a small figure in a flimsy coat and worn shoes with Ella tucked under her arm, traipsing from one town to another, one life to another; and she saw how Ella had simply looked out at everything around her with those clear blue-green eyes, as if perfectly resigned to whatever might happen next.

Fabia had placed her carefully in her Moses basket in the middle of all those other women's kitchen floors while she scrubbed and polished, tidied away, scraped stale food from stacks of dishes, loaded and unloaded dishwashers, ironed and folded clothes. And all the time, Ella had lain quietly, clasping and unclasping her little pink fists, opening and closing her eyes and murmuring to herself from time to time.

And now they were here in York – the final destination, Fabia hoped, at the end of their long journey. Just three weeks ago, she'd watched her daughter, fifteen years old now, half-child, half-woman, with wild brown hair and that steady gaze, stand-ing in the middle of the courtyard as the men lugged the boxes and shouted to one another and a little dog yapped.

She'd seen how Ella stood observing with her usual calm and serious expression, as if a part of her were somewhere else, somewhere far away and completely unreachable.

Fabia Moreno felt, and not for the first time, a stab of fear for her daughter. She wished that she would giggle and shriek and fidget and get impatient, even stamp her feet and complain, making unreasonable demands in the way that she saw other teenage girls doing.

There was always a part of Ella that seemed unreachable somehow, even to Fabia. You never knew quite what she was thinking. Always with her nose in a book.

And then, of course, there was the other thing, all the signs that Fabia knew to watch for in a daughter. The gift that all the women of her family had been born with, one way or another.

Seeing things, hearing things, feeling things. Tasting sounds and sensing shapes or the sudden crackle in the air, the colours a person made around them. Knowing who was arriving at the door before they were even there. Feeling your way into another's thoughts. Ella had this, she knew. But she wondered if Ella herself was aware of it yet.

Now she looked down at the top of Ella's head, her hair a wiry halo that blazed in the sunlight.

'You *are* holding on to this ladder, aren't you, *carina*?' she said, preparing to balance on one leg and reach her arms above her head to drive the last screw into the ceiling fixture.

Ella turned from gazing out of the window and grasped the stepladder with new determination.

'I didn't know you could do all this stuff, Mum,' she said.

'Neither did I.' Fabia laughed as the chandelier in her hands sent rainbows bouncing over the white walls. 'But what is it they say here? That funny thing. Don't tell me. Let me remember . . . *Sink . . . or swim*?'

Even now, almost sixteen years after arriving in England, she was still grappling with the language. She missed things out, forgot the correct sequence of the words. The vowels never seemed to feel quite right in her mouth somehow. And here in the North, she felt even clumsier. People here spoke in such a different way. Sometimes her head ached from concentrating so hard just to keep up with what they were saying.

It was so frustrating. She was an educated person, an intelligent person and yet she couldn't always make herself understood.

'Ooh, yes. We do need a new dress shop, something a bit different.' The pink-cheeked girl at Braithwaite's Fruit & Veg had smiled. It was the first shop in their new neighbourhood that Fabia had visited, just around the corner on Petergate. White tiled walls, swept floors, the produce stacked in crates lined with green baize or arranged in wicker baskets. Fabia had smiled approvingly and this girl had smiled back.

'Here on your holidays, then?' she'd said. 'Or something more permanent, like?'

'Oh, permanent. Most definitely.' These words had felt good in her mouth. And the girl herself reminded Fabia of a ripe fruit – a peach or perhaps a rosy apple – her bosom looking as if it might burst the stiff sheath of her green nylon overalls at any moment. She would look very lovely in something with a bit of corseting, Fabia thought. A sweetheart neckline. A full skirt. Something '50s style. Cotton. Perhaps blue or primrose yellow.

'Vintage, you say?' The girl was counting coins into her hand now. 'I do like all that old stuff. It's in all the magazines now, innit? I might have to pop in and 'ave a look.'

She'd slipped an extra peach into the brown paper bag and winked.

Fabia liked the hum and lilt of her talk, the ease of her body as she reached up to drop apples onto the scales suspended from the beam above her head, sending the silver dish bobbing and swaying.

'I make some of the dresses myself too,' said Fabia, 'and alterations. Because, well, perhaps you know that vintage is very hard to size. We also have shoes, handbags, scarves, jewellery, perfume . . .'

She stopped and felt herself blush at the sales pitch tripping out of her mouth. 'Oh, I'm sorry. Listen to me . . . Please. Come. See for yourself.'

She tried to hide her embarrassment, burrowing to the bottom of her canvas shopper, fishing out a flyer from the bundle and propping it against a pineapple. 'We have little opening. Not a party, exactly. Glass of wine, yes? And . . . how do you say it here? *Canapés*?'

'Oooh. Very nice,' said the girl, her cheeks dimpling again. 'Cana-what's its. Those snacky things, innit? Want to give me a few of your leaflets, then, luvvie? I'll put 'em on the counter.'

And as she left the shop, Fabia had felt a kind of fizz and crackle returning to her body after all the years of sadness. It was like throwing off a heavy blanket after a long illness and stretching her arms wide.

She'd done it. She was here. She and Ella. Finally, they could make their new beginning. She could almost believe that it was going to be all right.

She put back her head and laughed, opening her mouth and swallowing big lungfuls of the chilly air.

'Mum! What are you doing?' Ella was hanging about in the street, looking in a shop window at a mechanised life-size model of a man stirring a bowlful of fudge.

'Breathing it in, *carina*. Breathing it all in . . .'

Ella scowled. 'Well, all I can smell is this fudge. It's disgusting. I bet it's only the tourists that buy it.'

She glanced around her self-consciously, pushing her hands deeper into her pockets. But then she looked at Fabia and smiled, in the way that you might indulge a small child playing.

She feels it too, thought Fabia. She's relaxing a bit. She's going to be happy here.

Because, above all, Fabia wanted Ella to be happy.

All that first week, she'd busied herself, unpacking boxes for the shop and the flat, finding furniture, hanging curtains, cleaning, painting and tweaking.

She'd discovered that she could sand the old varnish from a table and paint it in smooth creamy strokes of duck-egg blue. She could glue the broken spindles of a chair or improvise a headboard from a piece of wood and a length of flowered fabric.

But she wished she could do more, spin a circle around them both, keep the happiness in and any badness out.

She watched Ella carefully, feeling relief on the days when she lost that far-off look, when she smiled or laughed or even put aside the book she'd buried herself in to help with painting a wall or emptying a box.

And then when Billy appeared in the shop, hovering in Ella's wake, his face splitting into that wide smile, Fabia felt her heart lift. At last, Ella had a friend. And so soon after they'd got here. This was a good sign. Perhaps this meant that she'd meet more nice young people. This friendly woman in the grocers, for example. Was she old enough to have a daughter? Someone around Ella's age?

She'd begun to believe that they were safe here. People were kind.

Stupid, Fabia. So naive. To trust. To relax in this way.

Because then, just a couple of days later, that awful man had come sniffing around, with his black coat, all grubby at the hem, and his eyes, tiny eyes, too deep-set in his face – never trust a man with too-small eyes, Madaar-Bozorg always said – looking into everything, picking up a handkerchief or a hat with the tips of his long white fingers, replacing each item with a look of distaste as if it were contaminated.

She'd felt her hand in her skirt pocket itching to leap out and grab his hands, to make those horrible probing fingers go still and quiet.

She'd had an almost overwhelming urge to pick up an embroidered cushion or a silk scarf and hold it up in front of his face so that she wouldn't have to look at that expression in his eyes for one minute longer.

But instead she'd smiled and smiled and laid her hand gently on his arm – he'd certainly liked that, hadn't he? – and she'd gestured towards the doorway, carefully, quietly, so that he wouldn't feel pressured, so that he wouldn't know, even for a second, that she was ushering him away, across the floor and out of the door. Away. Please. Leave us now. Watching as the last flick of his black coat disappeared around the corner like a rat's tail.

Fabia Moreno knew how to make a shop. She knew how to make a high waist and a concealed seam, how to drape a neckline or cut on the bias, how to sew stretch jersey, remove the scuff marks from a 1920s evening slipper or restore the nap of a blush-pink leather glove.

But she didn't know how to keep Ella safe, how to shield her from the prying fingers, the hard faces, the questions and looks, the words half-whispered behind the back of a hand or tossed over a shoulder, words made to cut you or hook you in.

Wherever they went, there was no getting away from those words, it seemed.

Foreigner. Dirty Arab. Osama Bin Laden. Terrorist cell. Excuse me, madam, may I see your papers? Passport? How long do you intend to stay here? Taking our jobs. Why don't you just go home?

What had this man said as he stood, holding her flyer between his long, wormy fingers? She tried to remember.

'I take it you have a permit for this little opening party. If you're going to serve alcohol, Mrs Moreno, well, you'll need certain permissions from my office. But I'm sure that can all be arranged . . .'

Fabia knew exactly what that meant.

'Oh,' she'd said, offering him her best smile. 'Thank you so much for advising me. I wouldn't want to cause your office any extra trouble, Councillor. In that case, I will offer my guests some very nice homemade lemonade.'

4

Plume of emerald-green feathers with Swarovski crystal clip. Bespoke stage costume jewellery. Paris. 1990s.

Jean Cushworth frowned at herself in the backlit salon mirror. Like this, with her hair sticking out in clumps all over her head, each clump wrapped in a piece of carefully folded tinfoil, she could see every wrinkle on her forehead. She moved in closer, trying not to look at the jowly bit under her chin, inspecting her crows' feet, which even ludicrously expensive pots of eye cream didn't seem to help anymore. She prodded the skin at her collarbones, noticing the way that it no longer sprang back under her fingers.

She watched this woman in the mirror, this woman who was herself and also strangely not herself, a woman she no longer recognised, and let out a long sigh. The woman in the mirror sighed, too, and she noticed now, along with the baggy skin under her eyes, a delicate web of lines at the corners of her mouth.

Jean Cushworth knew women with mouths like that. They were the main reason why, years ago, she'd finally managed to kick her thirty-Marlboro-Lights-a-day habit. Those women couldn't wear lipstick anymore without it creeping from the edges of their lips, giving them a slightly mad expression.

Now she saw that she too would very soon be one of those women.

Maybe she'd go for Botox, after all. Perhaps even full-on surgery. God knows, Graham could afford it. He owed her. That much was clear.

She thought of her mother and how she'd let herself go in the last decades of her life, the cardigans with the splotches of gravy down the front, her hair, the lustrous chestnut curls, her 'crowning glory' as she'd always called it, left to fade to a wiry grey thatch and hacked at every couple of months by that awful woman who came to the nursing home.

'Only seven pounds, she asks for,' her mother had announced jubilantly. 'Special OAP rate. And to think I've spent all that money in salons over the years. Yes, that's one good thing about getting older. You don't have to give a damn anymore.'

But Jean Cushworth did give a damn. She made a little grimace at the woman in the mirror and saw her mother – the raised eyebrows, the disapproving glare – grimace back at her.

No, she was not going to give in. She'd fight it just as long as she possibly could. She was never going to be like her mother.

Vincent, the colourist, was faffing over her now, adjusting the towel around her shoulders and then carefully unwrapping one of the foils.

He caught her eye in the mirror. 'Just seeing if you're cooked, Mrs C.'

She grimaced again and flicked through the pages of a magazine, lingering over the soft, spray-tanned curves of some young celebrity presenting her new baby to the camera. No laughter lines on *her* face, Jean noticed, despite the fact that this girl was smiling in that way they'd always told her you really never should, back in her own modelling days. It was a smile that bared all of the girl's perfectly straight white teeth.

Probably touched up, Jean thought. Lots of air-brushing. We never had any of *that* back then. We even did our own make-up.

Now Vincent was removing the foils, one by one, playing each strand of damp hair through his fingers, spreading it over the towel.

'Have you seen that there's someone new moved into that old boarded-up place on Grape Lane?' he was saying, 'A vintage dress shop. Vintage with "vintage-inspired bespoke". Apparently.'

He raised a provocative eyebrow.

'Oh, I haven't been down there in months,' Jean said. 'Not much reason to, really . . .'

Vincent brightened, relishing the opportunity to impart some new gossip.

'It's someone come up here from Down South. She's Italian, I think. She came in the other day with some flyers. Very lovely, she was. Terribly glamorous. A breath of fresh air, really. She's kitting the place out beautifully too. I had a little walk past there, bit of a nosy. Very stylish. Worth taking a look.'

Jean smiled at him sweetly. 'Oh, I'm sure it's lovely, if you like that sort of thing. Personally, I've never liked the idea of wearing,' she dropped her voice conspiratorially, '*someone else's cast-offs* . . . I mean, it might be all right for students and people with not much money to spend but . . .'

Vincent laughed. 'I know what you mean. Those dusty old places. Smell of mothballs and damp and old ladies' wee, most of 'em, don't they? Still, I don't think this place is going to be like that. No, it looks much classier. And vintage-style bespoke. That's the next big thing, really. I'm getting people asking for '40s up-dos and '60s asymmetric bobs. I love all that stuff. Good luck to her. Anything new in this place gets my vote, that's for sure.'

'I suppose,' said Jean, 'but then, are people in York actually ready for something new? I think most of us rather like this place the way things are.'

'So, Mamma, would you say that you're an actual witch? Or just sort of a pseudo one?'

Ella spun the screw-top jar of thread-ends on the kitchen table. She watched the bits of silk, blue-red-brown-yellow-white, blurring together.

Mamma's needle stopped moving. Her eyebrows shot up in an expression of alarm.

'What a funny thing to ask, *tesora*. A *witch*? Why would you think that?'

'Well, this, for instance. It's not exactly normal, is it?'

Ella held up the jar, shaking it so that the bits of thread jumped around.

'Ella. Stop that. Please –'

'Why?' Now that she'd started, Ella couldn't help herself. 'Why, Mamma? Why are all these bits of old thread so important? Why keep them at all?'

Mamma waved her hand dismissively.

'Ah. It's just a silly habit. Something Madaar-Bozorg and the aunts used to do. Each time I come to the end of my thread, I fasten it tight, snip it off and say, "Bless this house and keep us all from harm." Then I pop the snipped bit in the jar. I've been doing it for so long that I'm almost afraid to stop doing it now. You see? Nonsense, really.'

Ella banged the jar down on the table. 'So it's a kind of spell, then? Isn't it? That's what I'm saying.' She gave the jar a little tap, relishing Mamma's displeasure. 'And what about the words

32

you're embroidering, right now? The words you hide in the clothes . . . in the hems and the pockets. You used to tell me, when I was really little, that those were spells too. Words to give people luck or special powers.'

Mamma sighed and smoothed her fabric on the table.

'Again, Ella, habit. A thing I like to do. It makes me feel good about what I'm making for people. Something beautiful. Something . . . yes, well, *secret*. And I told you about these words a long time before we had a shop, when I used to make things as gifts for the people who'd been kind to us. I was teasing you. We were just playing together. And yes, I suppose the words *are* a kind of magic. But only in the way that I put peppermint leaves and rose petals in your bathwater . . . to help you relax, to help you have sweet dreams . . . or the way that I tell you stories, like Madaar-Bozorg and her sisters told them to me, to help you to understand things, see things in a different way. Or the way I make *torta* and bowls of pasta like your father used to do . . .'

She looked at Ella. 'I can see that I'm not convincing you. But you know, you could even say that the way we dress the shop window, to make a little bit of pleasure for our customers, is magic. Because the world is *full* of magic when you know where to look. It's in the river, the way it moves, and in that pot of basil on the windowsill, the way the leaves know exactly how to grow, how to create themselves . . . and,' she patted the silk on the table, 'it's in this fabric, here, the way it has a flow and a feeling all of its own when I move my needle through it . . . But really, *tesora*, this magic is not an "Abracadabra, I turn you into a frog, I make you disappear" kind of magic. This magic is more like . . . like *love*.'

'OK. I get that part.' Ella tried to hide her impatience. Something didn't feel quite right about this conversation. It was as if Mamma were weaving around them both a cocoon of soft colours – pastel blues, silvery pinks, a smudge of primrose-yellow – while somewhere underneath, she could feel a pulsing, a thrumming, something bolder – red vibrations, streaks of lightning-white and black jagged edges.

From the corners of the room, she imagined that she could hear voices and echoey laughter, insistent, repeating Mamma's words in a way that sounded almost mocking: *Abracadabra, abracadabra. Magic, magic, lu-uuurve magic.*

She shivered.

'But what I don't understand, Mum, is . . .' She stopped. She didn't want to say it out loud. It sounded stupid. Completely insane, in fact.

But it was too late. Now Mamma was looking at her with her head on one side in that way she always did when she was tuning in.

'Colours and feelings, *tesora*? Things you shouldn't really be able to know about someone but somehow you just do? Is that what you want to say?'

Ella shrugged. 'Maybe.'

She gave the jar on the table one last shove.

Mamma poked the needle through the lapel of her blouse, for safe-keeping. She folded her hands carefully on the table.

'I understand. You don't want to talk about it. It's scary, isn't it? When you first start to notice. I do remember that . . .'

Ella started to push back her chair. The legs made a scraping sound on the wooden floor.

'The Signals,' said Mamma. 'That's what I've always called them. I've wondered for a while now if you were starting to feel them too. You've heard people talk about sixth sense, I'm sure. And that's what we have – you and me and Madaar-Bozorg and her mother before that and probably her mother before that. You see, your mind, Ella, and your body are very powerful instruments. You should always listen to what they tell you about the world. They'll always serve you well . . .'

A crackle in the corner of the room. A shimmer of green in front of Mamma's face. A cold feeling creeping up her spine. Why couldn't she trust what Mamma was saying? It wasn't as if she didn't want to.

'Mamma?' she said and she hated the way that her voice came out, all small and thin and afraid.

'Yes, *tesora*?'

'What about the box under your bed?'

Mamma's face froze. She drew herself up straighter in her chair.

'What do you know about that?' she said, quickly. 'Ella, some things are very private, you know.'

A shudder, as if the room slipped for a second. A spark of orange, a jagged line of red. Mamma's green eyes reaching deep inside her.

'Yes, Mum. I know. I wasn't snooping, I promise.' She made a quick gesture. 'Honest. Cross my heart and hope to die . . .'

'Don't SAY that, Ella! I've told you before.'

She had to say it now. In another moment, Ella knew, Mamma would get up from the table and start banging pans around on the stove, turning her back to hide her anger.

'Well, don't tell me that magic is only about cooking and sewing and ... and *love*,' said Ella, the words blurting out of her mouth before she could stop them. 'Because that's not the whole truth, is it? I saw you opening that box when we were moving in here. I saw you taking out the candles and that big old book and a lot of other weird stuff ... I'm not a little girl anymore. You said we were going to make a new start here. So I wish you'd just tell me.'

Mamma sighed again, heavily. It was as if all the anger were seeping out of her. Ella felt it gently flowing away in long, muscular ripples.

'*Tesora*, you have to trust me,' she said, laying her hand over Ella's own. Her touch was warm, soothing. Ella felt a tongue of mauve light creeping through her fingers, reaching up as far as her elbows.

'Trust me, Ella-*issima*. What's in that box is *not* magic. It's just props. You know, staging. Just like my old stage costumes. Candles, an old scrapbook that I made as a girl. Cards – tarot, I-Ching, Goddess – I'll show you them all if you like. Old bags of herbs that Madaar-Bozorg gave me. But they are not something I play with anymore. Do you understand? They are part of the past. Part of the Old Ways, the Old Country. We don't need them. *You* do not need them. You have education, books, opportunities, so many ways to make the world bend in your direction. You can be anything you want to be. And we mustn't make ourselves different, Ella, anymore than we already are. This much I have learned – the hard way. So *carina*, you have to trust me ... You mustn't talk about magic or spells or any of these things to anyone else. Not Billy, not anyone at school, OK? Because they won't see it the way we do.'

Ella felt the cold glitter of Mamma's rings as she reached over the table, stroking her cheek, cupping her chin with her hand.

'Do you understand what I'm saying, Ella? *Do* you? We *have* to fit in here. Sink or swim.'

'Yes,' Ella muttered. 'OK, Mum. OK.'

5

Umbrella. Orange fabric (delicate, slight fray) with black Bakelite handle. 1930s?

That night, Ella slept deeply behind the old curtain that Mamma had rigged up to divide their bedroom into two separate halves.

The curtain was a faded rose colour, with shepherdesses and sheep wandering all over it in gold brocade.

'We can count these sheep,' Mamma had laughed, 'to help us sleep when bad dreams come.'

Ella dreamed of an autumn tide, its swell washing up against the stone walls of the city and in and out of the shop door. The water entered everywhere, smooth and brown as rippled silk. As it receded, it left behind a flotsam of jewels and feathers.

She felt herself rocked by the movement of the water. Her heart floated loose in her chest, like a water lily drifting above its long stem.

She lifted the hem of her nightdress and walked down the narrow stairs to the shop, over and over, over and over, the carpet squelching up between her toes.

The wrought-iron woman with her long, twisted hair had climbed down too, from her place high above the shop doorway, and she stood in the middle of the shop, smiling, her hair flowing over her shoulders and down over her bare feet, making miniature whirlpools on the wooden floor.

In the distance, Ella heard the Minster bells chime three o'clock. The woman pointed in the direction of the sound with her pale fingers.

'Listen,' she laughed. 'Sink or swim? Sink or swim?'

In the morning, there was no sign of Mamma. Ella poked her head around the dividing curtain. The bed looked as though it hadn't been slept in. She made her way down the shop stairs, rubbing at her eyes.

'Ta da!' Mamma turned to her, spreading her hands vaudeville style. 'The final touches. What do you think?'

Ella saw that the window was finished. The mannequin had her hand on her hip and her head tilted at an angle, as if she were listening to far-off music. She was wearing a 1930s black cocktail dress with hundreds of tiny pearl buttons down the back. At her feet, shawls and scarves, which Mamma had twisted and coiled to imitate waves, spilled in brilliant colours. She'd positioned her favourite art deco umbrella so that you could almost believe the wind had snatched it, just a moment ago, out of the mannequin's upturned hands, and from the ceiling she'd suspended a storm of paper leaves, each one turning gently on a single thread of silver.

Ella recognised the velvet hat stands, their haughty profiles newly adorned with plumes and headpieces. On the counter, a blue calfskin travelling case spilled sparkling necklaces and brooches.

She admired the new white labels, each inscribed meticulously in Mamma's flowing copperplate script: 'Sweet little 1930s ballerina brooch. £6', '1930s art deco crystal dress clips. Perfect for décolletage. £19', 'Delightful 1950s Trifari-style lizard brooch. £35'.

There were gowns arranged along rails at each side of the shop and silk kimonos floating from the ceiling, their sleeves and skirts pinned like the wings of butterflies.

'And, look,' Mamma said, unable to contain her excitement. 'Go on. Look at the fitting room, *tesora*.' She pointed to the alcove at the back of the shop where she'd hung an old theatre curtain with gold tassels and fringe. Ella moved the curtain aside and peered in.

There was an antique mirror propped against the wall at the precise angle to catch your reflection and throw it back at you in such a way that your neck and legs appeared longer. The walls of the fitting room were painted deep red and hung with some of Mamma's old publicity photos: a nineteen-year-old Fabia Moreno sporting a bikini made of green crystals with a plume of emerald feathers sprouting from her head; a poster for The Songbirds and their 'Sizzling, Scintillating, Sell-out Show' with Fabia at the centre of the line, caught forever in a high-kick, smiling and smiling; and this black-and-white close-up, Mamma's personal favourite, dark hair flowing over pale sculpted shoulders, eyes downcast, full lips and the tiniest, most tasteful hint of cleavage.

As a little girl, Ella had loved these pictures, constantly asking questions about them: 'Tell me again, Mamma, about Paris . . .'

Her dressing-up box had held bits of the old costumes.

Now, seeing them here on the changing room wall, she felt nervous, on edge in a way she couldn't really explain.

Mamma was arranging a pair of silver shoes on a small table, nesting their heels, one inside another, turning out their toes, as if they were requesting the next dance. She'd made little still-lives of some of the gloves and handbags and fan-shapes of the handkerchiefs and scarves.

'It's beautiful, Mum. Much better than our old place.'

Mamma stopped and picked up an elbow-length green silk glove, laying it along her forearm like a favourite pet.

'You think? You honestly think, *tesora*?'

Ella nodded. 'I do. It's brilliant. Very, very cool. Wicked.'

Mamma laughed that deep throaty laugh of hers. '*Wicked*? Ah, I like this new word. Wicked . . .' She snapped open a pearlescent plastic compact shaped like a shell and patted at the shadows under her eyes.

'Look at me! *Tsk*. What a sight. But we are finally ready, *tesora*. We can have our little opening. I thought that perhaps we could set out some glasses on this little table here. What about these lovely champagne saucers? For the lemonade, I mean?'

Ella nodded. 'Sure.'

'Now, of course,' Mamma smiled, 'all we need are some customers.'

She drew her cardigan – the blush-coloured cashmere that she always wore draped across her shoulders, just so – more closely around her.

'Mum, have you slept at all?'

'Not really, *tesora*. My mind was too busy. But it's done now.' She clapped her hands together. 'I am ready. Except coffee. I must have coffee.'

Ella followed her up the stairs.

'You have to sleep, Mum. It's still early. Why don't you lie down for a bit and I'll wake you in a couple of hours?'

Mamma turned mid-stair, frowning.

'Because you have to go to school, *tesora*.'

41

'Not today, Mum. It's Saturday.'

As she watched Mamma moving around the kitchen, selecting her favourite cups, delicate white porcelain with a gold rim, flicking stations on the radio, banging the filter of the coffee pot against the side of the sink to dislodge the old grounds, running water, Ella turned over the Mamma Problem in her mind.

She'd thought about it a lot over the past few years. Mamma's tendency to work all hours at something, to forget to sleep or eat. Her organisational brilliance when it came to sourcing vintage clothes at flea markets and fabrics from wholesalers all over the country, scouring eBay for bargains and transforming junkshop finds, coupled with her occasional inability to remember what day of the week it was.

Ella was different. She'd always liked to have a carefully-drawn out timetable of all her activities at school so that she could be sure that she'd packed her bag the night before with the right books and games kit, the envelopes with trip money or club money and even, where necessary, the right notes to the teacher, which she'd draft out carefully on the telephone pad and then ask Mamma to copy and sign in her own beautifully flowing handwriting.

'So organised,' Mamma would say, ruffling her hair. 'But really, *tesora*, you worry too much.'

To Ella, everything about Mamma was a kind of contradiction: the dramatic outfits and red lipstick against her desire to fit in; her love of everything that was brave and colourful and different – in dresses, food, languages, people, places – and her respect for British people and their very reserved and careful British ways; and, of course, the secret at the heart of it all, the thing that Ella alone knew, that Mamma was only pretending to be Italian.

She wondered how other people would react, here in this new, sleepy city, to the opening of Mamma's shop, her extravagant window displays, the photos in the fitting room and all her little eccentricities.

As Mamma pushed a strand of hair out of her eyes and yawned and stretched her arms wide, circling them to release the ache in her shoulder blades, Ella felt that surge of feeling again. She wanted to protect Mamma from the raised eyebrows and the bitchy gossip; but privately she wished that, this time, she'd just get a nice, quiet job – secretary or teaching assistant or something at least halfway normal – and then she immediately felt guilty for even thinking such things.

Now Mamma placed one of the white cups in her hand. Ella took a sip, savouring the slightly bitter flavour.

'To us,' Mamma said, raising her cup and then stooping to look out of the tiny kitchen window across the higgledy-piggledy rooftops, sparkling with frost, and the two stone angels with their tired faces that could just be glimpsed on a portion of the Minster walls. 'To us, *tesora*. To new beginnings –'

Below them, the shop bell jangled, making them both jump.

'*Dio mio*. It's not even eight o'clock.' Mamma pressed her lips together. 'Who can it be? I'm not properly dressed.'

Ella was already pulling on her jeans.

'It's Billy,' she said, flying to the bathroom mirror, scraping her hair back in an untidy knot. 'He said he'd come and help deliver flyers for you. Remember?' And then she stopped and looked Mamma up and down. 'And when are you ever not dressed, Mum?'

43

Mamma smiled. 'Well, he'd better come up and have some breakfast first.'

It was the first time that Billy had been up to the flat. He leaned in the open kitchen doorway looking awkward and much too tall.

Ella slathered butter and marmalade on slices of toast and tried not to look at him. It was funny to see him out of school uniform. He wore jeans and a blue T-shirt with some kind of band logo on it. He looked . . . Well, nice.

'It's very kind of you to do this, Billy,' Mamma said.

'Not at all, Mrs Moreno. I want to help.'

Ella felt his eyes wander over to her then. She couldn't stop the smile from starting at the corners of her mouth. But Mamma was watching.

'Ready, then?' Ella said, laying down her half-eaten toast.

Billy carried the box of flyers. They walked down Petergate, Ella shoving the flyers through letterboxes, Billy handing them out to people as they passed on their way to work.

'Lovely new shop,' he said, grinning, whenever he spotted someone he thought might be a potential customer. 'Opening today.'

'I could never do that,' Ella said, laughing. 'You really don't care, do you?'

'So, what do we do now?' he said, when the box was finally empty.

Ella shrugged. 'I suppose I'd better get back. You know, in case Mum needs me for anything.'

'OK.' Billy grinned that lopsided grin. 'You know, you look lovely. With your hair like that.'

She fingered a stray wisp of hair. She didn't know where to look.

'Had a nice time, *tesora*?' said Mamma, as Ella came carefully through the shop door.

'God, Mum. Leave it, will you?' Ella felt her face getting all hot again. 'He's just a friend. OK?'

'Of course, Ella-*issima*.' Mamma smiled that infuriating smile and returned to arranging earrings on a silver tray.

6

Housecoat of green cotton, embroidered with hummingbirds in red and yellow. Antique fabric. Circa 1900s. Hand-sewn in Tehran.

Fabia lay watching the shadows moving on the ceiling. She didn't need to reach for her watch under her pillow to know that it was very early.

From the other side of the curtain, she could hear the rise and fall of her daughter's breathing: a soft, even murmur. The sound soothed her, somehow; perhaps because, unlike so many other things in Fabia's forty-three years, it never changed. It never sounded like anything else.

She relaxed her mind and began to feel her way back along the delicate thread of other mornings in which she'd lain listening to her daughter in this way. It was like a necklace, each memory a coloured glass gem, the string reaching back into the past and forward into the future.

And now Fabia's mind began to whir again, making silent calculations, adding and subtracting columns of numbers. She was determined to get it right this time, absolutely determined that she wouldn't leave any room for things to slide.

Her previous shop had been little short of a disaster. Not enough money in Eastbourne. Not the right kind of money, anyway. And if she was really honest, she'd known that all along. She'd allowed herself to be convinced by the rental agent's talk of professional people, young couples, people in film and television and website design, just the right people to have a keen interest in vintage fashion, and how they were being squeezed out by rising property prices in Brighton into Eastbourne's affordable family-sized houses.

She'd seated herself patiently on one of the white plastic tulip-shaped chairs – a replica, she'd vaguely registered, of some mid-century designer – Jacobsen? Saarinen? – and let the young man with hair sculpted into a cartoon crest in the centre of his forehead talk her into a cheap six-month trial rental of a shop on Marine Drive.

The truth was, she'd been exhausted, sick of cleaning other people's kitchen floors, tired of the asides and the snide remarks. She needed a way out. She had a little money saved, and she knew about two things in this world: about clothes, and about how to make people feel good about themselves. It hadn't quite worked out that first time. But it had given her some breathing space, some time to see how it could all be done so much better.

Then the York shop had come up. The old friend of Enzo's, a chance remark, a few phone calls. It had been easy. So easy, really. And that, Fabia thought, was always a good sign. When the Universe was in the right alignment, as Maadar-Bozorg would say, everything moved effortlessly.

Now Fabia allowed herself a luxurious stretch. She was feeling something she hadn't felt in a long time. Trickles of blue and green, starred with intense points of silver and yellow. Excitement. Nerves. Anticipation.

She'd calculated that there was just enough left over from the move, the sale of old stock and the lease money paid up-front for them to get by for three months. After that, one could get loans, the lady at the bank had told her enthusiastically, even some kind of grant for women in business.

She'd smiled at Fabia across the lacquered desk, unfolding the leaflets in front of her.

But Fabia knew that all those things – loans, grants, special awards – meant negotiating with people, people like that Pike man, and she'd rather not tempt Fate that way. Once people started asking questions, looking into your accounts, wanting to know this, that and the other, you never knew where it would end. She'd learned that the hard way.

She wasn't afraid. She'd been in worse situations. Saturday's opening hadn't been too bad. A steady trickle of customers, sipping her homemade lemonade – at least that Pike man had saved her a little money – trying on the shoes, looking through the rails. She'd made a few sales too. So that was something. No, this was a good start. And at least she didn't have to spend her days with her head down other people's toilets anymore.

Outside the window, the city began to clatter into life. Fabia imagined the shopkeepers throwing open their metal shutters, the vans from the countryside trundling into the market, unloading crates of flowers and boxes of fruit onto the trestle tables with their striped awnings. Soon the narrow streets around the market would be a press of people and some of them would be making their way along the uneven pavements and into Grape Lane. She, Fabia, would be ready. She'd welcome them into the shop with a smile and she'd try not to watch too closely as they held up her dresses in front of the mirrors and cooed over her beautiful scarves and shoes and then, slowly, gently, she'd work out what it was that they really wanted.

But, for now, she'd just let herself lie here a little while longer.

She knew that when the Minster bells began to chime eight o'clock, Ida from the next-door café would swill the courtyard with a length of yellow hose, unwind a sun-faded canopy and set the tables and chairs out with a bad-tempered clatter.

'I'm not going to be doing this much longer,' she'd said, when Fabia went over to introduce herself. 'Terrible sciatica. All this standing and running around after folks. It's a young person's game. You're welcome to it, love. It's killing me.'

Fabia was sorry for old people in this country, whose families shirked their responsibilities. It was not like that in Iran.

She thought about Maadar-Bozorg sitting in her chair out on her tiny balcony and hoped that her cousin was remembering to take her to the pool for the Ladies Only swimming session. One day, Fabia thought, when things are different, I'll go back. I'll make a pool at the old village house where Madaar can swim whenever she wants and a new patio where she can grow her herbs and plants.

The walls of the house will be sparkling white and I'll have the old floorboards sanded and polished and the roof and the windows fixed and a proper bathroom put in. No one in my family could ever afford to do that. But I can, if I work hard enough.

It was thoughts like these that eased her guilt, but beneath these thoughts, her mind was busily working away.

She wondered if she would ever see the village and Maadar-Bozorg again. She wondered if she'd ever sit on the patio, resting her back on the sun-warmed wall, feeling the rough stone through her dress, watching the patterns made by the shadows on the old crazed concrete.

She thought of the summers they'd spent there, in the mountains, in the place where her grandmother had been born, and then a memory, something she hadn't thought of in a long time, began to focus itself in her mind. It was like looking down a long telescope, back into the past. One of those mornings of shimmering blue that happen only in the mountains.

She would have been eight, maybe nine, standing there on the terrace that ran the entire length of the house. It had been early, very early, before anyone else was up.

She was wearing her nightdress, thin white cotton, embroidered with tiny white roses. The stones of the terrace were already hot under her bare feet. There were strands of hair, damp with warmth, clinging to the nape of her neck and a trickle of moisture curled between her shoulder blades. She felt the air move around her as she stepped off the terrace onto the baking earth, cautiously, looking back over her shoulder at the shuttered house behind her, because she knew she shouldn't do this, not without her sandals. There might be scorpions, or even snakes.

Her eye had been caught by a pomegranate, round and fat and red, nestled in the pointed leaves of the nearest tree. There were so many trees in that garden – oranges and lemons, as well as the pomegranates – but it was pomegranate fruit that Fabia loved and this one was the biggest and reddest that she'd ever seen.

She reached up on her tiptoes, stretching her arm into the tree and her hand closed over it. It came away easily. When she held it in her palm it was heavy and perfect. Its burnished skin seemed to glow from the inside. She traced the shape of it with her thumb, feeling the smooth curves that ended in that funny, puckered star shape.

She stepped back onto the terrace, holding her prize in both hands. As she did, something moved in the corner of her eye. A flash. A flicker of something.

She stood still, listening.

From where she stood, the garden sloped downwards, through the groves of fruit trees, following the contours of the mountainside. Down there somewhere, Fabia knew, the gardener Hamid had a small hut. She had never seen it. She wasn't allowed to go down into that part of the garden, where the land was left uncultivated except for a few vegetables Hamid grew for himself.

Sometimes she would see the thin wisp of smoke from Hamid's cooking fire. She never went closer. She mustn't disturb Hamid's privacy, Madaar-Bozorg had told her.

But now she could hear something. Was it the sound of someone laughing or crying? She couldn't tell. Then that flash again, like sunlight reflecting off glass. Then the sound again – she was sure now that it was not laughter. A long moaning sound, that seemed to spread out through the still trees and disturb the air.

Should she call out, in case Hamid was down there and needed help? But Madaar-Bozorg said she mustn't make a nuisance of herself, and perhaps Hamid would be angry with her.

She stood there, listening, until the moaning sound subsided. Then she crept back indoors.

In the kitchen, she laid the pomegranate carefully on the wooden board and took a knife and a spoon from the drawer. She scored the skin of the fruit with the knife and broke it open, admiring the spill of glistening seeds, turning one on the tip of her finger like a red jewel. She took one half of the fruit and, as Madaar-Bozorg had shown her, she smacked at it with the back of the spoon, carefully, precisely, so that the seeds flew into the bowl, spattering their red juice.

She was just beginning to spoon the sharp-sweet seeds into her mouth when Madaar-Bozorg appeared at the back door, the door that led from the kitchen to the garden. She was wearing her cotton housecoat, the green one embroidered with hummingbirds, and her hair was loose down her back.

She tried to cover her surprise at seeing Fabia already at the table.

'Hello, little early bird,' she said, smiling, but Fabia could see that she was using the smile to hide something. Her hands fluttered to her hair, smoothing the parting, gathering it up at the nape of her neck. She didn't even seem to notice that Fabia was eating stolen pomegranate.

She walked quickly out of the room and Fabia noticed the crumbs of soil that fell from her feet onto the tiles. When she appeared again, she was dressed and in her sandals and her hair was pulled into a neat chignon.

They'd spent a lot of time at the house in the mountains, she and her grandmother. As Fabia grew older and began to understand things, she watched Hamid closely, noticing the way that he never met Madaar-Bozorg's gaze. How if she came into the garden, he would quietly slip away around the corner of the house or into the trees.

Sometimes when he was working near the house, Madaar-Bozorg would ask Fabia to take him a glass of lemonade, or a sweet cake or a plate of cut fruit. She would never take them herself. Hamid would smile at her, a beautiful smile, showing his white teeth. He would wipe his hands on his trousers and take the plate or the glass gratefully, almost reverently.

This was how she came to understand what passed between Hamid and her grandmother. That and, of course, The Signals.

Because Fabia noticed that whenever Hamid and Madaar-Bozorg were in one another's vicinity, something in the air changed suddenly. It was so strong that she could almost touch it – like static or that too-tight feeling just before the rain comes. And if she relaxed her mind and breathed deeply, she found that she could almost see it too – not in the usual way that she saw things but somewhere in the deepest parts of her mind. Squiggly lines that fizzed and jumped and crackled. Red, the colour of pomegranates; brown, the colour of the earth; and with the sharp green scent of leaves.

Fabia was careful not to go into the garden so early after that. Sometimes she would hear the creak of a floorboard or the squeaky hinge of the backdoor as Madaar-Bozorg let herself back into the house.

She loved her grandmother and questioned nothing. Things were as they were.

Fabia's mother had left when she was so little that she could hardly remember her.

The woman in the photograph on her bedside table was a stranger to her. Occasionally, she would take the photograph in her hands and hold it up very close, scrutinising this woman, her mother, for clues. Did she have her mother's nose or her eyes? Impossible to say. The photograph was black-and-white and a little blurry. The mysterious woman seemed to be turning away from the camera, as if she didn't want Fabia to really see her.

'Where *is* my mother?' she'd once asked, a long time ago, at her cousins' house.

'She's with the angels, now,' her aunt had replied, quick as a flash, crossing herself with her index finger, then bringing her hands together in the shape of a prayer. Madaar-Bozorg had actually snorted then, banging her teacup down on the table.

'Don't tell the child such nonsense,' she'd said, fiercely.

Later, she'd taken Fabia to a spot outside the city where they could look down on the grid of streets far below. She pointed to a huge tree, its leaves casting a circle of shade.

'This is where your mother is,' she'd said. 'Here. This is where I scattered her ashes. So the real answer to your question is that she is in the soil here, under our feet, and in the leaves of that tree, and in every blade of grass and tiny shoot and little flower that grows on this hillside. She's part of everything around us now. That's where to look for her. That's what happens to us when we die. We go back. We return to where we came from.'

Fabia had looked up at Madaar-Bozorg, seeing her strong profile against the sun, her sunglasses pushed up onto the top of her head, the slightly hooked nose, the high cheekbones and the way that she stood with her hands on her hips, as if daring the city below them, and she decided then that she'd never need any other kind of mother. She loved Madaar-Bozorg for her loud, low laugh, for the way that she wore a man's trousers to work in the garden, and for her hands, which were brown and lined and smelled of oregano and wild garlic.

She loved that the Madaar-Bozorg in the village was quite different from the one that most people saw in the city, elegantly dressed, twisting a string of pearls around her fingers. In the village house, she sang as she cooked or sat all day, sometimes on the terrace or in the cool shade of the patio, reading her books, writing her lecture notes, shielding her eyes with her hand and squinting into the quivering blue horizon.

And of course, it was Madaar-Bozorg who had first shown Fabia the magic in words. Fabia could see Madaar-Bozorg's sun browned finger running along the lines of poems or favourite chapters, sounding out the letters. She could still taste those words on her tongue, words like *mag-ni-ficent, por-tent, popp-y, yell-ow* and that strange word *snow*. The names of things: *table, kettle, leaf, river, star*. And her favourite words of all, the names of the goddesses in her storybooks: *Hestia, Demeter, Kali, Persephone, Ariadne, Inanna, Morrigan, Seshat, Selene*.

Now Fabia stretched her arm out from beneath the quilt, extending it as far as she could until her fingers almost touched the low attic ceiling. She moved her hand slowly, dreamily, tracing little circles in the air, watching the shadows made by her fingers on the sunlit walls.

She felt herself slip from that other earlier version of herself, back into her grown-up body.

Gradually, she became aware that Ella's breathing had changed. She turned her head and saw her daughter's face peering at her from behind the dividing curtain.

She was looking at her with that inquiring and ever-so-slightly disapproving expression, her eyes large in her face, her hair springing from the sides of her head in a tangle of fuzzy curls.

Fabia's hand fell to the bed with a dull thud. She thought of how she'd do anything – anything that she possibly could – to protect this sweet girl from the past, to keep that break in the fabric of their lives hidden from her forever, to weave a new story around her, in the way that Madaar had always done.

She must never know – her Ella-*issima*, her *tesora* – about the terrible thing that had torn through their lives, the dark gap that, on some days, still threatened to swallow her whole. No, she must mend it with invisible stitches, make it smooth again.

'Mum, what're you doing?' Ella had yanked the curtain right back now.

Fabia hoisted herself up, twisting her body, placing her feet neatly on the floor, one next to the other.

'Nothing,' she said, 'nothing at all. Just thinking about things. Coffee, *tesora*?'

7

Eau d'Esprit in original crystal bottle. Paris. House of Cacharel. 1955.

Mamma was busy with a customer. She threw Ella one of her Meaningful Looks and tilted her head silently in the direction of the fitting room.

The curtain twitched and the brass rings rattled across the rail as Mrs Cossington, Ella's geography teacher, strode purposefully towards the larger mirror in the centre of the shop floor. She stood, turning herself this way and that.

'But do you think it's really *me*?' she said, examining her reflection, extending her foot in its stout, brown lace-up shoe, pulling her shoulders back, patting her stomach.

Ella felt her cheeks get all hot again. Why did her face always have to give her away?

But here was Mrs Cossington, who'd merely raised an eyebrow at all her day-dreaming in class, the comets she'd drawn in the margins of her geography exercise book, their long tails tangling with the dates and letters. She hadn't made sarcastic comments, as other teachers might have done. Instead, she'd said quietly, tracing a comet's tail with her finger, 'Perhaps, Ella, we'll look at astronomy next, the planets, the earth's composition . . .'

'Oh, yes,' Mamma was saying. 'The colour, yes, most definitely. Let's see . . .' and she took a piece of scarlet fabric from the counter, folding it into a sash and smoothing and pinning it around Mrs Cossington's not inconsiderable ribcage.

'Yes, this gives it a certain line here, like this . . .' and Mamma traced a shape in the air with her hand. 'It lifts the décolleté here . . . and here . . . and then the skirt falls just right. It's much more . . . er, how do you say?'

'Flattering,' said Mrs Cossington, her mouth set straight. 'I think that's the word you're looking for, dear. You see, when you eventually reach my advanced age – and that, by the way, is *positively ancient* – you'll understand that your body does not go in at the places where it used to go in. Or, for that matter, out at the places where it used to go out.'

She twisted in the mirror to get a better look at her back.

'Yes, dear, you've performed a miracle. You've given me back a figure again. Quite, quite marvellous,' and she allowed herself a small smile.

'I can make these little alterations,' Mamma said, removing a pin from the corner of her mouth. 'We can remake this seam right here and have it ready for you to collect on Friday. Then on Saturday night . . .' She clapped her hands together. 'Ta-da!'

'Well, I don't know about that,' said Mrs Cossington, 'but I'll look a darn sight better than I ever thought I could at one of these gatherings. You know, I'd quite given up on the entire performance.'

And then, for the first time, she looked over at Ella, hovering just inside the door. 'Good morning, Ella. How are you?'

'Fine thanks, Miss,' Ella said, hardly daring to breathe. She had a feeling that Mrs Cossington might demand, any moment, that she tell her, *come on, sharpish now,* the population of Canada, or the exact circumference of the earth, something she was sure she couldn't possibly remember because she wouldn't have been listening.

Instead, Mrs Cossington beamed at her, the angles of her face softening in a way that Ella hadn't seen before.

'Ella, I've just discovered that your mother has a great talent,' she said and then she disappeared into the fitting room, swishing the velvet curtain after her.

Ella blushed to think of Mrs Cossington standing in their shop in only her underwear. She felt ashamed about imagining Mrs Cossington's white arms like uncooked puddings and her big bra that made the creaking noise when she bent over your desk to inspect your work.

She busied herself with folding and refolding a silk scarf printed with tiny poodles.

Mrs Cossington appeared again, still doing up the buttons on her thick, sludge-coloured tweed jacket.

'Now, my dear?' she said.

Mamma waved her hand, making that *tsk*-ing noise. 'Please. We can settle all that next Saturday, when you come in to collect. When you're happy that everything is just so,' she said, showing Mrs Cossington a slip of paper where she'd jotted, discreetly, the final figure. 'It's good?'

'*Very* good, my dear,' said Mrs Cossington, her eyes already roaming over the counter, the pyramid of soaps arranged like fondants, the branch of artificial blossom from which Mamma had hung earrings that sparkled like raindrops.

'Oh,' she breathed, 'I think I'll take these too,' crooking a cautious finger around a pair of green, cut-glass gems. 'I'm the little girl in the sweet shop today, dear. You've made me feel quite . . . quite *young* again.'

Mamma unhooked the earrings and held one of them to Mrs Cossington's left lobe, sizing her up as if she were an artist making a sketch.

'Yes, definitely your colour,' she said, holding up the hand mirror for her customer to admire the glint and gleam. '*Che bella!*'

Ella held her breath. When Mamma pronounced her verdict in this way – *Che bella! Che figura!* – it seemed to Ella that everything in the shop grew still for a moment. The velvet busts on the tables seemed to lean in closer, the hat stands nodded their feathered heads and the dresses hanging from the ceiling gave a little silken shiver of their wings. She could almost hear the rows of shoes clicking their heels together and the jackets on the rails elbowing one another, the gowns puffing out their skirts and passing a breathy whisper down the line in a flurry of silk and sateen: *che-bella-che-bella-che-bella-che-sei.*

Mrs Cossington, oblivious, was fishing for her purse in her voluminous black handbag as Mamma arranged the earrings in one of her best boxes, the kind she usually reserved for the semi-precious stones, wrapping it all in a crisp of pink tissue and tying the ribbon in an expert bow.

'May I?' Mamma said, unstopping one of the bottles on the counter as Mrs Cossington offered up, solemnly, the white insides of her wrists. The fragrance of sandalwood, cinnamon and rose filled the shop.

'When I lived in Paris,' Mamma smiled, 'they used to say that every woman needs a signature, a fragrance that lingers in the air when she leaves a room. Subtle, of course, so that no one can even say it's there . . .' She leaned in conspiratorially. 'Our secret weapon.' She smiled again. 'And this, I think, is yours, Mrs Cossington. *Eau d'Esprit*. Made for sixty years to very secret recipe by head of the famous Cacharel family himself. To me, it says: *This woman knows something. She is free spirit. She doesn't belong to nobody.* Live with it for a little. Find out how it suits you.'

Anybody, Ella thought, wincing. She doesn't belong to anybody. But Mrs Cossington seemed not to notice the slip. She was already lifting her wrist to her nose and breathing deeply. Her eyes, those eyes with their big, hooded lids that could dart all over a classroom and spy out a yawner or a doodler or someone fiddling with their phone at a hundred paces, now drooped a little and then finally closed. Her hand went to her bosom, which rose and fell in a sigh as if she were breathing in something at the very edge of memory. After a long moment, she opened her eyes again.

'Thank you, my dear,' she said, 'thank you.'

From her place just inside the door, Ella could see that the stockinged legs and jacketed arms of Mrs Cossington were stepping *quick-smart-now* into Grape Lane, but her head and her naked heart were somewhere else entirely.

This was Mamma's magic, of course, the great talent that Mrs Cossington had just discovered. Fabia Moreno could recognise the shape and scent of someone's private longing. She knew how to interpret people's dreams.

'She says you are a very good student,' Mamma was saying now. She put her hand to her heart in that dramatic way that Ella usually found so irritating.

'Really,' said Ella, trying not to look too surprised. 'Did she?'

'Yes. Today, Ella, you make me very proud.' And then Mamma raised an eyebrow. 'She said you like dreaming up stories more than you like geography. So like your father . . .'

The story of the sealskin

One of Ella's favourite stories was an old one that Mamma had been telling her since she was a very small girl. She knew every word by heart. But still, some evenings when dinner was over, and the dishes were put away and Mamma was settled on the sofa with her feet tucked up under her, Ella would say:

'Mamma, tell me again the story of the sealskin, the soulskin.'

And Mamma would put her head to one side, as if listening for something, and Ella would know that she was travelling back inside herself, back to the Old Country, hearing the waves washing in and out of Madaar-Bozorg's words as she wove the story of all stories.

Then she would begin:

'Once upon a time, in the land of long, hot summers and short, cold winters, where the corn grows high and golden, where the oranges glow like lanterns in the trees and are the sweetest and most delicious that you've ever tasted, there lived a sad and lonely man.

This man was not just a little sad, and not just a little lonely. The loneliness inside him was as deep as a well, and, when he tried to laugh, no sound came out of his mouth, only echoes from a dark place inside himself. People said that something terrible had happened to him, but no one knew for sure what it was.

Some tried to guess, of course, as people do, but the man kept himself to himself in a small house at the edge of the village and he wrapped his loneliness around him like a thick, black overcoat.

Like most of the men in the village, this man was a fisherman. He'd leave the harbour in his boat every morning, just as the sun was showing above the horizon and he'd return home every evening as the sun was setting, with a chill in his bones and a heavy heart. He'd watch the other men tying up their boats as their wives and sweethearts and children stood on the harbour wall, smiling and shouting out their names and welcoming them home. And each day his sadness grew darker and wider.

Soon he began to fish only at night so that he wouldn't have to feel the gap between his own life and the lives of other men, a gap that seemed to him to be as wide and bottomless as the sea itself.

One night, as he was making his way out to fish under the full moon, he rounded the dangerous rocks outside the harbour and came upon an incredible sight. At first, he thought he might be imagining it, that it was a will o' the wisp, an illusion rising up out of the sea spray and the moonlit mist to taunt his lonely heart.

Resting his oars, he let his boat drift in close, closer, closer until it was dangerously close to the clefts in the rocks. From this hiding place in the shadows, he watched. And truly, it was a sight to soothe his weary eyes.

There on the rocks were three women, their naked skins as white as milk in the moonlight. Their hair was loose around their shoulders and glittered – one red head of hair, one black, one golden – under the stars.

As he watched the women throwing up their arms to the night sky, swaying and dancing and singing together, the man felt his heart clattering in his chest like a rusty engine. He felt the black spaces inside him begin to melt away.

The sound of the women's voices and laughter drifted out to him across the water but it was the voice of the woman with long red hair that he heard most clearly. She was the youngest and, he thought, the most beautiful of the three. Her voice rang out across the water and reached all the way inside him, filling the dark spaces with light.

He felt all his sadness and loneliness fall away from him like an old wrinkled skin.

Quickly, soundlessly, he pulled his boat right up to the rocks and, trying not to splash in the shallows, he dropped to his hands and knees and crept ashore. There he saw another strange sight.

At the edge of the water was a heap of empty sealskins and he guessed that these belonged to the dancing women.

So it was true, the man thought to himself. All the tales that his grandmother had told him were true, after all. These women must be the selkies, the seal people, part human, part seal-spirit. His hand trembled over the pile of skins, his palm hot as if it were burning.

Without really knowing what he was doing, he quickly selected the most beautiful of the skins, the one that glinted at him with its fine red hairs, and rolled it up and stuffed it under his sweater where it felt soft and warm against his skin.

Then he waited.

And he waited.

And as the moon began to set, the women stopped dancing and climbed down over the rocks, one by one. Two of them slipped easily back into their sealskins and slithered and splashed into the sea.

But of course, the youngest woman, the woman with red hair to her waist and the voice like music, couldn't find her skin anywhere. As she searched, she cried out.

"Where is my skin, my sealskin?"

It was nowhere to be found.

It was then that the man stepped out from his hiding place.

"Beautiful lady," he said, "I want you to be my wife. Until this moment, I've been the saddest and loneliest man in the world, but you've sung away all my troubles."

He saw the look of horror pass over the selkie's face. She flushed with shame and clasped her arms around herself to shield herself from his gaze.

"No," she cried. "Of course I can't be your wife. I'm not of your kind. I'm of the Others, the sacred ones, the ones who live and sing beneath the waves."

But the man was insistent. He clasped the skin to him. Now that he'd found his happiness, he had no intention of ever letting it slip away.

"Be my wife," he said. "Live with me and I give you my word that in seven summers, I'll return your sealskin to you, and then you can choose to stay or go. It will be up to you to decide."

A long rippling sigh escaped from the young selkie's lips. She let her arms fall to her sides. She studied the man's face for a long time. He could see that she was thinking – and perhaps, he thought, she was a little curious about what life would be like among humankind.

Slowly, gradually, a smile appeared at the corners of her mouth as she looked him up and down.

"Very well, Fisherman," she said, "I will live with you for seven summers. But after that, I must return to my true home and be with my sisters."

The fisherman lifted the young seal woman into his boat and rowed her back to the village. Although his nets were empty, his heart beat proudly in his chest, for he knew that he'd landed himself the biggest catch of all.

Months passed in the village. The corn on the hillside grew tall under the hot sun, the oranges began to ripen and the man and the seal woman had a baby together, a little boy. The seal woman told her son stories, just as I'm telling you this one now, *tesora*, stories of a secret world under the sea where the people lived on sunlight and starlight and wove songs out of the ocean waves.

The seal woman tried to be happy. She really did try. She mended her husband's nets, whispering powerful charms into the knots, and his catch was always the best of the village, so they never went hungry.

But as the years passed, the young selkie's skin began to wrinkle, her hair began to come out in handfuls, the roundness of her hips and breasts began to wither away and she could no longer see very well to cook or clean or mend.

"Husband, you've kept my sealskin for seven long years and now it's time for you to honour your promise and return it to me," she said. "The eighth autumn is arriving."

"Wife, you must think I am a very stupid man!" said her husband, laughing. "If I ever give it back to you, you'll leave me all alone." He strode off into the night, slamming the door behind him.

The little boy loved his mother and was very afraid of losing her to the world beneath the waves but, at the same time, he couldn't watch silently as she suffered in this way. That night, as he was sleeping, he heard the wind and the water whispering to him.

He jumped out of bed and ran out into the night, scrambling over the rocks and through the rock pools. As he looked down into the waves, he saw a big bundle, clumsily tied with string, rolling out of a cave between two of the biggest rocks. He picked it up and held it to his chest, and gasped as he felt the strong scent of his mother unfolding itself all through him like the sea itself.

He ran back to the house and stumbled through the door where his mother was waiting for him. She snatched him up and snatched up the skin.

"Mother," he cried. "Don't leave me!"

But something older than herself, something older then the rocks and older even than the sea, was calling to her.

Holding the little boy by the hand, she staggered to the rocks, stepped into her sealskin and drew it up all around her. Already she could feel her strength returning. Now she dived down deep under the water, still clasping the boy tightly to her body, and the boy discovered that he too could breathe the water like air and swim with all the grace and slipperiness of the seals.

Seven days and nights passed and the boy lived among his mother's selkie-people. They danced and sang in their world under the waves and feasted on starlight and sunlight from plates of shell and drank the moon's reflections from goblets of pearl.

The seal woman's skin turned white again and her long, red hair shone more brightly than ever before. The little boy laughed to see how plump and soft she was becoming. He could no longer circle her wrist with his hand.

But on the seventh night, he noticed tears in his mother's eyes and knew that it was time for him to return to the upper world.

"Little one, my precious one, one day, many years from now, it will be your time to come and join us," his mother told him, guiding him up to the shore and sitting him gently on the rocks. "Until that time you'll live here in the world of people, of human beings," she told him. "But I'll never leave you."

And, sure enough, as the years passed, the boy became a man and well-known in the village as a poet and a singer and a teller of wonderful stories. And every evening, his nets were filled with fish.

Some people said that this was because as a very small boy he'd been dragged to the bottom of the sea in a terrible storm and he'd learned how to talk to the selkie-spirits.

Even today, you can see him, *tesora*, on moonlit nights, sitting on the rocks, talking softly into the waves. Some say that the seals come close to the shore at night to speak with him and that one particular female seal, with a pelt of shining silver, sings to him the songs and stories that he shares with the village people, like this story, *tesora*, that he once told to me and that now I'm telling to you. And perhaps, one day, you'll tell it to your own son or daughter . . .'

Then Mamma would let out a long sigh and rearrange herself against the cushions, stretching her legs out in front of her and yawning. 'And now, my Ella-*issima*, it's time for me – and you – to go to our beds.'

And Ella would allow herself to lean in a little, breathing in Mamma's favourite French perfume – irises, lilies, sandalwood – and the Marseille soap that she sold in the shop and something else, Mamma's own rich scent, that was impossible to define.

For a long time after Mamma had settled into her bed on the other side of the curtain, Ella would lie and imagine that she was drifting out to sea in a boat with stilled oars, feeling the slow lap of the waves, watching the stars.

8

Girl's grey school skirt, standard issue. Visible alterations made at hem and seam. Briggs School Uniform Suppliers. 2010.

They'd been in York for a couple of months. Ella was beginning to get used to the short, cold days, when the mist crept up from the river and rubbed itself through the narrow streets, like a giant cat with damp, grey fur.

Then suddenly, a March wind blew into the city, whipping the river into brown froth, sending people scurrying through the streets, their shopping bags filled like sails, and the pigeons flapping frantically under the eaves. In Museum Gardens, gusts of rain chased away the squirrels and the early tourists and battered the first beds of tulips. Even the gargoyles on the outside of the Minster seemed to hunker down on their carved plinths, and the stone angels tucked in their crumbling wings.

Mamma didn't like the wind. 'It makes me restless,' she grumbled, flicking through the rails of clothes in the shop, fingering the flimsy sleeves of her favourite dresses. 'When will spring arrive?'

'Ne'er cast a clout till May is out,' said Ida, scrubbing at one of the metal tables.

'May?' gasped Mamma. '*Dio mio*. We'll all be frozen half to death by then.' She made a little shudder as Ida plunged a mottled hand into her bucket of soapy water.

'You'll have to get used to it, luvvie,' Ida grinned. 'That's if you're going to make a go of it up 'ere.' She pounded at the padding of her shiny, red anorak. 'Yer need a bit more insulation, that's your trouble. Put a few more layers on yer. 'Ow about one of my nice scones?'

But Ella loved the wind. She loved how it slapped her cheeks and tangled in her hair, how it smelled of things rising and quickening. She loved to stand on the riverbank and stretch her arms out wide so that she could almost imagine she could fly.

'Have you been wearing your scarf?' said Mamma, when she came home from school with one of her sore throats. 'You haven't, have you? Your ears look all red.'

Ella wasn't fast enough to dodge Mamma's prying fingers.

'*Tesora!* You are like lump of ice!'

'Mum, stop it. I'm not a little kid anymore.'

But this time not even Maadar-Bozorg's famous gargle of sea salt, lavender and honey could soothe her throat. By evening, the fever had taken hold of her. It raged all over her body. It floated her up to the ceiling and shook her eyes in their sockets. Now she was too weak even to resist Mamma's special remedy of rosemary and sage.

Ella's voice came in squeaks and croaks. Mamma ignored her, basting her chest with the disgusting mixture, her lips set in a determined expression.

Ella submitted, exhausted. Now Mamma produced a boiled egg from her pocket and rolled it slowly up and down Ella's body – up each arm, down each leg. This was one of Mamma's favourite tricks. 'When all else fails,' she'd always said. Ella knew that Mamma would take the egg, now apparently filled with all the poison in Ella's body, and place it carefully in the freezer compartment of their battered old fridge, up against the ice-cube trays and the bottle of vodka.

'To take the heat away,' she said now. It was pointless to try to argue.

Finally, her hand resting light and cool on Ella's forehead, Mamma announced, 'We need a doctor. I'm going to go next door and ask Ida who to call.'

Ella nodded, feeling the heat rise up from her stomach and sweep over her in a red wave.

When the doctor arrived, he was not at all how doctors usually are. To begin with, he seemed very young. When Mamma pulled back the curtain, he crouched on his haunches at the side of her bed in a not-very-doctor-ish way and his face up close was smooth and clean-shaven, with a firm chin and eyes as twinkly as Billy's.

'Dr Carter,' he said, extending a hand. 'Very sorry to be making your acquaintance.' Then he smiled. A particularly twinkly, white-toothed smile.

'So,' he said, taking her wrist expertly between his fingers.

'May I?' he asked, before placing his stethoscope inside her nightdress, as if he were asking her for a waltz around the bedroom. Not very doctor-like at all.

'Tonsillitis,' he pronounced, after peering into her mouth. 'Nasty. Antibiotics. Necessary for this type of infection, I'm afraid.'

He pulled a prescription pad out of his bag. 'Is there someone who can get this for you, Mrs Moreno? She needs to start it right away.'

Mamma was biting her lip. 'I think . . . You see, we don't . . .'

'Not a problem. I'll take care of it.' He smiled again and put a hand on Mamma's sleeve. 'She'll be fine. I'll be back in about twenty minutes. Don't worry. I can see myself out.'

They heard his footsteps on the stairs and then the jangle of the shop door below. Mamma plumped Ella's pillow. Her hands were cool on Ella's skin.

'What a very nice man,' she said.

Ella closed her eyes. She listened to Mamma humming softly under her breath. Those words. Words from the Old Country. The notes shimmered behind her eyelids – silver and blue with pinpricks of red.

When she opened her eyes again, the luminous hands of her Betty Boop alarm clock, one of Mamma's more irritating eBay finds, pointed to half past midnight. She heard footsteps on the stairs again and felt the press of a cold flannel on her forehead.

A little while after that, she heard the shop bell again – it must be very late by now? – and the clink of glasses in the kitchen sink, then bare feet padding across the hallway and the swish and rustle of Mamma undressing in the dark, sliding herself into her own bed on the other side of the curtain.

'Mamma,' she tried to whisper, but her mouth made no sound and she floated on a flotsam of feathers.

Funny, Ella thought, how your body could be doing one thing – buttering a slice of toast or listening to Mrs Cossington going on about plate tectonics – when your mind was somewhere else entirely.

It was at times like this that The Signals would arrive, flying into her head like a flock of angry birds, all red beaks and green wings, like nothing she'd ever seen before – not with her ordinary eyes, anyway.

What did she mean by that, with her *ordinary* eyes? She didn't know, exactly. It was just that she had no idea where these images came from or how they got there, inside her mind. It was as if she were pressing up against the outside of her body and she could feel the air against her skin beginning to change its colour and texture.

She noticed that it always happened before something went wrong, or when someone was angry or upset, or especially when it was highly inconvenient, like in assemblies, for example.

She hated them. The strange swirling colours. The feelings.

'Nothing to worry about,' Mamma kept saying, in a highly irritating and matter-of-fact way, 'The Signals. Actually, they can come in very handy.'

But there were so many other questions Ella wanted to ask. How was she supposed to turn them off? Was that even possible? Would they start to come more and more often?

Only the other day, when she'd been at Katrina Cushworth's house, she'd felt them so strongly that she'd thought she was going to pass out, right there, in Katrina's hallway.

Because Flippin' Norah, here was the Big News. Ella finally had another new friend and the friend was even female.

Katrina Cushworth had blonde hair, one blue eye and one brown. And Flippin' Norah was something she would say. She'd been telling everyone that she and Ella were Inseparable. That was the word she used to her mother, who was Mrs Jean Cushworth, a Very Important Person in this city.

When Katrina said anything, it always seemed to begin with a Capital Letter.

Katrina Cushworth lived off The Mount in one of the biggest houses in the city. You walked out of the crooked arrangement of streets at the city centre, past the funny, lopsided shops and tearooms and the squat, little buildings with beams and mullioned windows, out over Lendal Bridge and up, way up past the station towards the racecourse. There, where the sky opened out, the houses changed to rows of grand Georgian terraces with large windows and glossy black railings or elegant stucco villas fronted with flights of stone steps. And Katrina's house was one of the largest and grandest of these.

Her garden was the size of a small park. There were enormous chestnut trees and swings and monkey bars. There was a funny little garden house too – Katrina called it the *summer house* – equipped with a massive TV and radio. Katrina had taken her out there that first afternoon. Let's get away from The Madhouse, is what she'd said. They'd carried everything out there – not what Ella would call a meal, exactly, but cupcakes and cookies and massive packets of crisps and those glass bottles of Coke, their outsides all filmy with cold, snacks that the housekeeper, Leonora, packed for them in a special wicker hamper.

'She's not a *servant*,' said Katrina. 'Blimey, you make it sound so medieval. It's just Leonora. I've known her since I was a baby. She used to be my nanny.'

But there was also Milton, a man with a sulky expression who drove Katrina and her mother around in a big silver BMW and lived in a flat above their garage.

'He's not a *chauffeur*,' said Katrina. 'Geez. He doesn't wear a cap with a crest, or anything. He's just our driver. And he carries all of Mum's shopping. Poor guy. Because boy, does she know how to shop.'

When Ella tried to think about how she and Katrina had become friends, she wasn't really sure how it had happened. Or even whether Katrina was really what you might call a friend. It wasn't as if Ella had ever had one before. Not a girlfriend, anyway. So how was she supposed to know?

'It's so nice,' Mamma said in that way that made Ella want to roll her eyes. 'We girls need friends, you know. Female friends. This is very important.'

It had all started a week ago with the note in Maths class.

'Pssssssst . . .'

The sound was like a small firework going off.

'Hey, Ella. Deaf as well as daft, are you? I'm trying to talk to you!'

The secret missive landed on the desk in front of her, a piece of paper torn from an exercise book and folded over and over until it was the size of a large hailstone. Ella dropped the paper into her lap, unfolding it one-handed under the desk and glancing down.

Mr O'Connor was one of those teachers who stood in front of the board and just rambled to himself. He probably wouldn't have noticed if she'd been flicking through a magazine in her lap, to be honest.

She smoothed out the paper. The handwriting was small and very round, the letters pressed deeply into the page:

'Today. After school. Meet me outside the girls' cloakrooms.'

Ella felt the hairs on the back of her neck where they were caught up into a tight ponytail, begin to prickle. She dug her fingernails into her palms and tried to catch Billy's eye. He always sat in the same place, right by the door. But today, he was crouched over his Maths book, his face screwed up in concentration.

He'd been told that if he didn't put some serious effort in, he was going to fail Maths. And he really needed to pass, Ella knew. Billy had got his heart set on university. History was his subject. It must be nice to know exactly what you wanted to do.

She glanced back quickly at Mr O'Connor, pretending to look interested in whatever it was he was saying about integers.

'Psssssssssssssst.'

This time, she'd have to turn round and look. And there was Katrina Cushworth, grinning straight at her, her face so open and her eyebrows raised in such an expectant way that Ella couldn't help herself from smiling too. The appointment was sealed. And with it, she thought to herself, she might as well give up any idea of keeping herself to herself. Anyone could see that Katrina Cushworth didn't operate like that.

Smile. Look them straight in the eye.

But she was also curious. What was it about this Katrina – or Kat as she liked to call herself, 'Because Katrina sounds so, well, as if you've got a broomstick up your bum, don't you think?' – that had led her to make the first move? She'd been circling slowly since Ella had first arrived at St Olave's, not altogether un-catlike, come to think of it. A little like the tabby cat Ella liked to watch from the shop window, skulking through the courtyard, circling its prey. Katrina had been sniffing her out, watching and waiting to see what she might do next.

At half past three that afternoon, Katrina was already slouched against the wall at the door to the girls' cloakrooms. Her hips were thrust forward in her too-short too-tight school skirt – you could see she'd altered it herself – and her left foot in its black leather court shoe ran up and down the back of her right leg.

As Ella came down the corridor, she saw Katrina yawn, stretching her legs and arms in a dramatically bored expression.

'Ready, then?'

Waiting but not waiting.

'No Billy, tonight?' said Katrina, pulling a fake, pouty expression.

Ella shook her head.

'I *am allowed* to have girlfriends, Billy,' she'd said to him earlier, when she explained that she wouldn't be walking home. 'It might be nice. I want to do girls' things too.'

'Fine,' said Billy, 'but *Katrina Cushworth*?' He made a face and minced off in the opposite direction, wrists flapping, knees together, bottom protruding at a comedy angle as if he were wearing Katrina's taken-in skirt and her shoes with the not-quite-regulation heels.

She knew his feelings were hurt.

'You know where I live, right?' Katrina was saying. 'It will take about ten more minutes to get there. I haven't got a lift today because Mum's out. As usual.'

'That's OK. I like walking.'

Ella kicked a pebble along the pavement in front of her. Secretly, she was relieved. The idea of sitting in the back of that car while that strange man drove them had seemed a bit creepy. Rain had started to fall, spotting her shoes and the sleeve of her coat.

As they passed up The Mount, she sneaked glances at pianos and dolls' houses artfully framed behind large sash windows. She admired perfectly sculpted box hedges and zinc tubs of topiary spirals and enormous wrought-iron door knockers.

Then they turned into a sweep of gravel driveway and tall trees that hung down to form a damp green tunnel. Between the dripping leaves, a house emerged, a white house that looked like a wedding cake with layers of windows stuck to its walls like jellied diamonds, and icing-sugar columns flanking the front door.

Katrina scowled. 'Home sweet home.'

Ella stood in the huge hallway, looking around. It was beautiful. She wanted to run her hands over the plaster borders that twined around the walls, their raised pattern of flowers and vines, or step between the coloured pools of light – ruby and emerald and sapphire – that fell across the polished floor from the stained glass windows on the landing high above her.

Then she stopped. She'd felt, very faintly, something cold rush through her, a clammy feeling that made her pull her coat closer around her.

Something on the very edge of her awareness began to vibrate, gently at first, then louder, louder. Blue and red squiggles. Hard, jagged white lines. The Signals. She blinked hard, trying to blank them out.

She turned and smiled at Katrina.

'It's a lovely house,' she said.

9

Necklace of rare blue Lucite beads with enclosures of gold confetti and seashells. 1950s.

Fabia slipped the dress from its hanger and held it up against her, smoothing the simple drape of the neckline over her shoulders. There was something about the texture of silk crepe that she loved. Yes, this one would be difficult to part with. Almost the right size too. A couple of extra darts here at the waist and it would be just perfect.

But grey. Enzo would have disapproved. She could see him now, almost as clearly as if he were standing right behind her, running his hand through his hair in that way he always did when he was thinking.

'But grey is elegant, Enzo. Sophisticated. Ready for any occasion . . . It goes anywhere. It's so easy.'

He would always shake his head. 'When I think about you, my darling, I think about colour. About *life*. The world is too full of grey, as it is. And grey is just too demure . . . too, *boring* for you.'

Now she returned the dress to its velvet-covered hanger. Such a nice shade, this particular grey too. Smoke-grey. Dove's wing. If she put it here, right by the door, people would see it as they came in and it would sell too quickly to be a temptation for her.

Money was tight this month. So many things Ella needed. School trips, books. But starting anything was always difficult. They were doing fine. Just fine.

She realised that her eyes were prickling with tears. She always thought of Enzo in times like this. Ridiculous. She needed to get a hold of herself.

She took a string of large blue beads from a bowl on the counter, and began running them through her fingers. Breathe, that's what Enzo would have said. *One, two, three, four . . .*

The shop door jangled and a blast of cold air bit her ankles. She whirled round.

'Fabia.'

A herringbone tweed jacket. A navy scarf. Blue eyes that were already twinkling at her.

'David. Hello. I –' She let the beads clatter into the bowl, smoothed her skirt with both hands, arranged her lips in a smile. 'How lovely to see you. I . . . I was just . . .'

He hovered, his hand still on the door. 'I'm not disturbing you, I hope?'

'No. No, not at all.' She heard her own voice, so bright and forced. To him, she must sound unwelcoming, but that wasn't what she felt.

'Come in. Please.' She was trying not to look at the enormous bouquet of lilies and greenery he was trailing casually from one hand. Now he turned them right side up, presenting them to her with a flourish.

'I just wanted you to have these.' He smiled. 'I don't . . . Well, I wasn't sure what to do. The other evening, you know. I – I wasn't sure how we left things –'

She felt the crackle of static in the air, the squiggles of yellow and blue that danced around him, the whispers gathering in the corners of the room.

She reached out and took the flowers. 'These are so *lovely*. Really. You are so kind.'

David raised an eyebrow. 'Not at all. The truth is, I had to see you . . . I –'

Fabia felt her throat tighten. She pressed a finger to her lips and then pointed upstairs. 'Ella and her friend . . .'

Was he blushing? Yes, it seemed that he was.

'I'm sorry,' he was shuffling his feet. She glanced down at his brown loafers. Beautifully polished, she couldn't help noticing.

'This isn't a good time, is it?' he was saying. 'I really should have thought. It's just that I was on my way home from work and . . . well . . .'

He pushed his hands into his pockets.

'No. Please don't apologise. But I must put these in water. They're beautiful. Lilies are my favourites, you know?'

He smiled again, raising his hands in a little gesture of help-lessness. 'I *didn't* know, of course. I just had a sort of . . . Well, an inkling, that you'd like them. But I'd better be off, then.' He nodded in the direction of the upstairs flat. 'I don't want to . . .'

'Yes,' she smiled. 'Exactly. But thank you. Thank you so much.'

She was already walking him towards the door. Her hand was on the door handle. Her voice sounded all silly and breathy. Her heart was hammering.

'Another time, perhaps?' He looked right at her then, searching her face. It was a real question, she realised. Not just something to say. He wanted to know.

She shook her head. 'I – Yes, I mean. Well, the truth is, I – I just don't know. I'm sorry . . .'

She watched his forehead crease.

'I've got this all wrong, haven't I?' he said. He looked utterly dejected. 'I think I'm making a bit of a fool of myself.'

In another moment, he'd be gone. Out of the door and across the courtyard, and that would be that.

She closed her eyes for a moment. This was a nice man. A kind man. And the other night had been . . . Well, more fun than she'd had in a long time. He'd come back clutching Ella's prescription in one hand and a bottle of wine in the other. 'This is terribly unprofessional, of course,' he'd said. 'But I rather thought you needed a drink. Doctor's orders.'

She'd had a little too much. She'd told him how worried she was about Ella. He'd put his arms around her. That was how these things always happened.

But it had been a nice thing, a true thing, hadn't it?

Now she met his eyes as he stood in the shop doorway. Before she realised what she was doing, she was putting a hand on his arm. She felt the warmth of him infuse her fingers.

'No. Not foolish,' she said. 'Not at all –'

She couldn't find any more words. She couldn't trust herself.

Instead, when he smiled again, she reached up and kissed him.

'So what's it like, then, at Katrina's place?'

Billy was sprawled across the sitting-room rug, supposedly doing Maths homework. 'Up at the Big 'Ouse.' He exaggerated the flatness of his vowels and mimed doffing his cap. 'Is it as posh as everyone says, then?'

Ella thought of Katrina's house, the echoing white hallway, the light falling through the stained glass windows. She thought of Katrina's bedroom, how she'd tried not to stare at the four-poster bed in the centre of the vast creamy-white rug, its frame draped with gauzy, pink curtains and fairy-lights; or the en suite bathroom with its mirrored wall and rows of luxurious bottles and jars and piles of softly folded white towels; how all the time, she'd felt Katrina's eyes on her, watching for her reactions.

Then she thought of the summer house with its perfectly tidied desk and the enormous flat-screen computer monitor and life-size studio photos of Katrina on the walls, soft-focused with bright, white backgrounds.

She thought of how large and full of creaks and echoes the house had felt and how there was no one to ask them about their day and what homework they had to do, just Leonora shuffling off into the shadows in her house slippers. She felt that cold, rushing feeling again and saw those jagged, white lines at the corners of her eyes.

'It's all right,' she said now, feeling Billy's eyes on her. 'It *is* very, *very* big. And expensive – you know, stuff everywhere – and in places it's all a bit pink . . . Well, I mean, *really* pink . . .'

She watched as Billy relished this information, rolling his eyes.

'It's sort of . . . sad. In spite of all the stuff and the pink. You know, it doesn't feel like a happy place. If that makes sense?'

'My mum went there once,' said Billy. 'Some garden party or something. She wasn't allowed to go inside. Well, only as far as the hallway and kitchen. She was working as a kind of waitress, wearing a right stupid get-up, if you ask me, like a kind of Victorian parlour maid's costume, handing out glasses of champagne and those tiny snack-things on trays. But she sneaked a look through the windows and she said the same thing . . . She said it was a very, *very* big house.'

Billy shook his head as if trying to make enough space in his mind to contain the idea of such a house.

'Not surprised it feels sad, though,' he said. 'What with the boy dying and everything.'

'What boy?'

'Hasn't she told you yet? Well, I suppose she doesn't want to talk about it much. Her brother. The older brother.'

'What happened?'

'Some horrible disease. Something to do with his kidneys. He went to St Olave's. I didn't know him. He was quite a few years older than us. It was awful. Towards the end, he started turning all yellow –'

Billy looked off into the corner of the room as if he were remembering something. 'And then, all of a sudden, he was dead. Gone. Just like that. Poor lad. Must've been four, five years ago now. We would've all still been at primary school.'

Then he turned to her, a wicked grin on his face.

'That house is probably full of ghosts . . . I mean, if Katrina were my sister, I'd definitely come back to haunt her.'

He flung himself at Ella, pinning her hands to the floor, tickling her under the ribs, putting his face up close to hers and making *whoo*-ing noises.

'Stop it, you idiot.' She pulled her hand free and swatted at him, laughing in spite of herself.

She was starting to hate how much she liked him doing that.

When Billy had come up to them in the dinner queue, just today, Katrina had sighed loudly.

'You do know that he thinks he owns you. Like a bag of flippin' marbles or something,' she'd said, as soon as he was out of earshot. 'You're far too good for him. Anyone can see that. Look at him. It's pathetic.'

Another time she'd said, 'He can't put you in his pocket like a prize conker, you know.'

Ella knew that wasn't fair. At least, not really.

But now, as Billy jumped up from the rug, his legs unfolding in that funny way of his, pulling her up after him, patting her down, pretending to straighten her shirt, she couldn't help wondering if he did think he had some sort of exclusive rights.

'What's up, El?' His forehead was all wrinkled and he was looking at her in that serious way of his.

She shrugged. 'Nothing.'

'OK. Better make a move. Walk me as far as the river?'

10

Blue silk dress with net petticoats. 1950s. Lovely detail at belt and décolleté. Can be altered to fit size 10–12.

Ella drew a corner of the velvet curtain across her body so that she wouldn't have to see. She hated looking at herself in the mirror. She hated the way that her body felt, the way her stomach pushed at the waistband of her school skirt, the way the soft flesh at the tops of her thighs rubbed together when she walked.

'Don't watch,' she said to Mamma, who was hovering outside the fitting room, her tape measure already draped around her neck.

The stupid blue dress hung on the ivory hook under Mamma's stage posters, taunting her.

It wasn't an Ella kind of dress. Ella avoided dresses at all costs. And it wasn't a Katrina kind of dress either. Katrina liked those American films, the ones with pink covers and hearts all over them, where girls carried fluffy dogs in their handbags and had perfectly groomed eyebrows. She wanted to look like the girls in all those Californian soaps, the shiny girls who drove shiny convertibles and flicked their shiny hair over their shoulders.

Ella had been brought up on Mamma's collection of box sets: all the Audrey Hepburns, Marilyn in *Some Like it Hot*, Anita Ekburg splashing in the Trevi Fountain, Sophia Loren.

But when she looked in the mirror, she didn't see how she could ever look like that. There was her hair, for a start. Long, dark and thick, it was always escaping whatever arrangement she devised for it. When she brushed it, it stood out from her head in a dark fuzz that seemed to crackle with static.

Ella made a face at herself in the mirror. She felt ridiculous for caring so much. But then she felt the panic beginning to rise in her, as if she were bursting out of her skin, as if her clothes couldn't hold her. She could barely swing her legs under the kitchen table anymore.

'A lovely young lass your Ella's making,' she'd heard Mrs Stubbs, the owner of the shoe shop on the corner say, collecting a new dress for her eldest daughter. 'Our Elizabeth just won't grow. I try to feed her up but she's all skin and bone.'

Ella vowed privately to eat even less. She hated being taller already than Mamma. She thought this was how Alice must have felt when she ate the cake and felt her body grow so big that it pressed against the walls of the house and she had to hang her elbow out of the bedroom window and her foot out of the front door.

It was hard not to draw attention to yourself at school when all you could feel were the boys' eyes on you as you walked down the corridor. It was doubly hard to fit in when you felt so different on the outside as well as the inside.

'You are blossoming, *tesora*, becoming a lovely, curvaceous young woman,' Mamma smiled.

But Ella wanted less, not more. Sometimes she'd prefer to disappear completely.

Then there was Billy. I mean, they were supposed to be friends, weren't they? That's what she'd thought at first. But then, more than just a few times it had happened now, on those afternoons after school. Either he'd jump on her, try to tickle her, just messing about. Or she'd turn to say something to him and his eyes would flick up guiltily to meet her face from where, she realised, he'd been staring at the top button of her blouse. It was as if he couldn't quite help it. She'd watch the colour creep over his face. He couldn't look her in the eye. Instead, he looked away, pretending to be thinking about an algebra problem or scribbling something in his tattered copy of *To Kill a Mockingbird*.

The worst thing was that she sort of liked how it made her feel. She liked that he looked at her in that way. She started to think about stupid things like whether she should wear lip gloss or whiten her teeth. She even thought – for about five minutes – about asking Mamma what to do with her hair. But that would be just the beginning, Ella knew. Mamma was desperate for any excuse to get her hands on her. And, so far, she'd always managed to avoid it. So why was she wasting time even caring about this stuff, all of a sudden? What the hell was wrong with her?

Katrina had given her a page torn out of *Mizz* magazine. She'd pulled it from her schoolbag just the other morning and watched as Ella scrutinised it.

'Cinder-Ella,' she'd said, all pleased with herself, 'You *shall* go to the ball.'

Ella read down the page again. The thin paper was already smudging between her fingers.

Breakfast:
Omelette made of two egg-whites.
Cup of tea, no milk.

Lunch:

Tin of tuna fish.

Apple.

Cup of hot water with 1/2 tsp. cider vinegar.

Dinner:

Small piece of fish or chicken breast.

Steamed vegetables.

Half a grapefruit.

Cup of hot water with 1/2 tsp. cider vinegar.

Ella thought of butter pooling on golden toast and Mamma's pasta with olive oil, rosemary and garlic. Maybe this was why she just kept on getting fatter? Clearly, other people didn't eat like she and Mamma did. Typical. Mamma was getting it all wrong again.

'Is this what you have for breakfast?' she asked Katrina, stabbing at the top of the page. 'This egg-white omelette thing?'

'Duh.' Katrina laughed. 'I don't do breakfast. Not since Project Party, anyway. If I did, I'd skip lunch or something. Mum's lost eight pounds in a week on this.' She tapped the page again. 'It does actually work. And you do go on about your weight quite a bit . . .'

Do I? Ella thought. Maybe she did. But it was all right for Katrina. She didn't need to worry. Not anymore, anyway. Not since Project Party. Katrina's Project – which seemed to involve not eating very much, a frenzy of fitness videos in the summer house and trying out various spray tans – had started shortly after they'd become friends. In fact, sometimes Ella thought that Katrina had only made friends with her *because* of the stupid party. It was going to be this enormous thing, hundreds of people, live bands, all for the stupid Royal Wedding.

'You're not seriously going, are you?' Billy had looked aghast. 'We should get rid of the lot of them, if you ask me. Spongers. Hangers on.'

'Mum says I've got to.' Ella shrugged. How could she even begin to explain all the reasons why they had to go? Ever since the invitation had come through the letterbox, all gold-edged creamy card and hand lettering, Mamma's order book had been filling up. Everyone needed a new dress, and no one wanted to look like anyone else.

Katrina had already bought hers online – well, three dresses to be exact. One was silver, skin tight and covered in tiny sequins. That's what Project Party was all about.

As quickly as Ella was acquiring new soft flesh, Katrina was elongating into long smooth lines. It was as if her body, which some people, definitely not Ella, might have described only a couple of weeks before as a bit on the plump side, was emerging from its cocoon. Her legs were long and perfect. Her arms were firm and shapely and didn't wobble when she raised them above her head. She herself was clearly pleased by this meta-morphosis and had become fond of running her finger around the waistband of her school skirt so that the elastic made a sat-isfying snap, or observing loudly to Ella, after making sure that she was certain to be overheard, that she bet Eddie Dickinson or Dean Silver over there could get one of their hands *around her entire waist*.

And Eddie or Dean or some other boy would, of course, always be happy to oblige, only to be batted away by Katrina, protesting that surely they hadn't thought she seriously meant it? She wouldn't have one of their sweaty paws within five hundred yards of her.

Now she looked at Ella from beneath her long mascaraed eyelashes. Katrina always wore mascara, although it was banned from school.

'What's up, cupcake? You won't be on that diet for long, anyway.'

'What do you mean?'

'Well, it's too much in your natures, isn't it? You Italians. All that food. You can't help yourselves.'

She spun away then, delivering her killer line over her shoulder: 'I wouldn't worry too much, anyway. Billy'll always fancy you.'

Now Ella pulled the blue dress up over her hips, tugging at the top of the bodice, yanking it up higher. It was beautiful, of course, if you liked that sort of thing, expertly cut to come in at the waist in a belt with a diamante buckle, and then one of those sticky-outy skirts with layers of stiff, net underskirt that swished as she moved.

She looked like one of those dress-up dolls she'd always hated as a child.

'Cornflower blue, *tesora*. It sets off your eyes,' Mamma said, poking her head around the curtain.

Ella wrinkled her nose. 'Mum, I feel like an idiot. It's just too . . . Oh, too . . . Too *something*, anyway. Can't I just wear my black one?'

Mamma sighed. 'You can wear whatever you want. I just thought you might like to try something different, a bit of colour . . .'

'Look Mum,' Ella took a breath, curling her hands into fists. 'I know what you're going to say. But do I *really* have to go to this party? I mean, Billy's not going. Lots of people at school aren't going. You know how much I hate that kind of thing.'

Mamma frowned. 'I don't understand. I thought this Katrina girl was a friend. A new friend. But then, you and Billy never seem to have anything nice to say about her . . .'

'I know.' Ella sighed. 'Billy really doesn't like her. But I feel a bit sorry for her, I suppose. She's very different when we're on our own. She talks to me about stuff. She needs someone to talk to. She's there in that huge house, all alone most of the time, with only this old servant woman who mutters and mumbles to herself. And I think there's a ghost –'

Mamma narrowed her eyes. 'What do you mean, ghost?'

'Oh, I don't know. Probably nothing. Except I get all these weird heebie-jeebie feelings when I go there.'

Ella started unfastening the belt buckle, ignoring Mamma's frown.

'So, Mum? You're not answering me. Do I really have to go?'

Mamma pressed her lips together. 'Oh, *tesora*, don't do this. You *know* that we have to go. *I* have to go. Because of all this . . .' Mamma swept her arm around the shop. 'Katrina's mother, this Mrs Cushworth, she has a lot of important friends, it seems. And we are new here. So, really, it is very kind of the Cushworths to invite us . . .'

'So is David going, then?'

Mamma looked away. She inserted the beaded end of a pin between her lips, crouched at Ella's feet and began to busy herself with the hem of the blue silk dress.

Ella snatched the skirt from Mamma's fingers.

'Mum! I'm not even going to wear this, anyway.'

Mamma got up again wearily. She took Ella gently by the shoulders and spun her around, helping her with the zip.

'Well, is he? Is he going? With you?'

Ella held her breath.

Finally, Mamma sighed. 'Would it be so terrible if he did, *tesora*? If he came to this party with you and I? Lord knows, he is a nice man and I could do with a friend . . .'

Ella didn't know what to say then. Everything she'd wanted to say, all the words that she'd been storing up, seemed to be stuck in her throat.

She felt guilty. Mean.

Because it was true. Mamma didn't seem to have any friends here. Not really. Customers, yes. But friends?

And Ella didn't really know if she was Katrina's friend either. Sometimes, Katrina was all over her.

'Like a rash,' said Billy, but Ella thought that the best way to describe Katrina's attentions, as she linked arms with Ella or invited her to admire a new T-shirt she'd just bought or listen to a new bit of gossip she'd just heard, was like an exotic climbing plant, an ivy or a vine, that sent its tendrils out in every direction. She was constantly seeking a foothold and, no matter how smooth-surfaced you made yourself, she'd find the chink.

She would stand in the playground and point, whispering loudly behind her hand about the other girls, until Ella felt her neck and ears tingle with shame.

'That one there, Lindi Cartwright, her dad's gone off with a girl who's only five years older than us.' She'd wink, nudging Ella in the ribs. 'A bit of a gold-digger, apparently. Well, that's what

93

they're all saying . . . Can't see what else she'd see in the old bug-ger. More fool him.'

Then, pointing over at another girl, 'See Big Barbara over there . . . OK, OK. Don't look so shocked. Even her brothers call her that . . . Big Babs. Big Baps. Well, her mum's been doing it with the postman. I mean, my God. Talk about original. The postman!' Her laughter rang out all over the yard. 'Well *what*? You're the only one who doesn't know. Just filling you in.'

Ella would dig her nails into her sticky palms, realising that this might be true, that Katrina was letting her in on the secrets that no one else would ever tell her. She didn't like Katrina's bitching but perhaps, she told herself, Katrina really didn't mean any harm. Perhaps she was just trying to include her.

Other times, Ella wouldn't see much of Katrina for days. She was always relieved when she could slip out of the school gate and fall in with Billy's lolloping stride.

'My lucky day, then, is it?' was all he ever said.

Now she scowled again and the girl in the mirror scowled back at her.

'Mum, I'm sorry. I'll wear the black. I like the black. It's more . . .' she searched for the right word.

'Boring? Predictable?' Mamma suggested, her eyes twinkling.

'*Dignified*, Mum. That was what I was going to say. Dignified. Maybe I *am* boring. Maybe I actually *like* not being noticed. I mean, not everyone can be like you.'

'Ella.' Mamma's voice sounded weary. 'I was just teasing. I didn't mean – I was just trying to help. This dress. I thought . . .'

Mamma's voice trailed off.

'Look, it doesn't matter, Mum. Please. Let's just leave it. The black will be fine. Really. I'm happy as I am.'

She already had her T-shirt over her head now. She bent and started pulling on her jeans. Mamma shook her head sadly, shaking out the skirt of the blue dress like the petals of a giant crumpled flower. She looked defeated.

Ella laid her hand on Mamma's arm.

'But thank you,' she said, stroking Mamma's sleeve, which was bottle-green silk today and freckled with tiny pink polka dots. 'But Mum, please. You've got to stop worrying about me.'

Mamma's wrist beneath the thin silk felt delicate, almost fragile. She smiled back at Ella but she looked as if all of the colour had drained out of her.

Ella had a sudden impulse. She lifted a pair of platform sandals from their stand, the straps covered in huge pink and yellow satin roses, their wedge heels clunking against one another. They were too big but she strapped them on anyway, rolling up the hems of her jeans.

'How about these?' she said to Mamma. 'Will I do now?'

Mamma's lips curved upwards and the dimple appeared in her cheek. She took a step backwards and pretended to examine Ella closely, her gaze travelling up and down, then she scooped up a handful of sparkling bracelets and pushed them up Ella's arms. She reached into a basket on one of the side tables and selected a jewelled velvet orchid, tucking it into Ella's hair.

Ella steadied herself on the platform soles and began to spin. Round and round she whirled, faster and faster. She felt her hair whipping her face.

'You're crazy!' Mamma laughed but she clapped her hands together and stamped her foot like a flamenco dancer and then she began to spin too.

In the dimness of the shuttered shop, Ella and Mamma spun together. The colours of the shop blurred around them. And as she whirled faster, Ella began to feel as if everything – all the difficult stuff, the never-fitting-in stuff and the Katrina stuff and the Billy stuff and the whispers and the meanness – was falling away. That if she could just keep on spinning, she'd leave it all behind. Forever.

Mamma's laughter floated up, all around them. She could feel Mamma's Signals fly in giddy ribbons of orange and yellow and cornflower blue.

For a moment, Ella forgot to think about the swell of her hips, the curve of her stomach. It was as if she was becoming another body, somebody different, some new possibility of herself. She felt all the worries, all the old stories melting away from her in a spill of words. For that moment, it felt as if she and Mamma could spin an entire new world.

11

Women's black sweater. Fits as oversized. Merino wool.

Fabia stood at the shop window, watching Ida scrubbing at her tables and stacking dirty cups and glasses on her tray. There was the man with the little dog again, his newspaper anchored by a mug of tea, his shoulders hunched into his overcoat, taking long drags of his cigarette. He came every day at around this time and Ida would greet him in her gruff way.

Fabia thought that he must be lonely. His face looked lined and tired. He fondled the ears of the little dog and shook his head over the newspaper, muttering to himself.

When Ella was at school and the shop was quiet, Fabia felt that way too. Sometimes she'd have conversations with Enzo in her head. She'd ask herself what he would do or say if he were here with her now, about this strange and beautiful child they'd made together.

And Madaar-Bozorg. Fabia wished that she could just call her. Sometimes she got as far as picking up the phone and dialling the first few digits of the code. But she knew that was hopeless. Madaar-Bozorg had become increasingly deaf in recent years but refused to succumb to what she saw as the indignity of a hearing aid.

'Why would I wear such an ugly thing?' she'd written in her last letter, in response to Fabia's carefully reasoned arguments. 'There's no one here who says anything worth listening to, anyway.'

'Speak up, dear,' she'd shouted when Fabia had called her on her birthday last year. 'You're not pronouncing your words properly. You've forgotten how to speak your own language.'

And Fabia knew that Madaar-Bozorg had her hand partially over the receiver. She'd never liked the telephone. Fabia pictured her, a tiny frail figure standing in the hallway of her ninth floor apartment, her hair still carefully brushed every morning and caught in a chignon at the nape of her neck, the string of pearls clasped firmly around her throat, as outside the balcony windows, the sounds of the new city clamoured and jostled against one another.

It was as if, with every year now, Maadar-Bozorg was slipping further away from her, the letters arriving less frequently, in a spidery Biro that was hard to decipher and the phone calls in which Fabia heard her own voice, bounced halfway around the world, echoing back at her down the line, unheard.

This was her choice, of course, the choice of the exile, the consequences of a decision she'd made all those years ago. No one but herself to blame. She'd chosen another life for herself, here on a separate continent. She'd left Maadar-Bozorg behind with nothing more than a kiss and a wave of the hand. She'd been in such a hurry. As a young woman, it had all been very simple. Keep moving.

Back then, her country, the Old Country, had seemed far too real, too constricting, while the rest of the world was vague, blurry, like a vast blue-green ocean. She'd fixed her eyes on the horizon and felt the surge of it launch her forwards, a current of cool, clean air coming up to meet her. And this current was progress, she'd told herself. She was part of history. She'd ride the eddy of it, follow it out, far out, as far as she could go.

Now she didn't answer to anyone. There was no man telling her what to do. She'd reinvented herself over and over, turning her back on the old ways, eventually adopting the name and language and customs of her European husband. To anyone else, she was Italian now. The candles lit on Sundays for the dead ancestors, the turns of phrase, the coffee made a certain way, Enzo's recipes of fish and pasta, the jokes, the pet names that extended even as far as the name that she'd taught her own daughter to call her: Mamma. Mamma-*issima*.

It was as if she had no real history anymore, her few remaining ties dissolving as quickly as an old lady's spidery handwriting.

So she couldn't start complaining, all these years later, that there was no one around to understand her. No, that was a weak way of thinking and she despised such weaknesses.

But she did, lately, feel very alone.

But now there was David. A sensible man, a kind man. Quite a surprise to have discovered this man, Fabia thought, just when she'd decided never to open her heart again.

To begin with, he wasn't her type. Not really. She'd always liked men with dark hair and dark eyes. Men like Enzo. She wasn't always sure how to be around this blonde English gentleman with his slightly crumpled jackets and funny manners, who acted always so carefully, as if she was made of china and might break under his hands.

It wasn't as if she couldn't talk to him. He was what people here liked to call a good listener. But he was a man, after all, and that meant that, if she ever told him something she was worried about, he'd suggest solutions, try to fix things. Fabia didn't know if there even *was* a solution or anything to be fixed.

Ella keeping herself to herself. Not going out anywhere except with Billy. And now this Katrina girl. She'd never brought her back here, to the shop. Wasn't that a little odd?

Her insistence on wearing black clothes all the time. Jeans, black sweater, black T-shirt. That plain black cocktail dress. Beautifully cut, of course. Chic, in its way, but so solemn, so severe. It worried her.

From all the colour and pattern in the shop, Ella would always select the simplest pieces. She pulled faces at Fabia's suggestions for jewellery and accessories. Just the other day, Fabia had held up some oversized pearls, a diamante brooch.

'Like Coco Chanel,' she'd suggested. 'Très chic. Not too much. Just a little bit of something against all this black. Something to brighten.'

Ella had just sighed. 'This is how I like it, Mum.'

She was spending so much time on her own in her room. Was this normal? Studying, so she said. This could hardly be something to complain about. Other mothers who came in the shop told her about how they had to bribe their teenage children to do homework or household chores. Despite the new dark cloud that seemed to cling to Ella and the solitary ways that she'd always preferred, Fabia couldn't say that she was ever anything except a good girl, so conscientious. So, why was she even worrying?

Maybe, Fabia thought – and this thought was like a spotlight cutting through the haziness in her mind – Ella was clever enough to really make something of her life in this new world. After all, this was Ella's country, her inheritance. It belonged to her in a way that it never would to Fabia. Maybe one day, Ella would be a nice lawyer or a doctor. Dr Moreno. She liked how that sounded. Enzo would have liked that. Maybe David could help Ella to make this happen.

Fabia felt her heart quieten then, her breathing become steadier. Yes, her Ella was clever and hardworking. Not like some of these other young people, wasting their time, making noise in the street, hanging around. As her mother, she would encourage this hard work. She would stop nagging all the time. She would be strong, strong as steel, so that Ella would have everything she needed to walk smoothly through this world. She would work even harder and put a little money by each week for Ella's future.

It was then that she heard it. A faint stirring in the air. A crackle under her fingers.

There's always another way, the voices whispered.

No, she said to herself. She might even have said it out loud. No, definitely not. Not that. Not spells and potions and Dumb Suppers. Not the summoning of spirits. All that Old World nonsense. She'd left it behind a long time ago. Well, apart from a few old habits. But they didn't count. Not really.

Go away, she hissed under her breath. Leave me alone.

The shop bell jangled, sending The Signals skittering across the room.

Fabia dropped the swathe of silk in her lap and met David's open grin. He was holding up a paper bag.

'Croissants. Proper freshly baked ones,' he said, 'and they're still warm. Any chance of a coffee?'

She was already there, putting her hand up to his face, pulling him down towards her so that she could kiss him.

He smelled of soap and aftershave and, very faintly, of the surgery's disinfectant. She breathed it in deeply.

12

Bracelet in the shape of a snake. White-gold, with red crystal eyes. Vintage Chanel in original box, 1956.

'How would you feel about us going out for the day, a little outing on Sunday? With David. He's offered to take us to the seaside.'

Mamma was biting her lip. Ella knew that every detail of her response was being scrutinised. She tried hard to make her face look interested – enthusiastic, even – but her cheeks felt as if they were made of rubber.

Over the past few weeks, she'd become used to the sound of the shop bell jangling in her dreams. Night after night, she'd half-hear it and in the morning she could never be sure if she actually had.

A few nights ago, she'd dreamed that she was drifting down the river on her back, her hair floating out all around her, watching stars falling across the sky and swooping like silver birds into the black water. She watched spires and stone turrets float by and felt the branches of the trees reach down to brush her face.

Then a bell rang out across the water, shattering the still surface into thousands of moving fragments. It was the sound of one of the party boats getting closer, the bell swinging and clattering through the dark, the water rushing under and against her in noisy waves. She twisted her hands in a clump of reeds and tried to hold on as the boat sent shockwaves through the water, threatening to sweep her away.

'Mamma,' she whispered. 'Mamma.'

She could see her then on the deck of the boat, leaning on the rail in her silver Marlene Dietrich number, the one that was backless all the way down to her hips. Dr Carter's arm was draped around her shoulders. The glass in her hand sent reflections bobbing and splitting.

Ella called again but Mamma couldn't hear her. Instead, the tinkling sound of her laughter floated out over the water and she saw Dr Carter pull her in closer so that her face tilted up to his. A neon sign flashed on, flashed off, streaking their faces with blue, gold.

The river washed through her and around her and she felt her teeth chatter inside her skull.

When she woke up, Mamma was singing in the kitchen, bobbing and dipping to Radio Two. Ella stood in the doorway, watching.

'*When the moon hits your eye . . . hmm-hm-hm . . . pizza pie, that's . . .*'

She turned with a flourish of the wooden spoon and tried to catch Ella up in the lilt of the chorus.

'Hmm-hm-hm, hmmm-hm-hm, hmm-hm-hm, *la-la-la, you're in lu-uurve . . .*'

She beat the spoon against her hip, dancing around the kitchen table, catching at Ella's hand, trying to twirl her under her arm.

Ella's arms and legs felt stiff, awkward. Her dream still clung to her, the tendrils of weed, the cold water.

She drew out a chair and poured herself some coffee from the pot.

'So you and Dr Carter – *David*.' Ella tried to keep any hint of sarcasm from her voice. 'Are you, you know, a thing? Is he, well –?'

The words she couldn't say felt like stones in her mouth but Mamma only smiled, the dimple in her left cheek deepening.

'Yes, *tesora*. I suppose you could say, well, that David is my friend. A good friend. I'm still getting to know him.'

Then her smile vanished. Her hips stopped moving, her arms fell to her sides and she stood perfectly still in the middle of the kitchen, looking at Ella with her big green eyes as if a thought had just occurred her.

'You know, Ella, there is something you need to remember,' she said, her face very solemn now. 'And that is that I will always, *always* love your father.'

Ella watched Mamma disappear then, watched her gaze travel far away, out into the air somewhere above her head, where she imagined that she could almost feel the shape of the past shimmering and pulsing for a moment.

Then, just as suddenly, she pulled herself back. 'But life goes on, *carissima*. We must go on, you and I . . . That's what your father always used to say to me, you know: "Don't look back, Fabia. Never look back. We can't always keep things as they are. We mustn't try to hold on to things." '

A flurry of red, a flicker of green wings. A voice taunting: *Hold on, hold on, hold on.*

Ella stood up quickly, pushing her chair back.

'How would I know what he'd say, Mum? I never even met him.'

She saw the hurt look on Mamma's face and immediately hated herself. She'd done it again, even though she'd tried so hard not to. Sometimes, these days, it felt as if she were playing a part in a film about someone else's life. She didn't even recognise herself anymore.

Dr Carter drove a BMW convertible. Black with tan leather upholstery. Mamma wore huge sunglasses and, because the roof was down, an embarrassing yellow headscarf covered with a large blue saddle-and-stirrup motif. Ella didn't care if it *was* vintage Hermés. She hoped no one from school would see them because, as if the yellow scarf wasn't bad enough, Mamma was drawing even more attention to herself. At every traffic light, she'd twist round in her seat and shout, 'OK, *tesora*?' at the top of her voice to make herself heard above the noise of the traffic.

At the junction with Scarcroft Road, David slowed for a red light and she saw Councillor Pike standing on the pavement, talking with Mr Braithwaite, that man from the grocers shop. Billy didn't like Mr Braithwaite all that much either. He said he had something to do with planning a new shopping centre on the edge of town. 'They've all got their hands in one another's pockets,' Billy said.

The wind whipped Pike's black overcoat around his ankles and flattened the thin fabric of his too-short trousers. Ella could see that Pike's face was thrust a little too close for Mr Braithwaite's comfort. He was jabbing the air angrily with one hand while the other tried to clutch at his coat as it flapped out around him.

Both men turned at the sound of David's revving engine.

'Good morning, Councillor!' Mamma shouted, clamping her scarf to her head, laughing into the wind. Pike raised an eyebrow and made a little mock bow in Mamma's direction. Ella slumped down further into her seat. Mamma's laughter caught in the wind, trailing behind her like a bright streamer. David put his hand out and touched her leg, chuckling.

'Fabia, go easy on the poor sod. You'll give him a heart attack.'

'Oh, I don't know. It might do him good . . .' Mamma winked and they both dissolved into more laughter.

Ella dug her nails deeper into her palms.

They drove out of the city, on and on, through endless lanes and fields. Ella thought she'd never seen so many fields, so much sky in one place. Mamma made Dr Carter stop a couple of times because she thought Ella was going to be sick. She was watching her nervously, all the time, in the rear view mirror, and she kept saying that Ella's face had gone greenish and then David would patiently pull over, while Ella reassured them that, no, really, she was fine. Mamma was terrified that she might ruin David's upholstery.

She watched the flat fields go by, the rows of corn just starting to bristle, the clusters of seagulls blown on the wind, lifting and scattering and settling again like clouds of white confetti.

They got out of the car at some small place – a village with an odd name – *Eastern-wold? Easing-wold?* – where they sat outside the pub in their coats and warmed their hands on white mugs of coffee.

'Awful coffee, isn't it?' said Dr Carter in a stage whisper and Mamma said it really wasn't that bad and then, after another sip, agreed with him that it was truly terrible and Ella watched them laugh and laugh as if sharing some amazingly funny joke.

She tried as hard as she could to smile. She knew that Mamma wanted her to be happy. She pushed her hands back in her pockets and clenched and unclenched them, trying to coax the warmth back into her stiffened fingers.

Lots of the people passing by the pub seemed to know David. They stopped and said hello and how are you and David said, these are my friends, Fabia and Ella, and Ella saw people trying to memorise their names, especially Mamma's, their lips moving without making a sound until they just gave up and smiled. David said that he used to work here before he moved to the city and that they were nice people. Very friendly.

At the promenade at Whitby, they ate what David called 'a fish and chip supper'. Even though it wasn't suppertime.

David brought out a blanket from the boot and spread it across their laps and Ella sat with the wind whipping her hair across her face, her eyes smarting with the cold, eating the hot chips right out of the paper. She noticed that Mamma didn't tell her off for licking the salt from her fingers.

What a lovely day it's been, Mamma said, over and over, on the way home, and Ella felt the empty space that had been growing inside her since that morning in the kitchen widen a little more.

Jean Cushworth was irritated. The wind was up and messing with her hair, which always put her in a bad mood, and one of her new shoes, the pair she'd bought online and now wondered if she should have sent back, was beginning to rub her heel painfully.

As she stepped off Grape Lane into the courtyard, the wind blew in her face and she had to stop and blink her eyelids very rapidly to free the specks of grit that might already be trapped behind her contact lenses. She felt her throat tighten. She knew now that she could be seen from inside the shop and this was not the kind of first impression that she liked to make.

When she could finally see properly again, she looked up at the gilt lettering – *Fabia Moreno*. Well, it certainly was a very exotic-sounding name.

She placed her hand on the door, noting the new sophisticated grey colour of the paint and the large brass knocker, which had been polished to a bright gleam.

'Good morning.'

A very attractive woman was coming around the counter to meet her. Early forties, probably, though you couldn't always tell. Long dark hair, her natural colour, Jean thought. Petite, but a bit on the curvy side. Lovely red dress, if you liked that kind of thing. Very Mediterranean.

'Good morning,' she said, pulling off her glove, extending her hand, 'Jean Cushworth. Lovely to meet you.'

Fabia Moreno smiled. She had enormous green eyes lined with dark kohl and a perfect smile outlined expertly in bright red lipstick.

'You're so very welcome here,' she said as Jean's eyes swept over the tables with their artful arrangements of coloured scarves and shoes, the shelves of handbags and the rails hung with silks and sprigged cottons and gowns with full skirts like exotic upturned blooms. 'I'll just let you have a little look and then if there's anything you need, just let me know'

Jean nodded. The truth was, she really didn't like this sort of thing. But everyone who was anyone was talking about this darn shop. Open now for only a couple of months and yet already there was a waiting list. Half of Jean's guests for the Royal Wedding Party were having their dresses made here, it seemed.

Later, at lunch with her friends in Betty's Café, Jean Cushworth would find herself flourishing a small white bag with black ribbon handles and the words 'Fabia Moreno' scrolled across it in gold lettering. The bag contained a large black box, which she would open so that Marge and Jen could admire the white-gold bracelet in the shape of a snake with chips of red crystal for eyes. She would try it on for them, turning her hand this way and that, so that they could see how it showed off her slender wrists, which as Fabia Moreno had commented immediately, were one of Jean's best features.

She would hear herself saying, 'Yes, I've ordered something bespoke. A bit glamorous. Well, you know, it's a simply *amazing* shop. Oh, and yes, of course she's coming to the party. Well, we'd already invited her. Her daughter's a friend of Katrina's, so she was coming anyway. But when I met the mother . . . She's so interesting, so *talented*. You must go and have a look. Tell her I sent you.'

'That bell is going to wear out soon,' said Mamma, as the door closed behind another customer. 'I can't keep up. At this rate, I'm going to have to get some help in.'

Mrs Cossington's dress had been a great success at the annual mayoral ball and that had brought in a flurry of customers. In fact, when Fabia had bumped into her in the street just the other day, she'd taken her to one side.

'I can't thank you enough, my dear,' she'd whispered. 'You've given me a new lease of life.'

She'd patted her hair which, Fabia couldn't help noticing, had been cut into a new style and coloured a rich chestnut, the green glass earrings sparkling above her coat collar.

'I'll be back, my dear,' she'd said, winking, 'and I just have to have more of that perfume!' Then she'd squeezed Fabia's hand. 'You're like a breath of fresh air in this town,' she'd said, looking her straight in the eye, and then she was on her way again, stepping over the cobblestones in what looked like a new pair of particularly elegant court shoes, leaving Fabia smiling to herself.

Now there was Jean Cushworth's Royal Wedding Party. All her friends, ordering dresses. In only three short months, Mamma had become very much in demand. Each evening now, she sat squinting under the lamp in the upstairs sitting room, altering a seam or a hem, or hunched over the sewing machine she'd set up on the kitchen table, its treadle producing a steady chant long into the night.

'I can help,' Ella said.

Mamma smoothed a stray tendril of hair from her cheek. 'Ah, *tesora*, thank you but I'm not having you cooped up here, ruining your eyesight. You're young. You should be out doing things after school, enjoying yourself, maybe joining something, making some nice new friends too. You know, it shouldn't all be about Billy, lovely as he is, or this Katrina girl . . .'

Ella looked away. She tried to hide her face from Mamma's scrutiny. The truth was that she'd been at St Olave's for three months now – a whole term – and she hadn't made any new friends. There was Katrina and there was Billy. When anyone new tried to talk to her in the playground or in between lessons, she felt her face get hot and she didn't know where to put her hands. She found herself imagining what they might be thinking about the new girl, the strange girl with the slightly funny way of talking, although she also knew that her words were already losing their southern sound, becoming more clipped in some places, more elongated in others. It was as if her lips and tongue were learning how to fit into this new place before the rest of her was ready.

'I like your hair. Lovely and dark, innit?' Lizzie Towcroft had said to her just the other day, holding out a paper bag full of sherbet. 'Go on. Just stick yer finger in then and give it a good ol' lick. That's right!'

Ella felt herself being watched carefully as her finger, covered in vivid orange powder, found its way to her mouth. The unexpectedly sharp taste, popping on her tongue, made her gasp and her nose wrinkle.

Lizzie giggled.

'Funny stuff, innit?'

'Sorry. I've never had it before.'

'Don't they have sherbet then, in the country where you come from?'

'I come from England, like you do,' Ella said. 'From the south, from Eastbourne. By the sea. Well, that's where I was born. They might have sherbet there. But I don't know. I never tasted it, anyway.'

'Do they all talk like you, down there, then? It's a bit posh, innit?' Lizzie said, grinning.

'I talk like this because my mum is – well – she lived in Paris before I was born. She speaks lots of languages. Her accent's all mixed-up,' Ella said.

She could feel her insides beginning to slither around. That familiar feeling, half-defiance, half-panic.

Lizzie's eyes were wide and shining. 'What about yer dad, then? Where does he come from?'

'My dad's dead,' Ella said. For a moment, it was almost satisfying to watch Lizzie's face turn red.

'Aw. Soz. No offence.'

Then her eyes lit up again. 'We'll have to teach you how to speak proper, just like we do up 'ere. Then you'll fit in better, right?'

She laughed a carefree laugh that seemed to force its way from her belly into her throat, her mouth opening to reveal her pink tongue and perfectly white teeth.

Ella wondered what would happen if she were to link arms with Lizzie, right there. She looked at Lizzie's wide hips, the soft swell of her stomach under her sweater, the way she carried herself with a lazy kind of confidence. She watched with fascination the way that Lizzie's mouth fell right open when she laughed, easily, unselfconsciously, so that you could see all the fillings in her teeth and the point of her tongue flicking across her lips. Being friends with Lizzie might be so simple, so straightforward. She sensed that if Lizzie decided that she liked you, then everyone would.

But then Lizzie stopped laughing. She was looking at Ella differently now, from under those hooded lids.

'What you gawping at?' she said. Her hand went up and she began to twirl and twirl a strand of her hair around her finger. 'Ohhhhhhhh,' she said, and the sound came out like a long release of air. 'Now I gerrit! You don't want to talk like the rest of us, do yer? Yer think I'm common, don't yer? Miss Fancy Pants. Miss Lah-di-dah, speaks all these languages, thinks she's too good for the rest of us. Except for that Katrina Cushworth, of course.'

112

She leaned in closer. 'Well, you know what you can do, Miss Fancy Pants?' she hissed. 'You can stick it.'

Before Ella could answer, before she could explain that this wasn't what she'd been thinking at all, Lizzie turned sharply on her heel and walked off in that slow easy roll of hers down the corridor.

For the rest of the day, throughout every lesson, Ella felt pairs of eyes boring into her.

She knew what they were all saying. *Miss Fancy Pants. Miss Up-Herself. Thinks she's so much better than the rest of us.* She'd heard it all before.

'No, *they* can stick it,' Katrina had laughed, when she'd heard what had happened. Why did that stuff never seem to bother her at all?

Ella wished that she could be like Mimi Parr or Lulu Barker, girls who seemed to make not-fitting-in an attitude, a kind of talent. They wore clothes bought from charity shops – geeky cardigans buttoned up to the neck and A-line skirts and old lady chunky-heeled shoes – and they did it with a kind of flair, a carefully cultivated air of eccentricity.

When everyone else was eating lunch in the school canteen, Mimi and Lola made picnic tea parties out on the playing-field to which only a chosen few girls were invited. They read poems to one other and played singles on an old portable record-player and danced under the trees, waving their arms in the air and closing their eyes.

That was how to be different, thought Ella. Different as cool. Different as something other people wanted to be a part of.

Once, only once, Mimi Parr had smiled at her, coming into the girls' toilets.

'I like your hair,' she'd said. 'Wild.'

For a whole day after that, Ella had liked her hair too. But the feeling had quickly faded, like a flower growing in the wrong kind of pot. There were too many other feelings, all pushing and jostling against it.

The story of Wolf Girl

'Once upon a time,' Ella wrote in her notebook, 'there was a young witch, a very powerful sorceress, who lived alone with her mother in a little flat above a shop in a half-hidden courtyard.

'By day, the witch was just like any other girl – except that she kept herself to herself and people thought she was strange, a bit too quiet, stuck-up even. They didn't know how she felt on the inside.

'She always wore black, but that was because it helped her to hide.

'Sometimes, in fact, the girl longed for colour – sunflower yellow or flame orange or cornflower blue. But black felt warm. Black felt impenetrable. She could pull it around her like a second skin and no one would ever get close enough to find out her secret.

'Because by night, while her mother lay sleeping, the girl sprouted thick fur on her legs and forearms. Her hair, already long and dark and wild, grew further down her back until it reached the floor. She leapt from her bedroom window and ran through the town, skirting the stone flanks of the Minster, taking the steps to the city walls in a single bound, moving swiftly from shadow to shadow, enjoying how the cobbles and the worn stone flags felt under her paws. Like this, taking the shape of the wolf, she could fly for miles out of the city, across fields and farmland.

'Sometimes, she'd scale rooftops and garden fences and peer through windows at people sleeping in their beds – people she knew, like Billy Vickers and Katrina Cushworth and the girl from Braithwaites and Lizzie Towcroft, who snored and wore fluffy, pink pyjamas – and she'd . . . she'd . . .'

Ella chewed on the end of her pen. What would she do? Put a curse on Lizzie so that her skin itched and her ears glowed bright red for the rest of her life? No, of course she wouldn't, although sometimes it was tempting. Maybe she'd weave a powerful love charm over the girl from Braithwaites so that a millionaire business man, passing by, would see her in the window and fall in love with her and she'd never have to weigh apples or sweep floors again? And Billy . . .? She felt her face flush.

She began again.

'And she'd breathe powerful charms into their ears so that they'd stir in their sleep and smell the scent of the old wild places in their dreams.'

That was better.

'But the Wolf Girl loved the woods, the fragrance of earth and wet leaves, the deep pools of darkness that waited between the trees, the cold, clear glint of the stars.

'She would run and run beyond the edge of the city and plunge deep into the woods to find the darkest places and she'd begin to gather twigs and branches to make a fire. Then she'd crouch on her powerful haunches beside it and breathe flame into the dead wood and as soon as the fire was leaping hot and high, she'd begin to sing.

'She'd call out the shapes from the flames and the spirits from the leaves and branches. She'd call out the song of the little owl and all the birds that nested here in the deepest parts of the wood, and the story of the moon that slept here in the arms of the trees. Finally, just before the sun began to rise, she'd sing the shape of her own true nature, the part of herself that she could never reveal in the light of day.

'As she sang, little by little, she'd feel herself returning to herself.'

Ella looked up from the page. An overfed pigeon strutted on the roof and, below her in the courtyard, the marmalade-coloured cat rolled in a patch of sunlight.

'There in the woods,' she wrote, 'the Wolf Girl never felt ugly or lonely and she never felt afraid. But she always knew that she had to return to the little flat above the shop and her other life in the city, hiding her wildness and her true nature.'

13

Dress with corseted bodice of gold satin brocade and ballerina-length skirt in gold tulle. Bespoke design by Fabia Moreno.

'Look at this.'

David waved the *Evening Press* at her from across the table. He was balanced precariously between two kitchen chairs, his long legs outstretched. He looked so uncomfortable, Fabia thought. There wasn't much room in here anymore. She needed the surface of the table for cutting out this new gown, and the other chairs were covered in metres of gold satin brocade and clouds of tulle.

Ella had retreated to the bedroom again, scribbling in a notebook, no doubt.

Fabia worried that perhaps David was already spending too much time here. He would often drop by on his way home from the surgery, and he always brought something for her: flowers, fresh coffee beans – 'Well, I drink enough of yours' – an almond cake fragrant with rosewater and, once, a beautiful goat's cheese wrapped in vine leaves. He seemed to know exactly what would please her.

'But really,' she said. 'There must be other things you need to do in the evenings. And I always have to be here, sewing. So you mustn't feel obliged . . .'

'Obliged?' He'd laughed. 'Fabia. Believe me, I really wouldn't be here if I didn't want to be.'

The truth was that she was getting much too used to seeing his face appear around the shop door, the sound of his voice on the landing.

But what about Ella? What did she think?

David moved a spool of ribbon carefully to one side and spread the newspaper on the only remaining patch of table, pointing at a notice picked out in bold type:

PUBLIC AUCTION
10:00AM
THURSDAY 21 MARCH
DODDINGTON HALL
THE EFFECTS OF THE LATE EUSTACIA BEDDOWES

'That's tomorrow,' Fabia looked up. 'I'm much, *much* too busy. And effects? Does this mean clothes?'

'Yes, might well do, among other stuff.' David grinned. 'The thing is, I'd heard that she'd passed away, Eustacia. She was a lovely woman. Very well-dressed. You'd have loved her.'

'So how did you know her?' Fabia laid down her scissors.

'Oh, the usual. I looked after her a couple of times when I worked out that way. She never married, never had children. She was fiercely intelligent, loved a good debate. She was interested in travel and gardening and women's rights and anthropology. She once told me that she'd wanted to be a botanist, had got herself a place at Oxford, but her father wouldn't let her go. Different times back then, I suppose. So she stayed at home, did lots of voluntary work and then, when her parents passed away, she finally got her freedom. She went all over the world – Africa, India, Vietnam – taking photographs, collecting rare plants, that kind of thing.'

Fabia nodded and rethreaded her needle. 'So, this Doddington Hall. Where is it, exactly?'

'Oh, it's a beautiful old place. Out in the Dales. Eustacia opened up the gardens to the public a few years ago. There's a picnic area and open-air concerts with fireworks in summer. There's even a regular bus service. But now I suppose they'll sell it all off to some fat cat property developer, who'll turn it into luxury apartments.'

Fabia winced as he took her precious scissors and started to snip around the notice.

'Here. It'll take you maybe an hour on the bus. Wish I could take you myself, but I've got a full surgery tomorrow.'

Fabia slipped the paper into her pocket.

'Thank you.' She shrugged. 'Maybe I'll manage to fit it in. She was elegant, you say, this Eustacia? What did she look like? Did she have amazing clothes?'

David smiled.

'Well, not that I know about these things,' he said, 'but I don't think you'd be disappointed, shall we say? Why not go and have a nosy? You deserve a morning off, God knows.'

'Don't mind *them*,' said Billy. 'They're a load of idiots, that's what they are. Novelty'll wear off, sooner or later.'

They were walking down by the river, throwing sticks from the bank, seeing whose would catch the current faster. *Laikin* is what Billy liked to call it, *laikin' out*. Ella tried the words silently on her tongue. It felt like licking an ice-lolly.

And then the words were out of her mouth before she could stop herself.

'But why do *you* bother with being my friend, Billy?' she said. 'I mean, it's not as if I'm Miss Popularity, is it?'

Billy stopped dead on the riverbank, a stick in his hand, staring at her. His face looked white, stunned.

'What kind of question is that?'

'Well, no one else seems to like me.' Ella hated the way her voice sounded in that moment. Silly, a whiny girl's voice, drifting down the riverbank.

A blackbird chirruped away above her head and it seemed almost to be mocking her, but she carried on.

'They all think I'm stuck-up! They think that I think that I'm better than them somehow. Except Katrina. And she doesn't count. But I'm right, aren't I?'

Billy looked down, kicking at a tussock of grass.

'I don't know,' he said. Ella thought he sounded irritated. 'I wouldn't know what they think. I mean, why's the grass green? Why's the sky blue? Why do you have to ask *why* all the time?'

But Ella felt suddenly reckless, as if she'd been pressing against some invisible wall and now it was beginning to give way beneath her fingers. She had to know. And Billy was the only one who could tell her.

'Well,' she said, 'for instance, why do we never go to *your* house? Are you *embarrassed* about me? Are you ashamed about being friends with the daughter of a – what is it they call people here? An *incomer*?'

Billy looked appalled. He flung his stick down and turned away from her. He ran a finger round the inside of his shirt collar and shifted from one foot to another. Then he turned back again.

'Is that really what you think?' he said, quietly. 'Because if that's it, then you *really* just don't know me at all!'

But Ella pressed on.

'Well, what is it, then? What's the big secret?'

Billy turned away and started walking. She ran to keep up with him.

'It's really very simple, El,' he was saying. 'My house isn't a place that you'd like very much.'

'But how do you know?' she heard herself protesting. 'Why does everyone always assume that they know what I'm thinking?'

'I don't. I don't assume anything. I just don't know how to explain it to you. But it's not because I'm ashamed of you, all right?' Billy said, beginning to scramble up the riverbank away from her. 'If anything, El, it's that I'm a bit ashamed of *them*, and that doesn't exactly make me feel good about myself. My mum left school when she was fourteen. My dad's worked in a factory all his life. My brothers are big, stupid uneducated bruisers, the lot of 'em. It's not what you're used to. You'd have nothing at all to talk to them about.'

Ella tried to scramble up after him. She didn't know whether to feel angry – what did he mean, that she wouldn't be able to talk to his family? – or embarrassed that she'd gone too far. Why did she always have to spoil things?

'I'm sorry, Billy, I didn't mean to . . . I just started to think –'

'Well, *don't*,' said Billy. 'Try *not* to think, why don't you? How's that for a new idea? If you ask *me*, maybe you do *too much* thinking . . . Always making up stories when there's nothing there. Always scribbling things down in that little notebook of yours.'

He stopped at the top of the bank, offering her his hand and then, when she took it, hauling her up so hard that she thought her arm might come out of its socket.

'I'm sorry,' she said. Her hand was still in his. He was kneading it between his fingers. She saw that he was shaking.

14

Scarf by Chanel. 1965.
Cream silk with black motif.

The Dales bus pulled off the main road and up a long gravel driveway. Fabia felt a flicker of that old excitement. Sale day. It was a long time since she'd been to one of these things. It meant the prospect of a bargain – maybe even a real find. There was nothing she loved more than the opportunity for a good rummage through other people's wardrobes.

Often it was only jumble-sale stuff. Nylon eiderdowns and faded curtains, napkins and crocheted table runners, dented packing cases full of yellowed linen sheets, perhaps the odd 60s cocktail dress in rayon or chiffon. But occasionally there was something that was truly precious.

Today might be one of those days. The bus wheezed through the stone archway that marked the main entrance to the park and Fabia imagined the young Eustacia, striding out along the driveway, perhaps with a sketchbook or a picnic basket under her arm.

As the bus braked sharply and the house came into view, she pictured how Eustacia might have looked as a young woman, before the War, draped over the stone balustrade of the terrace. She saw her in her mind's eye as a haughty beauty with one of those English rose complexions, her slim figure swathed in an evening gown of green silk.

She assessed the graceful proportions of the Hall, its large windows, which looked out onto the park, the discreet details of the porticos, and felt sure that Eustacia would have been a person of great taste, with at least a couple of lovely pieces stashed away from her earlier years. There would be jewellery, most definitely jewellery, one or two dresses, handbags and perhaps some favourite shoes.

She jumped off the bottom step of the bus and followed the cardboard signs that had been taped up on pillars and tree trunks to direct the auction-goers. She passed through a gate into what she guessed were the kitchen gardens. They were neat and well-stocked, laid out in that very English way. A hedge of lavender brushed her legs, releasing its pungent scent, and bees busied themselves along a wall of roses and honeysuckle.

An austere, suited woman – Fabia wondered why the women from the auction houses always dressed in that rather unflattering way – flashed her a professional smile.

'Sign and then print your name here, please.'

She held out her clipboard and a pen and then presented Fabia with a catalogue and a number printed on a large piece of white card.

Fabia followed the line of people through a series of sparse rooms and stone corridors, emerging in an impressive marble-columned hall. She shivered, drawing her jacket around her.

The room echoed with subdued voices. Rows of chairs had been arranged between the columns. People were craning their necks to admire the fine plasterwork of the ceiling. The sun cast stripes of light across the polished stone floor through tall, perfectly symmetrical windows.

Fabia settled herself towards the front, where she'd be able to see the lots more clearly. She flicked through the catalogue, marking in pencil the items that seemed most promising.

She noticed that almost everyone else here seemed to be dressed in tweed or those ugly, green quilted jackets. She brushed a piece of lint from her favourite red jacket. She felt a bit like a teenager again among these grown-up, stern women with their hair sprayed into stiff helmets and their sensible brogue shoes.

The auction moved very quickly. An assistant carried each item carefully from a small anteroom and laid it on a table draped with a plush scarlet cloth. Fabia raised her card and made bids on a number of things – a pearl choker with a crystal clasp, a set of luggage by Louis Vuitton, a 1930s toilet case in pink leather with silk lining, a camel coat with a fake fur collar by Jaeger.

But every time, the bidding went higher than she'd anticipated. She knew her limits. What she was waiting for came right at the end. *Lot 108: Various accessories including fans, rings, gloves, belts and scarves.* Fabia knew that the real treasures were to be found among the 'various'. Things got bundled together and sometimes, just sometimes, a real gem would get overlooked.

She waved her card.

'Fifteen pounds. Any advances on fifteen pounds?' The auctioneer looked weary now. People were already beginning to get up from their seats, drifting away.

'Fifteen pounds to the beautiful lady in red.' The auctioneer flashed her a smile.

A few heads turned in her direction. A woman several rows in front swivelled round in her chair and appraised Fabia over the tops of her glasses.

Afterwards, tea was served from two enormous stainless steel urns in one of the drawing rooms. Fabia busied herself with examining the detail of the wallpaper, a stunning yellow

Chinese silk. She fiddled with her phone, pretending to listen to messages so that no one would try to talk to her.

Finally, when the queue for tea had dwindled, she took her cup and perched carefully on the edge of a window seat upholstered in blue brocade, looking out over the hazy vista of the park. A few more minutes and she'd be able to leave without drawing further attention to herself, make arrangements to pay for and collect her box of treasures. She couldn't wait to hold them in her hands, to be able to look at them more closely.

She began to imagine again what the young Eustacia must have felt as she sat here. Would there have been suitors, local young men, standing fidgeting in the middle of this room? Had anyone asked for her hand? Then, later, Fabia thought, Eustacia would have sat here with her aging father, the one who'd denied her an education and confined her to this very luxurious cage. What would they have said to one another? She imagined them sitting in those striped wingback chairs, either side of the fireplace. And, of course, finally Eustacia would have sat here alone, looking back on her life, wondering as we all do in the end, what she might have done differently.

A young woman approached and wedged herself in at the opposite end of the window seat, tucking her feet up under her, balancing her teacup precariously in her lap. She smiled at Fabia.

'I couldn't help but notice your beautiful outfit,' she said, extending a hand. 'Hello, I'm Sylvia. A cousin of Eustacia's. Officially, great-cousin, twice removed. We're dying out, you see. Practically none of us left.'

She smiled again, a dazzling smile that made her face dimple. She wore jeans and a floaty top, a pink cashmere cardigan – a good one, Fabia thought, but a little rubbed at the cuffs – and strings of mala beads, rose quartz and turquoise and aquamarine, with a pendant which Fabia recognised as the hand of Fatima, a sign of good luck back in the Old Country.

The young woman's hair was cut very short, giving her the look of a mischievous elf.

Fabia took her outstretched hand, decorated in large silver rings.

'Fabia Moreno,' she said. 'Very pleased to meet you.'

'Ah,' said Sylvia, 'Fabia. I knew it. I *knew* you were someone interesting. You have the lovely new shop in York, don't you? The one in Grape Lane. My sister's been telling me all about it. How *exciting*.'

She set the teacup, which Fabia was relieved to see was already empty, on the floor and sprang to her feet.

'Would you like to come with me? There's something I'd like to show you.'

She was already on the move, weaving through the packed room, looking back over her shoulder at Fabia, gesturing for her to follow.

Fabia followed. They walked very quickly through a warren of corridors, past walls covered in oil paintings and portraits and mahogany tables arranged with Chinese vases and silver trinket boxes.

Sylvia came to a stop at the foot of a staircase, resting her hand on the polished banister.

'Servants' stairs,' she laughed in her high, lilting voice. 'As children we used to sneak down here and into the pantry. Midnight feasts. We were terrible. We ate everything in sight.'

'You used to stay here?' said Fabia, surprised. She hadn't thought of the Hall as a family house with children clattering down the corridors. It seemed so quiet, so elegant, so restrained in that English way. Not at all child-friendly.

'Oh, yes, we were here, off and on, all the time. Mummy and Daddy were away such a lot, you see. Shipped us off here for the summers. But we loved it. A children's paradise. Trees to climb and a house full of staff to indulge our every whim. And, of course, Eustacia. She was such fun. We were always just a little bit scared of her – which was probably a very good thing – but she had such a sense of adventure, always inventing things for us to do, expeditions, indoors and out, projects, challenges . . .'

Sylvia laughed again, but Fabia saw her eyes well with sudden tears.

'Oh, I'm so sorry,' she said. 'I didn't mean to . . .'

'Oh, goodness, you didn't. She had such a good innings. She was ready to go. She told me only last month that she didn't want to linger.'

Sylvia sniffed and fished a tissue from the sleeve of her cardigan and began to take the stairs, two at a time.

'It's just that I miss her so much. It can't ever be the same!'

They reached the top of the stairs and she took a key from the back pocket of her jeans and inserted it into a door, pushing it open.

'Come in, come in. That's right. Here's what I wanted you to see.'

Fabia allowed herself to be ushered into a large, bright room. It was painted a soft shade of green and one wall consisted almost entirely of window, through which the light poured, settling in a kind of miasma over the polished floorboards and the furniture.

There was a large bed with a simple white coverlet and, above it, a mural painted in delicate strokes, almost Japanese in style – hummingbirds and butterflies hovering between pointed green leaves.

'Eustacia's room,' said Sylvia. 'She painted this wall herself. I wish there was some way I could keep it. It breaks my heart to think of it fading or someone papering over it when the house gets sold.'

'So lovely,' Fabia breathed, moving in closer, noticing the orange beaks of the hummingbirds and the care with which each wingtip had been picked out in gold. She thought for a moment of Madaar-Bozorg, standing in the kitchen in her housecoat embroidered with red and green wings.

Sylvia had already crossed the room and was wrestling with the lock on another door.

'This is her dressing room,' she said. 'I think you'll like it.'

Fabia stepped through into a sudden spill of colour. From floor to ceiling, the room was lined with cupboards, which Sylvia was now throwing open with a series of theatrical flourishes, revealing rails of garments and shelves of belts and scarves and shoes.

'My goodness,' Fabia gasped. Instinctively, she moved closer, running her hands over one of the rails, lifting out a dress of creamy lace.

'One of her favourites,' said Sylvia, approvingly.

Fabia checked herself, sliding the dress back into its place.

'I'm sorry. How rude of me.'

'Oh, she'd love you to look,' said Sylvia. 'Do. Please do. Everything is here. From the '30s onwards, she kept everything.'

She slid open a drawer in a little rosewood cabinet in the centre of the room and took out a large leather-bound notebook.

'You see,' she said, leafing through the pages, 'She catalogued it all. Every detail. What she bought, where it was made and then each time she wore it. She was like that. A great collector of things – plants, paintings, clothes.'

'Is this her?' Fabia peered at a black and white photograph in a silver frame – a young woman, with a face and demeanour not very different at all from the one that she'd imagined, posed in a conservatory next to a large potted palm. She was small and slim and her dark hair was bobbed in the fashionable style of the era, finishing at her jawline and carefully waved. She looked directly at the camera with a steady, open gaze and her chin was ever so slightly raised in what Fabia imagined as carefully concealed defiance. She wore a pair of beautifully cut trousers and a crisp white shirt, a tie and a silver tie-pin. She leaned on a silver-topped cane.

'Yes,' said Sylvia. 'That's Eustacia on her twentieth birthday. Isn't she something?'

'She certainly is,' Fabia breathed. 'I think she and my grandmother would definitely have got on.'

Sylvia was holding the notebook open at the last completed page.

'Her last entry was just a few weeks ago. Look . . .'

Fabia leaned forward to decipher the small, precise handwriting.

'Silk scarf. Vintage Chanel. Cream with black motif.'

Fabia's heart skipped a beat. She traced her finger across the careful columns and read: 'From Fabia Moreno, York. 26/1/11. Just like the one I once lost in Delhi.'

Fabia looked at Sylvia, puzzled.

'Eustacia came to my shop?' she said, making a mental scan of every one of her recent customers over the age of 60. 'I don't remember . . .'

'No,' said Sylvia. 'It was my sister. Cammy. Sorry, Camilla. Cammy is just what we call her in the family, you know. And the scarf. Well, in fact, we buried Eustacia in it. She loved it. It reminded her of a time when she was very happy.'

At the edge of Fabia's memory something stirred. Of course. It was very soon after she'd opened. The first week, perhaps. The scarf with its outsized Chanel motif, the bold interlocking 'C's. She remembered folding it carefully in pink tissue for that lovely young woman, the one with the baby in the pram. She'd admired the woman's woollen pea coat – sky-blue with gilt buttons – and her fat, contented baby in her stripy knitted cap who'd gurgled and babbled.

'It's a birthday present,' the woman had said. 'For my elderly cousin. I wish I could bring her here. She'd love your shop. But she's just too frail these days.'

'Of *course*.' said Fabia. 'I *do* remember Camilla. I *do*! Well, *imagine*!'

Sylvia was watching her with her bright eyes, her head tilted to one side.

'I've made a decision,' she said. 'I want you to go through and choose.'

She gestured to the walls of clothes.

'It's what Eustacia would have wanted,' she said. 'Someone who'll truly appreciate them. She'd have loved to visit your shop. When we gave her the scarf and told her about you, she made Cammy describe the shop and everything in it in great detail. We knew she didn't have much time left, then.' Her eyes glistened again. 'But that scarf gave her such pleasure. When we were thinking about what to do with all this stuff, Cammy did suggest you as a possible solution, but I just didn't know what I thought about it. You see, I'd never met you. But now that I have . . .'

'Oh,' said Fabia, swallowing. 'It's so kind. But I couldn't. Really, you don't know what you're saying. I just couldn't . . .'

'Couldn't you?' laughed Sylvia. 'And I do know what I'm saying, I can assure you. We've debated it, Cammy and I. It's a mammoth task, going through it all. There are some things, obviously, that we'd like to keep for ourselves but the rest . . .'

She lowered her voice conspiratorially.

'No one really knows about all these things, either,' she said. 'We kept this room locked. The thought of that horrible man from Christie's going through her lovely things.' She shuddered. 'No, better that they go to someone like you.'

'But I couldn't possibly buy them from you,' said Fabia, embarrassed. 'I just couldn't pay you what they're worth.'

'Oh, no! I'm so sorry. How perfectly awful of me.'

Sylvia clapped her small suntanned hand to her mouth. The tiny bells on her bracelets jingled.

'I should have been clearer. It's a gift, you see. A gift from Eustacia to you. You can keep some and sell some. Because wouldn't it be wonderful if someone else were able to really enjoy them? Eustacia would have loved that. Cammy and I, we don't really have much use for this kind of thing. Most of them wouldn't fit us, anyway. Eustacia was so petite. Just like you. And as you can see, I'm a bit of an old hippie, to be honest.'

She gestured towards her beaded flip-flops, the frayed edges of her skinny jeans.

'But *you*, Fabia, you'll be able to find the perfect owners for these things. You'll just know, won't you?'

15

Day or cocktail dress. Unusual design with detachable sleeves in mustard mohair/merino mix. Label reads 'Selfridges'. Originally purchased by Eustacia Beddowes, London, 1949.

It had taken an entire week for Fabia to go through Eustacia's clothes, selecting the items that she felt she could sell, packing them carefully in layers of tissue, copying the relevant entries – dates, names, details – from Eustacia's notebook and labelling each garment carefully.

In the evenings, when the shop was closed, David had patiently driven her back and forth between York and Doddington Hall, the back seat of his car stacked with boxes.

Now she stood in the shop, the dresses and shoes and coats spread out all around her, draped on the backs of chairs and over the counter.

She still couldn't quite believe it.

'How will I ever part with any of them?' she'd said to Sylvia. 'They're all so precious.'

'Well, you must keep whatever you want for yourself, of course,' Sylvia had laughed. 'They're yours now.'

So Fabia began the process of trying on everything she could. There was the cream lace tea gown, of course, the one that had seemed to leap from the rail in Eustacia's dressing room and into her hands.

It was made in two pieces: the silk underslip, cut on the bias, and then the exquisite lace – *'handmade by nuns in the South of France,'* Eustacia had recorded carefully – draped from the shoulder and gathered into a diamond-shaped panel at the waist, the back cut into a deep 'V'. As she stepped into it, she felt the silk whisper around her shoulders. It smelled very faintly of something vaguely familiar – roses, perhaps, or was it jasmine? The sweet powdery scent of a summer's evening – and, as the silk fell over her head and upstretched arms and settled into place, it made a small sighing sound. It fitted her perfectly.

Then there was the taffeta evening gown in bold chevron stripes of black and beige; and a stylish trouser suit in lightweight black wool, the high-waisted trousers finished sailor-style with double rows of large black buttons.

As she stepped into them, she felt little ripples in the air, The Signals shimmering at the nape of her neck and the insides of her elbows.

These are yours, they whispered, *yours, yours* . . .

Fabia had never really been a trousers person before, but she was surprised to find that this elegant 1950s style, which Eustacia had clearly favoured, elongated her legs and swished around her ankles when she tried them with wedges or platform heels. They made her walk differently somehow, hold herself straighter, taller.

Then there were the pieces that she instantly coveted, but that didn't suit her at all. The Balenciaga double-breasted day coat, for instance, its textured white cotton cut in a wide A-line and lined with navy wool. Fabia put her hands into the large patch pockets and turned in front of the mirror to admire the back. The sleeves were much too long, even when she turned back the cuffs. Matronly, that was the word. Eustacia had been athletic in build – these made-to-measure couture pieces could have been worn by a prima ballerina – while Fabia had softly rounded curves.

She sighed and laid the coat carefully to one side.

And here was the mustard mohair day dress, described in Eustacia's entry for 1949: '*Bought in Selfridges, London, for lunch with R.*'

Fabia imagined Eustacia poised elegantly in an overstuffed chair among gigantic potted ferns, peering over a silver cake stand arranged with tiny sandwiches and *petits fours*, perhaps in the salon of The Ritz or The Savoy.

Because it was that kind of dress. A dress made for sipping tea from bone china cups. It had a high-necked bodice, cut to skim the figure, a broad belt in contrasting black wool and a surprisingly full skirt for the time. No austerity measures here, thought Fabia. The sleeves could even be detached from the bodice to create a cocktail silhouette through an ingenious arrangement of concealed buttons. But mustard was definitely not Fabia's colour. She stood in front of the mirror, grimacing.

There was an Ossie Clark 'Lamborghini' trouser suit in black embroidered satin that looked a little like a Japanese lacquer print. '*Celia Birtwell fabric*,' Eustacia had noted in her journal, and alongside it she'd pasted a magazine cutting of Twiggy wearing the exact same suit, labelling it: '*Vogue, 1968.*'

Fabia ran the fabric through her fingers. It reminded her a little of the mural that Eustacia had painted above her bed at

Doddington – hummingbirds and delicate bamboo trellises intertwined with chrysanthemum blossoms and butterflies.

Fabia knew that the suit wouldn't fit her – the slender cut of the jacket, the slim-hipped trousers. She didn't even try them on. She wondered, though, where she could source similar fabrics to reproduce this piece for her vintage-inspired line. She could think of several customers who would love this look in their size.

She imagined Eustacia standing in her dressing room at Doddington, a tumble of scarves and shoes spilling around her, slipping her arms into the silk sleeves of this jacket, fastening up her hair.

The shop doorbell jangled, startling her out of her reverie.

'Hello. Are you open?'

A young woman – she might be in her early twenties – stood uncertainly in the doorway, looking at the open boxes on the floor and the layers of dresses and trousers draped over the counter.

'Of course.' Fabia smiled. 'Come in. Please excuse the mess. We don't usually look like this. I'm just finding homes for all these lovely new things.'

The woman stepped forwards, her fingers instinctively reaching for the satin trousers in Fabia's hands.

'Oh, these are beautiful,' she breathed. 'Perfect. Just perfect. Just exactly what I was looking for . . .'

'Well,' Fabia smiled, appraising the young woman's figure. 'Why don't you try them on? I'll just hang them here in the fitting room for you while you look around.'

The woman's eyes were already roving over the shop, sizing up one garment and then another with appreciative gasps. Her hands wandered over the rails, fingering the dresses in bright cottons with full net underskirts, inspecting the soles of a pair of green leather platform sandals, opening and closing the gilt clasp of a velvet evening bag.

Fabia watched discreetly as she continued to work her way through Eustacia's treasures, shaking out a crease, smoothing a sleeve, tweaking a collar, slipping each garment onto its padded hanger.

She noticed immediately that her new customer had an eye for clothes. She bent carefully, almost reverently, to inspect the detail of a pocket or a hem. She was dressed in a mixture of high-street and vintage – the black pencil skirt and leather biker jacket were definitely high-street, but she'd tied a vintage scarf jauntily at her neck and her red shoes had pointed toes and an unmistakable 1950s heel.

Her long dark hair was swept up in a fabulous beehive effect, which showed off a single streak dyed shimmering blue.

'Are you looking for anything in particular?' Fabia asked. 'I have all this new stock too that I'm only just unpacking.'

Her customer turned and smiled.

'Oh, goodness,' she laughed and Fabia noticed the high, breathy lilt to her voice. 'Don't make it any harder for me. I can't choose as it is!'

Then she added, blushing slightly, 'I absolutely *love* your dress, though.'

Fabia glanced down and realised that she was still wearing the mustard wool day dress.

'Oh,' she said, 'and it just doesn't suit me at all. I wish it did. I was just trying it on. But *you*, however . . .' She put her head to one side, running her eyes up and down the young woman again. 'Definitely. You *must* try it.'

A few moments later, Fabia was helping her customer fasten the dress and pinning a large gilt-plumed brooch at her left shoulder.

'There.' She stood back admiringly. 'It could do with a few little alterations. It's slightly too large on the hips. But that's no problem, I could do that for you. And something like this brooch would be just the right finishing touch, don't you think? It looks wonderful with your shoes.'

The young woman nodded, transfixed by her image in the mirror. She ran her hands over her hips, testing the nap of the fabric.

'It's so soft. It feels well . . . like nothing I've ever worn before.' Her face flushed. 'But . . . Umm. How much is it, please?'

Fabia began carefully inserting her marker pins at strategic points along the bodice. Priceless, she wanted to say. A unique piece that could fetch a couple of thousand.

'For you, how does sixty pounds sound?' she said. That was the exact price of Ella's next school trip.

The woman smiled, trying to cover her surprise. 'Yes, please. I'll take it.'

'So, do you live in York?' Fabia finished pinning and stepped back to check the result.

'Yes,' said the young woman. 'And I've been past lots of times since you opened. I'm a guide, you see. I do those awful ghost tours. *Spooky Stories*. You might have seen the sign. Most of the time, I'm dressed up like the Bride of Frankenstein in some hideous wig and outfit. This is my day off. I couldn't wait to come in and have a look around.'

Fabia nodded.

'I think I might have seen you,' she said. 'What an interesting job.'

'Well, it is if you don't mind trying to squeeze a tip out of a load of bored tourists who just want to know where Guy Fawkes lived.' She pulled a face. 'I've been doing it ever since I left uni. It was supposed to be a stop-gap but, you know . . .'

She shrugged.

That explained it, Fabia thought to herself. There was a kind of sadness hanging around this young woman's shoulders. Despite the brilliant streak in her hair and her bright red shoes, her Signals were pale, washed-out greys and browns.

'What do you *really* want to do?' she said, smiling at her in the mirror.

The young woman looked startled.

'It's such a long time since anyone asked me that,' she said, fidgeting with a loose strand of her hair. 'I don't know. That's the problem. Something . . . Well, this is going to sound so . . . so *adolescent* . . . but I've always wanted to do something *creative* . . . to *make* things.'

'Of course,' said Fabia. 'And to me, if you don't mind my saying so, you look like a very creative person. When you walked in, I thought that about you right away. Your lovely hair, your shoes, your scarf. All so beautiful. *Bellissima*. You make me very . . . very *curious* about you.' She smiled again, teasingly. 'In fact, I bet you could do whatever you wanted to do.'

The woman's cheeks coloured again.

'Well, actually, what I really love is baking,' she said. 'Special cakes for celebrations, little cupcakes . . . making tea parties with vintage cups and saucers and beautiful linens. I mean, I really don't know why I'm even telling you this. But that's what I'd really love to do, if I could choose . . .'

'Oh, and you're already so very sure that you can't?' said Fabia, raising an eyebrow.

The woman paused and turned away from the mirror, meeting Fabia's eyes properly for the first time. Fabia could feel her turning the thought over inside her mind. She laid her hand lightly on the woman's back.

'Just slip out of this and leave it on the hanger for me,' she said, quietly. 'I can have it ready by next Monday.'

When the girl emerged from the fitting room, she put out her hand shyly.

'I'm Amanda, by the way,' she said. 'Well, actually, Mandy. And I really want to thank you –'

'I'll see you on Monday, Mandy,' Fabia smiled, ringing the money through her clunky, old-fashioned till. 'Why not bring me one of your cupcakes? I'd love to try one.'

It was strange, the way that things worked out, thought Fabia, at the end of that week, as she stood stirring risotto in the tiny kitchen.

It was as if Eustacia's clothes were choosing their new owners. She almost didn't have to do anything. She just listened quietly and let the clothes decide.

'This is going to sound a bit silly,' she said to David and Ella, as they ran hunks of bread over their scraped-clean plates, 'but it's almost as if a little bit of Eustacia herself is in those clothes. A bit of her appetite for life, her *joie de vivre*. I can feel people becoming inspired, just by putting them on.'

She told them about Mandy, who had already been back to the shop, presenting her with a box containing a bite-sized cupcake, topped with a butterfly crafted from spun sugar.

'She's already got a new fizz about her,' she said. 'She's full of energy, full of new plans. I told her that the woman who used to own that dress would have followed her heart's desire, no matter what.'

'And who else, then?' David leaned back in his chair. 'There are others too, I'm guessing?'

Fabia told them about the woman in her sixties who had lost her husband last year to a long illness. She'd stepped into the shop in a drab, camel-coloured coat and she'd fingered the silk of one of Eustacia's blouses – midnight blue, seed-pearl buttons – with such longing that Fabia had urged her to try it on, even though she'd secretly earmarked it for herself.

As she'd watched this woman turn in front of the mirror, the blouse tucked into the high waistband of a pair of black wide-legged trousers, she'd known this had been the right thing to do. A slow, soft smile began to creep over the woman's face and then she put up a hand to stifle a giggle.

'I look almost glamorous, like Katharine Hepburn. I can't believe that's me,' she'd said, so that Fabia couldn't resist asking permission to play a little. She'd rolled back the woman's fringe, pinning it with a small diamante clip, and placed a long tortoiseshell cigarette holder between her fingers. Her customer couldn't stop smiling.

Then there was Mrs Stubbs, the owner of the shoe shop across the street. Fabia passed it almost every day. Its windows were full of brown lace-ups and Mary Janes with cushioned soles and rubber heels. 'Built for comfort,' said the slogan across the top of one of the displays.

'I could never wear something like that. Not me,' Mrs Stubbs had joked, on her first visit to Fabia's shop, watching her daughter try on an Yves Saint Laurent 1970s dogstooth suit with generously cut palazzo pants and fitted cropped jacket. But when she'd dropped in to pick up her daughter's alterations, Fabia had seized her moment.

'I was just thinking of you,' she'd said, holding up one of Eustacia's gowns, a loose, drop-waist shift in plum-coloured crepe with a very plain boat neck. 'You know, for your little family celebration . . . I thought it was just the thing.'

'For me?' Mrs Stubbs had frowned. 'Really? I don't do dresses as a rule. They never fit me right, dear. You see, I'm all out of proportion.'

'Tsk. What nonsense,' Fabia smiled. 'I think it's perfect for you. And so easy to wear, so very *comfortable*. With some lovely flats, of course.' She held up a pair of soft-soled metallic slippers. 'Or perhaps a very slight kitten heel.'

'Well,' said Mrs Stubbs, looking at her watch. 'I've got time. I suppose there's no harm in trying it on.'

In front of the mirror, she'd turned and breathed, running her fingers over the fabric of the sleeves, pointing her toes in the sparkling slippers. 'I don't know what to say. I'd never have thought . . . I mean, quite honestly, I feel twenty years younger!'

Ella listened to Mamma telling the story of Mrs Stubbs. She sipped surreptitiously at her glass of wine. That was one good thing about David, she supposed. He always insisted on pouring her a very small glass. Well, when it wasn't a school night, anyway.

'So, Mum, what words have you chosen for all these customers?' she said, playfully.

Fabia's hand stopped in mid-air on its way to gathering up a plate. She let it fall to her lap.

'I haven't, yet,' she said, frowning, giving Ella one of her Meaningful Looks and then nodding at the glass in her hand, 'Haven't you had enough of that already?'

'What do you mean? What words?' David said, smiling at the look that he'd seen pass between them. 'What's this all about?'

'Oh, it's just a little thing I do.' Fabia was annoyed now, beginning to noisily gather up the plates and cutlery. 'A little sales thing. You know . . .'

'No,' said David, his eyes twinkling. 'I don't know. I'm not following . . .'

Ella grinned.

'Mum thinks of a word for each customer. She holds the person in her mind like this . . .'

Ella drew herself up in her chair and demonstrated gazing off regally into the distance, humming an 'Om' sound and bringing the tips of her fingers and thumbs together.

'Then *abracadabra!*' She clicked her fingers. 'She gets it. The totem word. The little bit of magic. She sews it into their clothes.'

'Really?' said David. 'A totem, you say? How very intriguing . . .'

Fabia could see that he was stifling a laugh.

'Yes, and she sews it *in a hidden place*. One they'll never see. A seam or a hem or –'

'*Sssh* now, Ella,' Fabia cut in. 'You're making me look silly. I'm sure David doesn't want to hear about this.' She rolled her eyes at him. 'It's just a bit of silly nonsense, from when Ella was a little girl.'

She began piling the plates in the sink, spinning the hot tap, releasing a fierce jet of water and steam. As she turned back to the table, wiping her hands on a tea towel, she tried not to meet Ella's eye.

'It's a game Ella and I used to play. She'd try to think of a word that would describe a particular person. Then we'd embroider it onto a dress –'

'Always nice words, of course,' said Ella, helpfully.

'Yes,' said Fabia, regaining her composure. 'Always beautiful words. And – it sounds so silly, really – but when Ella was very young, I'd tell her that the words were a kind of spell, a magic charm. *Eccola*. A bit of magic for a little girl.'

Now she risked a glance in Ella's direction. She saw her daughter's expression waver for a moment. She was sure that she must be picking up on The Signals she was sending: Red. Stop. Danger. A single tongue of flame. The air crackled with it.

Finally she saw Ella catch it, the rising heat, the faint smell of smoke in the room.

Fabia turned away, opening the fridge, letting its white hum cool her.

'Now, who'd like some of this *torta*?'

16

Bolt of white linen with loops attached, to be strung as canopy or awning. Birds embroidered at each corner. Some sun damage.

Fabia flexed her toes against the warm enamel of the bath. She noticed with displeasure that her nail varnish was chipped and that a reddish lump had appeared on the side of her big toe – a bunion?

She took the block of Marseille soap and rubbed rich streaks of lather over her arms and shoulders, pausing at her collarbone, taking a deep breath of the scent. The truth was that she was getting old. Tonight, she *felt* old. There was a new aching in her bones, a longing that even the warm water couldn't dissolve.

She looked down at the soft fold of her belly, took a pinch of pink flesh between her finger and thumb and let out a sigh. In fact, she'd never before been afraid of getting older. As a girl, Madaar-Bozorg had always told her that it was a good thing to acquire your years. She'd spoken of her own age as something she wore with pride on her body, tracing the tiny silver scars on her thighs, the delicate network of stretchmarks on her stomach, the wrinkles around her eyes.

But it was different here, Fabia thought. Day after day, she saw her customers turn in front of the mirror, holding their stomachs in, poking at the cushioning over their hips or the loose skin of their upper arms with annoyance, even anger. She had to work especially hard to convince them of their beauty, smoothing a seam, inserting a dart or pinning a brooch – and then choosing the right words, of course, to stitch into a waist or a pocket so that the wearer would be infused with new confidence.

She arched her back, let her eyes close and her head sink backwards until her face was just below the surface of the water. She listened to the roar of water in her ears, the drip-drip of the tap and a clanking and shuddering in the old pipework far below her.

An image swam up to her then. Something she hadn't remembered in a long time. A group of women waiting in the courtyard of the Jobrani sisters' house in Tehran, their scarves pushed back from their heads, their hair uncovered, chattering eagerly among themselves.

Every Tuesday the women would come, standing and waiting under the white linen awning that Mahdokht, the youngest of Madaar-Bozorg's sisters, would string from two poles. Inside, in the large cool living room, the three sisters would spread their cloth across the tiled floor, rolls of silk and cotton and brocade spilling over the geometric patterns of the tiles, and their customers – one by one – would enter and stand before the long mirrored wall, cooing with delight as three pairs of hands snipped and pinned the fabric around them, tweaking it here, draping it there, until it hung just right.

As a girl, Fabia loved to stand in the doorway and listen to the women in the courtyard. She felt the crackle of excitement that leapt between them as they anticipated their new garments – a dress or a shawl – or whatever it might be that the sisters would decide to make for them. It was there, peering into the dim cavern of that living room, that Fabia first learned of the power in the cloth, and the magic in the words that Talayeh, Mahdokht and especially her beloved Madaar, whose given name was Zohreh, would select for each woman.

She'd watch as the sisters took it in turns to close their eyes, breathe deeply and let the words come. In those days, one of them might whisper a phrase in a customer's ear as she stood in front of the mirror. At such times, Fabia would see the woman's face light up, or crumple in puzzlement so that Madaar, the eldest of the sisters, would lay a hand on her arm saying, 'It will all become clear to you, *habibeh*. Don't worry. Hold these words close to you and their meaning will make itself known. Perhaps tonight when you're sleeping, perhaps tomorrow – perhaps even next month. But you will know soon. You will *know*.'

Fabia would watch each woman leave the house carrying herself a little taller, reciting a word under her breath or fingering the sleeve or the neckline of a finished garment. And she would know that the three sisters had somehow reached inside each woman and drawn out a single, fragile thread, something that, over days and weeks, would become stronger, more resonant, unravelling into the future.

But then there was the day when a man had strode through the courtyard, sending the women scattering, hastily covering their heads. Mahdokht, the youngest aunt, who was always the most nervous, dropped the glass into which she was pouring coffee and watched helpless, unable to move as the liquid spread its stain over a length of blue silk and over the red and yellow tiles on the floor.

But Madaar-Bozorg had stood her ground. She'd faced the man squarely, her hands with their jewelled fingers pressed firmly to her hips, as he made his complaint about how they'd filled his wife's head with nonsense, how she was no longer satisfied and would not keep his house, how she had ideas, crazy ideas, that he could never allow to happen, how they'd wrecked his marriage, made him a laughing stock.

Fabia watched from her place in the shadows as Madaar-Bozorg listened, her head on one side, her lips in their crimson lipstick pressed firmly together. Then she heard her say, slowly: 'Oh, pull yourself together, man. You ought to be ashamed of yourself – coming here, causing a scene, frightening these poor women, suggesting such ridiculous things. I thought you were an intelligent man, a rational man, a man of science . . . What do you think we are, my sisters and I? A bunch of witches?'

She gestured behind her at the rolls of cloth, the table heaped with spools of silk and magazine cuttings. 'We make clothes, beautiful clothes, that's all. Clothes that women want to wear. This is 1966, in case you hadn't noticed.'

The man had gone away, ashamed. He had even, Fabia seemed to remember, begged Madaar-Bozorg's forgiveness. He'd got carried away, he said, by silly talk of magic words and totems.

But things had changed a little after that. There were fewer women waiting in the courtyard the next Tuesday morning and Madaar had focused more on her university work, her teaching and the writing of her academic book, a study of the role of women in Iranian folklore.

Now Fabia opened her eyes and reached up, loosening the hair from its coil at the nape of her neck, letting it fan out around her, tickling her shoulders. She thought of Ella's outburst earlier that evening – how it was all a bit of a game to her, something secret and forbidden and therefore endlessly interesting – and how powerful it must make her feel to hint at things that she knew Fabia didn't want David know.

Because Ella, this girl who had grown up in a very different place, far away from that courtyard full of waiting women, could never understand the places in Fabia's heart where fear curled, cold and gelid. And David, a logical man, a real English gentleman, could never be expected to understand these things either. Magic words, charms, the whisper of silk against skin, a hand caressed by the lining of a pocket, the secret weight of a hem.

She thrust herself up through the water, reaching for her towel. No, there really were some things better kept to herself. She couldn't believe now that she'd risked so much when Ella was younger. She hadn't thought ahead about the questions Ella might ask, the conclusions she might jump to, here in such a different time and place.

Fabia stood and opened the tiny bathroom window, letting the cool night air slap her cheeks and the fragrant steam escape. She rubbed at her legs with the rough towel, feeling the strength return to her calves and ankles, enjoying the cool of the lino floor. Yes, some things were hers to keep close, for Ella's own good. To keep Ella safe.

She wiped at the mist-covered mirror and looked at her face reflected there. A woman smiled back at her, a woman who had lived. And yes, she thought, she liked the new lines around her eyes, the creases at the corner of her mouth.

She cupped the warm skin of her belly in both hands and smiled.

*

Mamma picked up the letter from the mat and slipped her fingernail under the flap.

'Oh no,' she said and then, '*Catzo*!'

It was Saturday morning. David had stopped by between errands and was balancing on a stepladder, his arms stretched above his head, replacing a bulb in the chandelier. He laughed and the stepladder began to shudder, the chandelier swinging precariously in his hands.

'I don't even know what you're saying, Fabia, but I know that it's very rude.'

Mamma pulled a face. Today, in her little powder blue suit with the peplum jacket and short neat skirt, Ella thought that she could easily pass for a schoolgirl.

'Agh. It's one of my regular suppliers. He's let me down about the foiled silk I ordered,' she sighed. 'He's saying he can't get hold of it but I need it for Jean Cushworth's gown! *Dio mio*. I have to have that dress ready for next Friday. Saturday morning at the very latest. *Disastro*!'

Ella stepped out from the doorway.

'Mrs Cushworth? Katrina's mother?'

'Yes.' Mamma grimaced, mimicking a regal voice and pose. '"I want only the very best," she says to me. "It has to be very special, better than any of the dresses you're making for the other ladies . . . I have a certain . . . how can I put it, without you thinking me frightfully arrogant? There is a certain *expectation* from people in this town. One mustn't *disappoint* . . ."'

'Well, can she choose a different fabric? A different colour, perhaps?'

Mamma laughed. 'David, you obviously don't know women. When we make up our minds there's no changing! I really don't want to disappoint her. She's brought me a lot of business already.'

Then her face suddenly brightened.

'I could go to the wholesalers myself and pick up the silk. I've been making do for a while now with so many of my little bits and pieces. I wonder . . .'

'We could make a day of it,' said David. 'Monday's my day off.'

Mamma clasped her hands together.

'What fun! Ella could come with us. Would you like a trip to London, *carina*?'

Ella screwed up her face.

'Honestly, Mum. What are you like? I can't just take a day off school. You have to get special permission from Mrs Tillotson. And I'd miss stuff. I'd have to catch up. I'll be fine here on my own, though. Go. Have a great time.'

As she turned away, she caught Mamma's expression of dismay reflected in the shop window.

'Such a good girl. *Too* good,' she said to David, shaking her head.

But Ella knew that she wasn't that good. She had her own reasons for staying behind. She thought about them all the time now. She couldn't stop thinking about them.

On Monday, when the bell rang for the end of school, she turned down the corridor past the girls' cloakrooms, and there was Katrina, leaning on the wall, hips forward, shoulders back, a smile playing at the corner of her mouth.

'Hi, Ella,' she said, flashing a smile. 'I saw your mum at the station this morning. With *David* . . .'

Ella felt prickles of irritation tingle down her arms at the thought this seemed to imply: that it was a bit of a joke, the idea of her mother and Dr Carter going anywhere together.

'I thought I'd come home with you,' she said. 'Keep you company, so you won't be all lonesome. Besides, I've never been to your place.'

Ella's heart plunged. They were out of the door now and heading across the playground where she could see Billy hovering by the school gates. He saw Katrina and instantly, like an automatic reflex, his head snapped down and he started to walk off, his hands in his pockets, staring determinedly at the ground.

'Billy! Wait a minute!'

Ella turned and glared at Katrina.

Katrina raised an eyebrow. 'Oh, right. Like that, is it?' A smile hovered at the corner of her mouth.

When they reached the shop and Billy had helped Ella wrestle with the complicated door locks, Katrina ran ahead of them, up the stairs into the flat and began to walk into each of the rooms, picking up a book here, a trinket box there, saying, 'How *sweet*!' and 'So *tiny*. How *abso-lutely darling*!'

Ella exchanged a look with Billy and went into the kitchen. She banged the coffee filter loudly against the sink, scattering damp coffee grounds.

Katrina appeared in the doorway. 'What on earth are you doing?'

'Making coffee. What does it look like?'

'Um, honestly? Like you're brewing up some weird kind of spell in the sink,' said Katrina, wrinkling her nose. 'Smells awful!'

'Right then, I'm off.' Billy shoved his hands into his pockets.

Ella's heart banged in her chest. 'But we only just got here . . .'

'Things to do, people to see,' said Billy. 'I'll leave you ladies to it.'

'I'll see you off then,' Ella said, perhaps a bit too quickly. 'I mean, I'll have to unlock the door and lock it again behind you.'

She followed him down the stairs and, while she fumbled with the keys once more – middle latch, top and bottom bolts – Billy hissed at her under his breath.

'God, El, how can you stand her?'

'Oh, do I have a choice? I hadn't noticed.'

'Here, I'll do that.' He slipped the key out of her hand. His fingers were firm and warm and sent little jolts of feeling through her.

The door gave way. The bell jangled.

'Well, then. Be seeing you,' he said, winking. 'Don't forget to have fun.'

'Billy –'

He turned, expectantly.

'Oh, it's nothing. Doesn't matter . . .'

She watched him cross the courtyard, under the low archway. She felt flat, limp, like a party balloon with the air gone out of her. What had she even been thinking, anyway?

And then, as she stood there, Billy's head suddenly reappeared around the far wall, a clown's head without a body, eyes crossed, mouth pulled askew, tongue waggling.

She stuck her tongue out back at him, sensing the strange new pull of feeling between them. He'd known she would still be standing here, watching.

This wasn't at all like the usual kind of Signals, colours and movements in the air around her that she could tune into. This was something that came from inside her. It felt as if she and

SOPHIE NICHOLLS

Billy were attached to opposite ends of a piece of elastic, each of them tugging in their own direction, straining as the elastic got tighter and tighter, wondering exactly how far it would stretch before snapping them back hard.

The bottom stair creaked. Katrina was standing there, her back turned, running her hands up and down her sides, wriggling her body as if held in the grip of a comedy embrace, making fake kissing sounds.

'Oh, get lost, Katrina,' Ella sighed.

Later, as they sat at the kitchen table, sharing the *timballo*, the round cake of pasta, cheese, sausage and rich tomato sauce that Mamma had left, Katrina prodded the air with her knife.

'Don't you ever get sick of it?'

'Sick of what, exactly?'

'Oh, you know. Life in general. Being an only child. Not that I'm a proper "only", you know. I mean, you've probably heard that there was . . . I mean, I had . . .'

Ella waited. She watched Katrina lay down her fork and scrutinise her plate. When she looked up again, she said, 'What really bugs me is the way that my mum – well, mine and yours are the same, probably – are always going off with someone. All that business . . .' She pursed her lips, making more air kisses.

'Mine doesn't,' Ella said. 'It's the first time she's ever been anywhere without me.'

'Well, mine does it all the time.' Katrina frowned. 'And I hate it. It's always Mr So-and-So this, Mr So-and-So that. Katrina, *sweetheart*, I *must* introduce you to my new friend, Mr So-and-So. Lately, it's that awful Pike person. You know the one.'

She squinted her eyes and combed her hair across her forehead with her fingers in imitation of Pike's greasy fringe.

'Yes,' Ella said. 'He came in the shop.' She felt a stab of fear at the sound of the name, remembered those eyes slithering over her.

'Really?' said Katrina, suddenly interested. 'What was he doing in a dress shop, for God's sake? Did he buy anything?'

'I don't think so.' Ella formed her words carefully, realising her mistake. 'It was just when we first got here . . . something about the Council. That's what he does, isn't it?'

'He'd be trying it on with your mum, probably. Eyeing her up,' Katrina said. 'He's a snake. But I hear that your mum's not stupid enough to get mixed up with someone like that, whereas mine's got no common sense. There's always bloody someone. It's so embarrassing – she's like a teenager. And then there's all the committee meetings. Committee for this, Circle for that . . . so that she can feel important, I suppose.'

'But what about your dad?'

'Oh, my so-called *father*,' said Katrina, rolling her eyes. 'An idiot,' she said. 'Completely clueless. Wouldn't know what she was up to from one minute to the next. Even if he did, he wouldn't be interested. He's old enough to be *her* father and he's almost always in France or America or Hong-bloody-Kong, selling his stupid equipment.'

'What kind of equipment?'

'Oh, I don't flippin' know, do I? Stuff for making your lights go on and off, watering your garden automatically and air-conditioning and heating. Stupid. Totally ridiculous. But all Terribly Important, of course.'

Katrina chased a piece of penne around her plate, trying to spear it with her fork.

'What is this stuff, anyway? It's weird.'

'It's *timballo*, which means drum. You take a bowl and you line it with *penne* pasta – you know, it's called that because it's shaped like feathers . . . Well, actually, like little quills – and then you put all these different things in – meat and peas and more pasta and cheese sauce and tomato sauce – and then –'

'Blimey. I don't need the bloody recipe!' Katrina pushed her plate away, rudely. 'It tastes funny. Too many flavours. It's kind of confusing my taste buds. And it'll be *packed* with calories.'

She dabbed at the corner of her mouth with her finger where a bead of tomato sauce clung on.

'No, I can't wait to get out of this place, for good. Do something useful.'

'Like what?'

She shrugged. 'I don't know. Just *something*. *Any*thing.'

'I quite like it in York, actually,' Ella said.

'Well, you've only just flippin' got here,' said Katrina and then her eyes lit up meanly. 'And, of course, you've got *Billy-boy* following you everywhere like a lovesick puppy. I mean, who wouldn't stick around for *that*?'

'Oh, shut up,' Ella said, scraping her chair back from the table, clattering plates together. 'Just. *Shut. Up.*'

17

Small charm in the shape of an owl. Sterling silver. Hallmarked.

When Katrina had left, trailing her veiled insults and bad jokes, Ella stretched herself across the sofa, flicking through TV channels.

It was true, what she'd told Katrina. This was the first time that she could ever remember that she'd been home alone without Mamma. Mamma had always been on the protective side. 'In your face', is what Katrina would say.

'Will you have a good old snoop, then?' Katrina had asked. 'That's what I do. You know, when I'm bored and on my own. It's amazing what you find out.'

Ella tried not to think about Mamma's box in its hiding place under the bed but the more she wanted to resist, the stronger its pull became. She knew, anyway, that she'd been thinking about taking a look since Mamma had left that morning.

It was the book that intrigued her the most. She'd seen Mamma turning the pages, the well-thumbed paper whispering under her fingers. She hadn't been close enough to see anything clearly – but it looked, from where she'd been standing, as if every part of the paper was covered in tiny handwriting, along with sketches and diagrams. A recipe book, Mamma had said, but it didn't look much like one. And if it was, why didn't she keep it in the kitchen along with her Elizabeth David and the faded red Larousse?

Her phone bleeped with a text message: *On 7pm train. Home 10ish. Love M xxx*

OK xxxxxxxxxxxxxxxxxxxxxxxx she texted back.

Not much time left, then.

She pressed the 'mute' button on the remote and watched as a woman in a sombrero stood with her feet planted firmly in a turquoise ocean, throwing her arms around and miming her excitement at the glittering water.

She would look. Just one look, she promised herself. Five minutes.

She went into the bedroom and knelt by Mamma's bed, feeling into the gap for something box-shaped.

It was gone.

She threw back the duvet and pressed her cheek to the dusty floorboards. Nothing. Only shadows, fluff and a crumpled tissue imprinted with red lipstick.

She dragged a chair from the kitchen and clambered up, feeling with her hands along the top of the wardrobe. It wasn't there, either. She looked through Mamma's drawer, her hands moving through the layers of silk and lace, being careful not to leave anything disturbed.

So Mamma *was* hiding something, after all. She must have moved the box right after they'd had that conversation.

Ella clenched her fists. She clattered down the stairs and went through the boxes under the shop counter, the reels of gift ribbon, the neatly folded piles of tissue paper. She peered into the musty cupboard under the stairs where Mamma kept the mop and bucket and shelves of cleaning supplies.

She ran back up the stairs again, taking them two at a time, and slipped her hand under Mamma's pillow. Her fingers closed over something. She drew out a single tarot card, a picture of a woman sitting on a throne in pale blue robes, with a large cross around her neck and some kind of strange horned crown on her head. Her face was inked with a serene expression and she held what looked like a scroll in her hands. Behind her, between two pillars, was a pattern of palm leaves and pomegranates, their skins split to reveal glistening red seeds. At the woman's feet was written: THE HIGH PRIESTESS.

Ella felt her heart banging against her ribs. Her skin felt hot and tight with frustration. What did that even *mean*?

The card seemed to quiver slightly in her hands and she thought she could almost feel the air stirring around her again, and hear voices, somewhere out there beyond the corners of the room, laughing and laughing at her.

She threw the card on the bed and then, thinking better of it, replaced it carefully under Mamma's pillow, smoothing the quilt.

But later as she lay in bed with her book, the words swimming in front of her, she couldn't shake the feeling that she was being laughed at, tricked in some way. It wasn't fair. What was it that she wasn't allowed to know?

She let her eyes close, let her mind contract to that still, quiet point and then let herself drift backwards inside her mind, back to the day when she'd first seen the book.

She'd been standing in the doorway of the bedroom, just a few days after they'd arrived here, watching Mamma stoop over the bed, the book lying on the quilt in front of her. She could just glimpse flashes of colour and hear a crackling sound, like dry leaves, as Mamma carefully turned the pages.

'Mamma?'

She saw Mamma whip round, her tight, forced smile, the way that she'd closed the book with a snap.

'Mamma, what are you doing?'

'Oh, just looking at a few old things, *tesora*. Things I've found in all these boxes. Things I haven't seen in ages. Be a darling, would you. Put some coffee on for me? I'm exhausted.'

Then, as she'd turned to leave the room, Ella had seen, through the chink in the door jamb, Mamma kneeling by the bed, lifting the quilt, pressing the floorboards with the flats of her hands, the faint creak of wood.

That was it. That was Mamma's hiding place. It all made sense now. She threw off her covers and scrabbled on her hands and knees under Mamma's bed, feeling along the edges of the painted floorboards for a break, a gap, a loose nail. Her fingers butted up against a splintered edge. She pulled the quilt impatiently over her head and peered into the darkness, levering with her fingernails. There was a groaning sound as one of the boards came up in her hand, revealing what she could just make out as a long narrow cavity.

She put her hand in, carefully at first because the dark space made her cringe, thinking of the scratching sounds she sometimes heard at night – mice perhaps, or even something worse – her fingers closed around a long flat box and she lifted it out, running her hand over the red, cloth-covered surface that was slightly grainy with dust.

Even though she knew that she was alone in the flat, she couldn't help looking quickly over her shoulder before setting the book in the middle of the rug. She felt the air gathering again, bunching up all around her, heard those voices, half-real, half-imagined: *She's here, she's here, she'shereshe'shereshe'shere.*

She lifted the lid. Yes, here it was. The book.

It was a strange book, its covers made from two rectangular pieces of board, covered with green watermarked silk and tied together with thick black ribbon. The cover was stained in places, marked with grease and age, and the pages were thick and uneven. At certain points between the pages, scraps of fabric and what looked like the edges of dress-making patterns poked out.

Ella's fingers fumbled with the ribbon. She felt her heart banging again, noticed that her hands were trembling slightly as she opened the cover, turned to the first page and read the inscription:

This book belongs to:
Zohreh Jobrani
~~Farah Jobrani~~
Fabia Moreno

The first name – Madaar-Bozorg's name – was written in small, neat cursive handwriting, the ink faded to a brownish-black. Ella recognised the style – although the writing had been firmer, less spidery back then – from all the blue airmail envelopes with the exotic stamps that had arrived intermittently through the letterbox throughout her childhood.

The names beneath it were added in what Ella immediately knew as Mamma's own confident copperplate. And Farah, of course, was her mother's original birth name, her given name from the Old Country, carefully scored out here with the tip of her fountain pen.

She turned the pages again, noticing the faint rustling in the corners of the room and the way that the air stirred over the backs of her hands like the beating of a thousand tiny wings.

Here was one of Mamma's sketches, a red tea gown with a sweetheart neckline, a few tiny red beads stitched to the page, a scrap of red silk.

Then the notes, scribbled in the margins: *Red: ruby, scarlet, vermilion. Look for a good red fabric with a warm orange base, rather than blue. This sample from Borowicks of Berwick Street, London. Variations – remake from red wedding sari, edged with gold lace? Chinoiserie – too stiff?*

She flipped forward in the book again, stopping at a page that shimmered with green – a green feather, sewn to the paper with carefully matched embroidery silk, a short length of sequin trim in emerald, a little pouch made of bottle-green satin with a card spool of glittery green thread tucked inside it. A picture cut from a magazine, showing a model wearing a green pillbox hat at a jaunty angle, a large peacock plume falling half over her face. *Vogue 1948*, Mamma had written underneath. *Use dyed ostrich feathers?*

Samples, sketches, ideas. Nothing here to be hidden away, surely? Why all the secrecy?

She turned back to the front of the book, which seemed to be written mainly by Madaar-Bozorg, with Mamma's notes squeezed into the margins.

'*The story of the selkie*,' she read, fingering a folded pattern in translucent paper, one edge stitched to the page. She pulled at it carefully and it concertinaed outwards, forming the shape of what looked to her untrained eye, like a bodice. But, she'd never seen Mamma use a pattern. She always cut the cloth directly on the table, her scissors snipping swiftly, barely hesitating as she formed the shapes that she would piece together.

Ella held the pattern up to the light, squinting to make out the miniscule writing that covered it: '*Once upon a time,*' she read, '*in the land of long hot summers and short cold winters, where the corn grows high and golden, where the oranges glow like lanterns in the trees and the bread is the sweetest and most delicious that you've ever tasted, there lived a sad and lonely man.*'

She smiled to herself, thinking of the many times she'd heard those same words from Mamma's lips. Carefully, she folded the pattern back into place, imagining Mamma as a little girl, her head resting on her grandmother's shoulder, as Madaar-Bozorg told her this same story of the sealskin.

But still, this wasn't magic. Certainly not secret. It didn't explain why Mamma was hiding this book away. Her fingers moved between the pages more hastily now, looking for clues.

'*Placement of charms,*' she read, finding a well-thumbed page. '*The effect of a particular word can be augmented by combining it with a particular charm, or by placing it in a certain position in the garment. Placement at the collar, for example, can give extra confidence, helping the wearer to hold her head high. Placement at the hem can have a grounding effect. (Consider also the insole of a shoe.) The edge of a sleeve can assist with interactions with others and ease relationships.*

'*The combination of charm placement with chosen totem words and particularly colour should also be considered carefully. Some colours – red, for example – are often powerful enough and need no further help. We should aim for subtlety and comfort for the wearer. Over time, this will have the appropriate effect.*

'Before use, charms should be "cleansed" by placing them on a windowsill in sunlight or moonlight, by burying them in complete darkness or passing them through the flame of a red candle.'

In complete darkness, thought Ella, thinking of the gap under the floorboards. She reached back into the box. And yes, here was bundle of red candles tied with a white ribbon and here a small screw-top jar. The contents rattled against one another – charms, the little brass and silver weights that Mamma liked to sew into the hems of lighter weight fabrics, so that they hung just so. Ella tipped a handful onto her palm: an owl, not much larger than her little fingernail, but still perfect in its detail, with eyes and beak and tufted ears; a lucky horse-shoe; a pair of angels' wings.

This *was* more interesting. She'd been right. It was magic. Everyday magic, maybe, but magic just the same. Mamma's charms and words were more than a game. Madaar-Bozorg, at least, seemed to think of them as spells.

Ella had never seen anything lying around on a window-sill – although now she thought about it, it was certainly true that Mamma liked to sit in a patch of sunlight to do her most delicate work, what she called 'finishing', the last point in the fitting or alteration of a garment. She'd angle her chair to catch the sun or, when the weather was warm enough, she liked to sit outside.

Her heart fluttered in her chest as she turned to the next page.

*'**Words**,'* Madaar-Bozorg had written, the letters fiercely underlined. *'The best words are not chosen. They choose them-selves. While working on the garment, try to relax your mind and focus only on the feel of the fabric, the movement of your fingers. Let the words find you.'*

Underneath, in tiny cramped script, she'd made a list of dates and details:

'*19 June 1953 – blue scarf, both hems – open your heart.*

'*6 July 1953 – yellow silk gown, interlining at décolleté – courage, a sunlit hour.*

'*18 September 1953 – embroidered housecoat, hem – patience.*

'*29 February 1954 – red wool suit, jacket pocket lining – carry your truth.*'

At the end of this list, in large capitals she'd added: *'I EVENTUALLY CONCLUDED THAT WORDS SHOULD NOT BE RECORDED ANYWHERE BUT IN THE CLOTHES THEMSELVES.'*

Ella shivered. Was she imagining the little breeze that seemed to blow quite suddenly through the chinks in the old wooden window frame and whirl around the room? She felt a cool touch on her cheek.

It was clear that Madaar-Bozorg had believed in the power of these charms and word spells, that she'd passed them down to Mamma. So why was Mamma so determined to keep these things hidden from *her*? Why did she go on insisting that it wasn't magic? She felt that hot bead of anger bubble up in her again. It wasn't fair. Didn't Mamma trust her? It wasn't as if she was a child anymore. Why couldn't Mamma just explain these things instead of being all cloak and dagger about it?

She closed the book, tying the black ribbons in a precise bow, returning it and the jar and the candles to the box, replacing the lid, being careful to wipe away her finger-marks from the film of dust.

She lay staring up at the ceiling for a long time, watching the patch of orange from the next door café's security light waver over the pale plaster. She counted the Minster bells chiming the hour – ten and then eleven . . .

Just as she was drifting down that familiar wide black river, the stars swooping down to touch her face, she heard the jingle of the shop bell far below her and the sound of Mamma's muffled laughter. She dug her nails into the palms of her hands, tucked her knees up under her and dived deeper into the cloudy darkness.

When Ella woke up the next morning, Mamma was already in the kitchen, peering at her reflection in the kettle, patting and primping her newly cropped hair.

'Blimey,' Ella said, still feeling cross. 'That's drastic.'

Mamma spun round and crossed the kitchen, flinging her arms wide. '*Tesora*. There you are. Were you OK? You weren't too lonely? I had *such a lovely time*! Next time, you have to come with us!'

Her eyes were more luminescent than ever in her small heart-shaped face, newly framed by the short dark hair.

Ella let herself be hugged.

'Are you all right, Ella? Has something happened?'

She shook her head, helping herself to a piece of toast, buttering it fiercely.

Mamma bent over the toaster, examining her reflection one more time. She fingered a strand of hair.

'It was just – how do you say? – an *impulse*? We were walking past a salon and I thought, well, I haven't done anything with it in so long, so I thought, why not cut it all off! Be modern! Be brave!' Her voice was higher than usual, coming out in little breathy gasps.

Ella remembered all the evenings that she'd taken the tortoiseshell comb to Mamma's hair, moving her arm down its
shining length, feeling its softness stroking the backs of her
hands, the rhythmic motion calming her.

'It's lovely, Mum,' she relented. 'It's cool. It really suits you.'

Everything was changing so fast.

18

Apron, vinyl-coated cotton with slogan. British Home Stores.

'Want to come with me somewhere?'

She had her head out of the window, letting the afternoon sun, reflected off the rooftops, wash her face clean. A pigeon basking in the guttering rattled upwards in a hiccup of feathers.

Billy was standing in the courtyard, shielding his eyes from the sun, squinting up at her. 'Well, then. Are you coming with me or not?'

'Give me five minutes.' She rushed to the bathroom to clean her teeth and tidy her hair. She'd started doing this lately. Whenever Billy called for her, she felt her stomach flip. It was like having a goldfish swimming around her insides. Really very annoying.

She often caught herself wondering if Billy preferred her hair like this, or like this instead, arranging it this way or that, and pinching colour into her cheeks in the freckled bathroom mirror, a tip she'd read in one of Katrina's mum's magazines.

'Where are you off to, Billy?' she could hear Mamma calling from downstairs. 'Where are you taking my daughter? I need to know.'

Billy was pacing up and down the courtyard, jumpy with impatience. He tapped his nose with his finger. 'It's a surprise, Mrs Moreno,' he said, 'Don't make me give it away.'

'Well, you be careful.' Mamma summoned her sternest tone, 'I'm holding you responsible, young man.'

Billy had crept under Mamma's skin somehow, in that way he had. The quick grin, the winks and nudges, they worked on you sideways, like he had a magic all of his own.

As she stood watching them throw words back and forth, easily, fluently, like sunlight across the cobblestones, she wondered what *her* magic was. No one ever seemed to respond to her in that way.

Billy produced a mock swagger. 'Now you *know* you can trust me, Mrs Moreno. What am I going to do, anyway? Shove 'er in the river?'

'Who knows? I wouldn't put it past you.'

He was still chuckling to himself as they turned out of the courtyard to join the polite push of Saturday shoppers along the narrow streets.

'I want to show you something,' he said. 'Something I bet you've never seen before.'

'What? Why can't you tell me now? I hate surprises.'

But he refused to be drawn.

They reached the cool damp of the trees that fringed the approach to the riverbank. The new leaves hung down in shimmering tassels, almost touching her face.

'Seen them yet?'

In among the trees and over the grassy banks, the geese were honking louder then she'd ever heard, picking up their webbed feet in a proud and determined march, making short-sightedly for the river.

'You don't need to be scared of them,' Billy had told her before. 'They're all mouth and no trousers, geese. Their eyes are on the side of their heads so they can't see in front of them at all.'

171

He'd demonstrated by clapping his hands in front of a hissing beak. 'See. Can't see in front of their faces. Most people don't realise that.'

This morning, the geese seemed unusually determined. A woman hurried past on the riverside path with a bag of shopping and swerved to avoid a convoy, sticking out their sinewy necks and snapping their wings.

As Ella looked more closely, she suddenly saw the reason why. In front of them, in a doddery line, several fluffy goslings tottered towards the water.

Billy grinned. 'Want to get closer?'

They found a place on the grassy bank that was still unsplattered by goose droppings and watched. She rested her back on a tree trunk, feeling the roughness of the bark through the material of her blouse. The heat was already gathering just above the river's surface. Flies hovered in the shimmer, like stray sequins. The hawthorns and chestnuts were draped with fat loops of pink and white blossom like feather boas, and when she closed her eyes for a moment she could see the sun stamped on the insides of her eyelids in a perfect disc of gold.

'Look. These ones here have only got one,' said Billy as a mother and father goose urged their single gosling in front of them.

'Like me, I suppose.' Ella wondered if it was only her imagination that saw the expression in the eyes of these geese parents, the way they walked more hesitantly and quietly, a little apart from the other more raucous families.

'Those over there are more like me and my brothers, then,' laughed Billy, watching a group of six or seven jostling one another into the water. 'Speaking of which,' he added, 'let's go.'

'Where?' she said, 'Where are we going now?'

Her limbs were heavy and drowsy. She didn't want to move.

'Well, I thought you wanted to come? Didn't you? Have a cup of tea with Mum? She's desperate to meet *you*, I can tell you!'

So this, Ella thought, was what Billy had meant. Mrs Vickers poured tea from a huge brown pot, the glaze crazed from years of just-boiled water. Ella balanced the cup and saucer on her knee in the dark front room and sipped carefully.

She really didn't like tea. She'd only tried it a couple of times before and she thought that it tasted like perfume, tart and chemical on her tongue. The milk looked faintly sickening, making white whorls across the top of the pale brown liquid. She was used to black coffee in tiny cupfuls, hot sips of fragrant steam.

'We've heard a lot about you, dear.' Mrs Vickers was smiling. She had a kind face, grey hair scooped up into a bun on the top of her head from which wisps escaped and floated around her cheeks like a fuzzy halo. The sun coming in through the window made this halo of hair flare and shimmer so that she seemed almost to glow.

She looked more like a grandmother than a mother, Ella thought. She wore a wipe-down apron, bright pink and printed with the words, 'KEEP CALM AND EAT CAKE.' Underneath it, her body looked soft and floury, like a well-baked loaf.

'All those stories. Billy tells them to me sometimes,' she said. 'I love to hear them. I've always liked a good story.'

'You should come into the shop some time, Mrs Vickers. I'm sure my mum would love to meet you.'

Mrs Vickers looked amused. 'Now what would I be doing in a posh shop like your mum's? I wouldn't know where to put myself.'

Ella asked if she could use the bathroom. It was a small room built on the back of the kitchen, smelling of bleach and cold.

She pressed her cheek against the cool of the wall. Her hands felt clammy and her heart pounded in her chest. She wasn't sure why.

Mrs Vickers had said that the shop was posh. Ella had always thought that 'posh' was for people like Katrina, with wedding-cake houses and gardens the size of parks. She didn't want to be posh. That was just one more way of being different, wasn't it?

She bent over the sink to pat water onto her cheeks. Behind the taps, a plastic beaker bristled with toothbrushes, so many that they didn't all quite fit. On a small painted wooden chest, several sets of razors and shaving brushes were laid out, each on a neatly folded towel.

On the back of the door hung a set of greasy overalls and a scrubbed enamel bath, which she guessed was for Billy's brothers to wash outside in the yard. The proper bath was so large and deep that she thought she might be able to float on her back in it, her hands hardly touching the sides at all. At the bottom of the bath were two coarse and crinkly black hairs, left behind by the bathwater. Yes, Billy's house was a house full of men.

When she emerged from the bathroom, the front room had filled up with them. Billy perched on a small wooden footstool while two large men spread themselves across the settee and another leaned in the doorway.

The seated men stood up as she came in and nodded their heads.

'Well, now, this must be the loveliness that's sent our Billy a bit soft,' said one, his face creasing with a familiar grin, and he took Ella's hand and bowed so low that his head nearly touched his knees. 'Pleased to make your acquaintance.'

'Don't mind Tommy, love. He's just messing about.' Another brother held out his hand to her. 'Billy's always been soft. But I'm Chris, his much more handsome other brother.'

Billy sprung up from the stool and made as if to punch Chris in the leg, but Tommy's hand shot out from his side and pulled Billy into a headlock so that all he could do was flail his arms around, muttering, 'Gerrof, Tommy, gerrof,' under his breath.

'Get on with you,' Billy's mum said. 'You're only embarrassing the poor girl.'

The older man, Billy's father, rolled his eyes heavenward, smiled and took Ella's hand in both of his. She noticed that he didn't have the wide grin of Billy and Tommy. His eyes were quiet and watchful. 'Nice to meet you, love.'

'C'mon then. Get yourselves washed and sorted,' said Mrs Vickers, 'There isn't room for all of you in here. We're trying to have a civilised conversation.'

Without another word, the men stretched themselves and moved off. Their boots clattered up the narrow hall and stairs and Ella watched Mrs Vickers wince as doors banged and floorboards creaked overhead.

'What a great lot of 'em!' She said as if she was suddenly surprised to find herself here in this house with all these men and couldn't quite remember where they'd come from.

Ella crumbled Mrs Vickers' cake between her fingers, a buttery sponge that left a white film of icing sugar on the willow pattern plate. She wiped her hands on the starched napkin and swirled cold tea in the cup and tried to say the right things in the right places and not say anything that sounded posh. All the time, she felt Billy watching her from his stool in the corner, his head cocked to one side.

Mr Vickers joined them again, his face pink and clean-shaven, his hair combed back from his forehead.

'So, Ella,' he said. 'Billy tells us you were down on the south coast before coming up 'ere. What was that like?'

'It was, erm . . . *nice*, I think,' she said, searching for an image or a phrase where she could find a foothold, something real to say. 'I liked the sea. I used to swim. But I like it here too, very much.'

'I hear there's a lot of trouble down there, lately,' said Mr Vickers, clearing his throat, watching her intently. 'On the coast. Problems with the workers at the docks, in the packing houses, the factories and so forth.' He nodded to himself. 'Yes, trouble, so we've heard through the Union. Things getting a bit hairy down there, to say the least.' And he looked at her again, a long searching look.

'I don't know, Mr Vickers. I suppose I wouldn't really know much about that . . .' She could feel a dark gap like a stain beginning to spread itself inside her.

''Course you wouldn't, love,' said Mrs Vickers, fixing her husband with a look. She cleared her throat. 'So you like to swim, you say. Well, Billy, now the weather's warming up a bit, you'll have to take Ella to the swimming platform.'

She turned to Ella, the light sparking the silver threads in her hair again.

'Yes, you might like that, love. I used to be a real one for swimming in the river when I was a girl.'

Then her face clouded over.

'Oh, but of course, what am I saying? Billy, you'll have to check with Mrs Moreno first. Yes, ask your mum, love. She might not want you going there. Better to ask her.'

Later, Billy walked her back home over the bridge.

'My idiot brothers,' he said, shaking his head. 'I did try to warn you. But you know they were only having a laugh, with what they said and everything, don't you?'

A pair of geese flew low over their heads, so low that Ella could feel the movement of the air made by their wings.

The evening was warm and spread out all around them. The surface of the river was smooth, the water moving beneath them like one long muscle.

She tipped back her head and felt the sky fall into her.

'Of course,' she said. 'Don't be silly.'

She didn't like to admit it, even to herself, but Jean Cushworth was feeling more than a little annoyed by the Moreno woman.

First, and it was undeniable now, she seemed to have got her claws into David Carter.

He'd caused quite a stir among her circle of ladies when he'd joined the local surgery as the new partner. Some of them, discovering that he was still unmarried, had taken to making quite crude jokes, remarking on his bedside manner, that kind of thing. Some of them, she was convinced, had even invented various aches and pains as an excuse to unbutton their blouses and have him pay them some attention. Sad, really.

But now she felt a nip of jealousy. She was willing to admit to that. For so long, she'd been looking for something more. And, yes, she may occasionally have toyed with the idea of David Carter.

Nothing serious, of course. She hadn't made a fool of herself over it. No one else would ever have known. It was only that he'd begun to feature quite prominently in her private afternoon fantasies.

For over a year now, the combination of her anti-depressant – a very low dose – and her lunchtime glass of wine meant that, most afternoons, she found it necessary to take herself off for a little lie-down. She'd pull the curtains and tell Leonora that she mustn't be disturbed and then she'd be perfectly free to abandon herself to a kind of half-dream in which the ordinary world receded for a while and she became her younger, more carefree self.

Lately, she'd found herself looking forward to this time, when she had nothing to do but sink into a mound of soft pillows and let her mind roam untethered. Sometimes it seemed as if this afternoon dream world was more real to her than any other. It was certainly much more enjoyable.

Now, especially since her last consultation with David Carter, she'd particularly liked running a certain scenario in her mind where she would perch on the edge of his desk, which she'd noted was large and sturdy and covered in embossed leather, and begin to unbutton her dress. David Carter – 'Please, call me Dave,' he'd purr – would bury his face between her breasts, inhale the expensive scent that she always applied at the base of her throat and begin to kiss her neck.

Just thinking about this now made her heart beat faster and she felt a hot flush – part pleasure, part embarrassment – or maybe it was just her hormones. Perhaps she really did need to make another appointment, after all. Get herself checked out properly.

She moved restlessly on the pillows, trying to find a more comfortable position, but she couldn't get the image of Fabia Moreno out of her mind.

She'd been shocked when Katrina arrived home, full of the news. Katrina had been quite bursting with it, almost desperate to tell her, with such a particular look on her face that Jean even wondered for a moment if her daughter knew what she was thinking.

She'd made out, of course, that she wasn't the least bit interested in a schoolgirl's gossip, but she'd felt as if a hand had gripped her insides and was twisting slowly.

No, Fabia Moreno didn't waste much time. Jean Cushworth had met her type before. Ambitious, determined, used to getting what she wanted. It was all really quite irritating.

So imagine how she'd felt today, visiting the shop for a fitting, to discover that the woman had this new haircut – short, very short – which, there was no denying it, made her look even more ravishing.

What annoyed Jean Cushworth more than anything about this was that both Vincent and James had been trying to persuade her to cut her hair shorter for the last year or so. Long hair can be terribly aging, Mrs C. Maybe it's time for a change. It will lift your face. You'd love it. And so much easier to look after . . . On and on, until she was forced to get quite snappy with them.

Her hair was her thing, her crowning glory. All her life, everyone had said so. She couldn't imagine what it would feel like not to be able to put up her hand and feel it there, silky and reassuring, or move her head at the right moment and feel it swing around her shoulders like the women in the shampoo adverts.

But Vincent had said those words and now they couldn't be unsaid. *Beyond a certain age* . . . She didn't like that at all. The idea of doing something bold and dramatic, something *new*, had its appeal. When she brushed her hair at night, she'd gather it in a handful at the nape of her neck, letting it loop below her cheekbones, trying to imagine what it would look like.

But the Moreno woman had got there first. If Jean decided to go shorter now, it would only ever look like imitation.

Maybe it really was true, what Graham had told her.

'The thing is, darling,' he'd drawled, slurping at a glass of his precious Chateau Neuf with that maddening expression on his face, 'you never do know what you want, do you? You always want what you didn't choose. You always think you should have done, *could* have done X, Y, Z, instead of focusing on what you *do* have, right in front of your pretty little nose and what you can make happen, if you only put your mind to it. You're scared, that's all, and you don't know how to be happy and you can't bloody admit it, so you make everyone else, Katrina and I included, bloody miserable. You never want anything until the minute that someone else tells you that you can't have it. If I were to take up with some young nubile thing, you'd suddenly want *me* again, not because you love me – I'm completely aware that you don't – but just because you wouldn't want anyone else to have me . . . Darling, why don't you just start being honest with yourself?'

Now she hoisted herself up on the bed, taking the sheaf of menus from the bedside table, noticing crossly that her new gel manicure was already beginning to peel away at the cuticles.

She tried to think of the party, casting her eye down the catering company's suggestions. There wasn't a thing she could find fault with, really. Canapés, buffet, drinks. It was all perfect.

She regretted now that she'd asked Fabia Moreno to design her dress. She'd already invited her, of course, and now she and David were almost certain to come together. She'd have to watch them making eyes at one another while Graham strutted around looking awful in his jeans and trainers – because she could never persuade him to dress up for anything – boring the pants off everyone with his corny jokes and endless chatter about his toys and gadgets and investments.

There'd be Pike, of course, but he didn't really count. She should have put an end to that, long ago. She didn't really know why she hadn't. He followed her around like a little yapping dog. It was embarrassing. It made her despise him. Although he was very attentive, in a way that Graham could never seem to be bothered with anymore, he wasn't exactly what she'd call interesting.

Jean let her mind drift back then, as she'd developed the habit of doing. She saw herself as a girl of eighteen, in a pale pink dress, standing on the terrace of her family home, Waring Park – and what had happened to that, of course, her inheritance? Her useless father had drunk it all away, that's what. But she could still remember how she'd felt, that evening, waiting for the guests to arrive, the air fragrant with jasmine and roses and the way that new dress had felt, the silk clinging at her breasts and swirling around her ankles. She could almost imagine that it was made of rose petals.

Everyone had admired her that night. She'd danced and danced and drunk too much champagne and handsome Bobby

Phelps had walked her out to the tennis courts and kissed her, a long lingering kiss. Her first. What had happened to Bobby? Married? Divorced? She couldn't remember.

And suddenly it seemed that she couldn't remember what had happened to anything. Thirty years or more. Gone. Just like that evening, it had all slipped through her fingers. And Laurence, her beloved boy. She could see him now, his hair wet from the shower after football, the dark curls stuck to his scalp making his green eyes appear even more luminous, and his body just beginning to fill out. It wasn't fair, that he'd been taken away from her. None of it was fair.

Here she was, with hair that wasn't even a real colour anymore and a body that was starting to sag, lying on a bed with the curtains drawn in the middle of the day. A solitary tear ran down her cheek. She pulled the quilt up around her. She felt ice-cold, almost numb. She couldn't even cry properly.

Finally, she flung the quilt off and fished in the back of the bedside cabinet. Her fingers touched the smooth glass of the bottle.

Hurriedly now, her hand trembling, she unscrewed the top, pressed the bottle to her lips and gulped.

The liquid warmed her instantly. She could feel it spreading through her insides. She took another gulp and then another.

19

Women's swimming costume, black lycra with white stripe down each side.

'Hey, Ella, can you do this, then?'

She was pressing her thumbnail into the stem of a daisy, slowly, carefully so as not to split it right through. She squinted upwards, shielding her eyes from the sun. Billy was dangling above her, head first over the river, the rope twisted deftly around his foot.

'Look, no hands!' He shimmied his arms up and down like clumsy wings.

'All right. My turn.' She stood up and began unbuttoning her skirt, easing her blouse over her head. She had her swimming costume on underneath but now, feeling Billy's eyes on her, she felt awkward, suddenly shy.

She busied herself making a neat bundle of her clothes, weighting them with a clean stone, resisting the urge to fiddle with the straps on her costume.

Billy had swung the rope back in and stood holding it for her above the swimming platform. Her toes sank in the warm mud and then gripped the slippery boards.

'Put one hand here, like this,' Billy said, placing her left hand on the rope, 'Then, once you've got some swing on it, pull down hard and aim your feet above your head. That way, you can flip yourself upside down.'

Ella looked at the river. It would be cool, clear and cool, down there under the water. She put the rope between her legs and swung it back across the platform, bracing her toes against the edge. Then she flew.

She let the pull of the rope take her out over the water, higher, higher. She felt the braided strands stretch and pull against one another, the creaking sound as the rope took and held her weight for a moment. She held her breath, feeling for the moment of stillness where her body, she knew, would hang perfectly in balance before beginning the return and, in this gap, she aimed her feet for the sky, slipping her foot easily into the loop, letting her head hang down.

For that one moment, she felt herself suspended there, her face inches from the surface. The river opened to her like a dimly lit room. She could just make out the shapes down there moving.

She let go of the rope, she let her foot slip from the loop. Just time to stretch out her arms and enter the water like an arrow, feeling the cold break over her body in a long green gasp.

She let the water take her deeper, gradually opening her eyes. There was a second sky down here, mud and silt, drifting like clouds. She tucked in her knees and crouched for a moment, looking up at the rectangles of light wobbling above her head, feeling the cool enter her bones. Only then, with her heart throbbing in her head, she pushed up and burst through the surface, re-entering the world.

The first thing she saw were Billy's white toes gripping the edge of the platform, his stricken face peering down into the water.

'For God's sake, Ella. What did you do that for? I thought for a minute you weren't coming back up!'

He grabbed her arms and hauled her up onto the platform where she lay on her back, looking up through the canopy of leaves, panting and laughing.

'Well, I'm glad *you* think it's funny, you mad loon,' said Billy, starting to pull his clothes back on. She could see that he was furious. 'You almost gave me a heart attack.'

She arched her back against the slippery planks, felt the tautness in her legs and arms and ran her tongue over the roof of her mouth, tasting the river again.

'Sorry,' she said, but she couldn't stop herself. The word burst out of her mouth in a big shudder of laughter. It was as if the water had opened her up and the sound was pouring out of her, taking hold of her ribs, her chest, her stomach. She hugged her knees to her chest and rocked back and forth on the boards, wheezing and laughing.

'Forgiven me yet?' Ella watched Billy's back as he strode along the river path, slashing at the tall grass with a stick as he went.

He turned and stuck the stick in the ground, folding his arms across his chest.

'Depends,' he said, grinning. 'But you'd better watch it. I'm gonna get you back. Honestly, Ella, I thought that was it. I was thinking about what I was going to tell your poor mum!'

Ella adjusted the towel she'd rolled in the crook of her elbow. Her limbs were still crackling with excitement but underneath the fizz of orange and blue there was a warm glow spreading through her legs and arms, the way that she always felt when she'd been in the water, as if the edges of her body were dissolving.

'I'm sorry,' she said.

'No, you're not.' Billy ran his hand through his hair, scattering water droplets.

Below them, on the river, a shiny white motorboat sent waves slapping against the bank. The man at the wheel saluted them, while a woman in large black sunglasses draped herself over the rail, squinting into the sunlight.

'Tourists,' said Billy. 'They get earlier every year. You'll see, El. By June, you won't be able to move down here. The whole place'll be full of picnickers, screaming kids and boats cruising up and down, churning everything up, making a racket.'

Ella frowned. It was hard to imagine that right now, with the shadows dappling the surface of the water. They'd seen no one else all afternoon.

'Yeah, and of course there's the new Boat Club. We've got your mate Katrina's mum to thank for that. Load of toffee-nosed idiots paddling around, pretending they know what they're doing, scaring away all the wildlife.'

As they rounded a bend in the path, he gestured to a newly painted sign: *York Boat Club. Private Members Only.*

'There was a petition, of course. People have been coming here for the last hundred years or more, swimming in the river, not bothering anyone. It's not private land. It's supposed to belong to everyone. But look how they've fenced it off. There's all kinds of birds here – kingfishers, I even saw a heron once, out on the mud – but that won't last long. Thousands of signatures, they got. But that Pike was in on it. Made sure Mrs Jean Cushworth had her way.'

He shook his head and slapped the sign with the end of his stick, leaving a spatter of wet soil on the glossy white and blue paintwork. 'They'll ruin everything that's good about the place and then they'll move on. Idiots, the lot of 'em.'

'Well, who do we have here?'

The voice was a menacing purr, drifting over to them from the other side of the new fence. Ella froze. Even without his black raincoat, she'd have recognised the man anywhere, the way that he thrust his chin forward as he walked, the way that, even now, he was looking at her, his eyes travelling up and down her body, taking her all in.

'Billy, lad. What're you up to, then?' Pike stood with his arms folded, his feet in their shiny black lace-up shoes planted wide apart.

'Taking a walk, Councillor. You know. Just enjoying the scenery.' Billy smiled his most charming smile but Ella could see the faint pulsing at his throat, the tension in the set of his shoulders.

'Well, as long as that's *all* that you're doing . . .' Pike smirked, then chuckled softly to himself. He turned to Ella. 'You want to watch him, my dear. He can be trouble, so I've heard, him and his brothers.'

His eyes travelled up and down her body again. 'Been swimming, have you?' he said, nodding at her wet hair, the towel under her arm. 'I imagine you're a strong swimmer . . .' He smiled at her again, the tip of his tongue darting over his thin lips.

Billy made a grab for her hand. 'C'mon, El. It's getting late. We'd better make a move.'

Pike nodded at them and turned away from the fence, smoothing his shirt against his chest, still smiling.

But even as she followed Billy, who was walking faster now, his stick slashing more fiercely at the grass, his towel trailing in the dirt behind him, she could feel Pike's eyes following her, burrowing between her shoulder blades. She could see in her mind's eye the way that he'd looked at her legs, that hungry look, his mouth parting slightly, the way that he didn't bother to try to hide the fact that he was looking, or the smile that quivered on his lips.

'Bloody pervert.' Billy jabbed at the ground with his stick, then flung it as hard as he could away from him.

Ella walked faster until she was level with him and could loop her arm through his.

'You're right. He's an idiot,' she said. 'So don't let him get to you. I certainly won't. Come on. Let's go and get an ice cream. My treat. I owe you.'

The story of the river

'You know, they used to say, in the town where Madaar-Bozorg was born,' said Fabia, threading her needle with silver embroidery cotton, 'which is a place where the corn is watered each year by a wide river and where tall flowers grow all over the grassy banks, that there was once a very beautiful young woman.

They said that her face was like an open flower and her waist was as supple as a green stem. She could dance like the fast-flowing river and she could sing like the birds on its banks. Any man who set eyes on her wanted to have her as his wife, but she couldn't marry because her father couldn't afford a dowry.

A rich man, passing through the town, decided to seduce her anyway. He told her that he'd no interest in cattle and cornfields. He'd enough gold of his own, enough to make more bracelets than she could ever wear on both arms. The young woman, who knew nothing at all of the world outside the village, gave herself to him with a trusting heart. She lived with him in a house by the river, with windows that shone with reflections of the water. With the next harvest moon, her belly grew round and tight as a drum and she gave birth to twin daughters.

A few years passed and the young woman was happy. She sat on the riverbank and played with her daughters. The first words they learned were the names of the flowers that grew there in the long grasses and the songs of the birds that swooped low over the water.

But then the rich man told her that he was returning to the lands he came from. His father had ordered him to make a marriage of convenience that would secure the family's fortunes for generations to come.

"I'll take the girls with me," he said. "They'll be cared for and they'll have every opportunity. I'll make fine marriages for them and they'll grow up to be fine women, not the wives of fishermen or farmers."

The young woman tore at her hair and ran her fingernails down her cheeks. She begged him and shrieked at him. She went mad with the thought that she would lose her cherished daughters. She felt as if her heart was a water-snail's shell, pulled out of her chest and dashed against the river stones by this man she'd so foolishly allowed herself to love.

That night, in a craze of grief, she tucked a daughter beneath each arm, ran to the river and dived deep into the middle of the current. The children drowned and the young woman drowned with them. Their bodies sank to the bottom of the river where the hungry fish picked their bones clean.

The rich man returned to his family and married the woman who'd been chosen for him. He was secretly very relieved that his father would never need to know anything about his secret family.

For seven days and seven nights, the soul of the young woman sat on the bottom of the river. On the eighth day, it flew from the cool darkness up, up into the light again. It shimmered in a haze of purest white over the surface of the water. It tried to shape itself into a body – into arms and legs and a mouth and fingers – but gradually, as the sun rose, it faded away.

And so they say that now, on any night of the year, you can see the young woman walking the banks of the river. Her hair flows down her back like weeds and her clothes are soaked with tears. She crouches on the riverbank and stirs the water with her long, white fingers. She's looking for the shapes of her dead daughters' souls.

When the river is full and ready to burst its banks, they say that the river woman must be wailing and crying for her daughters and that the river can no longer hold all her tears.

This is why young girls must never go near the river after dark, for the river woman may think they are her own lost children and tuck them into the folds of her watery cloak, carrying them away with her into the shadowy depths.'

'I don't want you going there, Ella. *Basta*. That's final,' said Mamma. 'What will people think of me? That I'm a no-good mother with a daughter running wild all over the place?'

Ella folded her arms across her chest.

'Mum, why are you listening to what one of your silly, stuck-up customers says? What do they know? Everyone else goes there.'

Fabia raised her eyebrow. 'My customers are stuck-up now, are they? Well, young lady, I need my customers, every one of them. Have you ever stopped to think that without my customers we wouldn't have food on the table or this roof over our heads? Hmm?' Then she sighed. 'Anyway, Ella. There are some things . . . some things . . . You know, it's far, far too easy to get a reputation when you're a girl.'

'A *reputation*?'

Fabia saw the anger flash in Ella's eyes. Despite herself, she felt a strange kind of relief. Hadn't she been waiting for Ella to push against her a little? Hadn't she wanted her to start being less of a good girl?

'We're not living in one of your 1950s fantasies, Mum,' Ella was saying. 'Well, *you* can if you want, but I don't see why I have to. Anyway, I don't understand you. You're always saying yourself that women can do everything men can, only better . . .'

Fabia sighed. She picked up a string of green glass beads and wound them around her finger.

'You know, *tesora,*' she said, slowly, 'you are right. You are so, so right. But I also know another thing, something I have learned myself, the hard way. It is different for boys. It is different for Billy. And that is just how it is. Infuriating? Yes. Unfair? Oh, yes. But it's how things are . . . So we have to be a little bit clever. If you hang around in a swimming costume down by the river, on your own with a boy, people like Mrs Moffat will see you and they will talk. They will come in here and make their little jokes, their little comments to me. All very careful, all very *by the way.* But is that *really* what you want?'

She reached out to touch Ella's arm but Ella shook her away.

'Anyway, David says that you can catch all kinds of diseases from river water – There are rats down there, rats with germs. And green slimy stuff . . . How do you say?'

Behind her, on cue, the shop door jangled and David appeared, swinging his doctor's bag.

'Algae,' he said. 'Green slimy stuff. Sorry to be a party pooper, Ella. It's just that I treated a young man, friend of Billy's I believe, just the other week for a particularly nasty skin condition. Told me he'd been playing down on that platform they've got rigged up down there –'

Ella sighed. 'I don't know anyone else who's been ill.'

'Well,' David pressed on. 'I've been thinking, you know, since your mum mentioned it, and I've had an idea.' He turned to Fabia, beaming. 'I might have come up with a solution.'

There was something about David that refused to be sulked at, thought Fabia. She watched Ella try to hold on to the tight little ball of her anger but David just smiled and smiled. His face shone with a sense of his own usefulness. 'I've a surprise for you. I think you'll like it.'

20

Beach kaftan. Original Pucci. 1967. Small repair at left-side seam.

It was typical. Just typical, Jean Cushworth grumbled to herself. These ridiculous communal changing-rooms. They were everywhere now. You were just expected to be accommodating, to do away with your decorum. She was going to have a word with the manager, make her feelings known.

It wasn't that she was ashamed of her body. Not exactly. But there was always that awkward moment when you had to let the towel drop. You had to fiddle with your bra behind your back and your skin was still damp so everything took more time, but you tried to do it all as quickly as you could because perhaps you didn't exactly want to show your breasts and your bare backside to all and sundry.

She'd been balancing on one leg, stepping into her knickers, at the precise moment when the Morenos appeared. Fabia hadn't missed a beat, of course. Jean noticed that she didn't do that thing that so many other women do of surreptitiously looking you up and down, comparing.

No, she'd kept her eyes on Jean's face and smiled that sickeningly beautiful smile.

'How lovely to see you,' Jean said, reaching for her bra, pulling her shirt over her head as quickly as she could. 'I didn't know you were members here.'

The girl hung back a little, looking nervously around the changing-room.

'We're just guests at the moment,' Fabia explained. 'David very kindly arranged it for us. Well, for Ella, really.'

She was wearing a kaftan covered in enormous swirls of colour – pink and turquoise and yellow – that stopped at the top of her tanned thighs. She's lucky she has that kind of skin, thought Jean. Olive. Always has colour. She was suddenly even more self-conscious of her own pallid flesh.

Fabia adjusted the strap of the beach bag on her shoulder. Her arms clacked with thick Perspex bangles.

'That's quite an outfit!' Jean said, realising that she was staring, her gaze travelling all the way down Fabia's legs to her feet in a pair of turquoise wedges with cork platform heels.

'Oh, you know,' smiled Fabia, apparently unfazed. 'I'm doing the 60s thing today. The smallest hint of sunshine always brings it out in me. Anyway, how are you, Jean? How are the preparations for the party? You must be so busy.'

That was what she did, thought Jean. She was good at it too. Always interested. Knew what to say and when to say it. Remembered every detail. But it meant that you never learned anything about her. She didn't give anything away.

And the girl. There was just something about her that was quite unnerving. She was a pretty little thing, Jean thought. No denying that. But she seemed so awkward, so uncomfortable in her own skin. Jean noticed that she'd disappeared into another bay of lockers to get changed, tucking herself carefully away from view.

When she appeared again she was wearing possibly the most ugly swimsuit that Jean could imagine. One of those black sports

Speedo things, for goodness' sake, with the high neck and ugly flashes down the side.

She clutched her towel to her front, self-consciously. Really, she couldn't be any more different from her mother.

What was it about that girl? Jean couldn't put her finger on it. The way she looked at you with those enormous eyes. Were they green or blue? She couldn't quite remember. You felt it go straight through you.

Ella dives deeper. Fingers, elbows, feet. Flickers of white in the turquoise water.

At the bottom of the pool, everything recedes. There's only the faint hum of the filters, the fresh scent of cleaned water.

Down here, she's no longer a girl but a woman with long hair that flows out all around her. Sometimes she's a bird flying across the blue bottom. Red beak and green tail feathers. Wake of pink petals. Fish-bird, bird-fish. Swimming above her shadow.

Again and again, she returns here, hanging her jeans and T-shirt in the locker, balling her socks in her shoes, putting on the blue water.

Sometimes she floats motionless for long minutes on her back. Clouds float too over the sky's curve, making a map like the world photographed from space. Another part of her, the deeper part, the part of her mind that goes quiet and then quieter, that can shrink to its own still centre, looks out from her eyes, unspools itself, floats out over the surface of the water.

The sky rolls above her, a gigantic eyeball veined with white. What does the sky see?

This. She. Lick of salt and roar of water.

If only she could stay here forever.

I wonder, Ella scribbled in her notebook, what it feels like to wake up in the morning and remember that today is the day that you marry a prince? Katrina says that she'd Rather Kill Herself. No one would dare to talk to you anymore or tell you Anything Interesting.

Billy says that the Royal Family was invented by the toffs to keep other people in their place. Chase the lot of 'em out of Buckingham Palace and turn it into something useful. Like what, for instance? Oh, a hospital or a university. Something like that. Yes, he'd like to think of all those oil paintings of stuffy old blokes in ruffs and pantaloons tossed on a gigantic bonfire. Mrs Queen stacking shelves or sitting at a checkout. Mr Queen doing people's gardens.

Billy, of course, hadn't been invited to Katrina's party. Instead, he was going to a Not The Royal Wedding Party in the pub at the end of his road, which sounded like a lot more fun.

Mamma had been up half the night for weeks with all the orders. There were so many parties and dinners and fêtes and none of her ladies could be seen wearing anything the slightest bit similar. But everyone wanted the same. Very full skirt or very, very fitted skirt, absolutely nothing in between.

'How will they walk in that?' Billy said, staring in disbelief at a tight sheath dress in red silk.

'I know. And it's shorter, always shorter, can you make it shorter?' laughed Mamma.

'All this fuss,' Billy said, 'and it's going to pour it down, anyway. They'll all need wellies and raincoats.'

It had rained all week. The shop in the courtyard groaned and creaked as the floorboards and rafters expanded, contracted.

Between downpours, the cobbles shimmered under clouds of midges. The wood in the window frames swelled until they couldn't be opened and the bathroom taps ran brown with river water, streaking the towels with rusty marks. There was a kind of clammy vapour to everything, even inside the shop, so that Mamma began to worry about the fabrics.

'It reminds me of home,' she said. 'The rainy season. Everything warm and wet for weeks.'

Ella was surprised to hear Mamma talk of 'home' in that way. For as long as she could remember, she'd avoided it, expertly brushing off Ella's questions.

Most people presumed she was Italian. Some guessed she was Middle Eastern, born in France. By now, Mamma's real story had been lost somewhere in the layers and layers of all the other stories she told, so that even Ella didn't know where it really began.

And yet, in recent weeks, there had been changes.

Just little things, but Ella noticed them.

The letters in blue airmail envelopes that had always seemed to find their way to wherever they were living, seemed to be coming with more regularity. Ella had picked them up from Mamma's dressing-table and tried, a few times now, to decipher the thin pages but, of course, they were written by Madaar-Bozorg, so she couldn't understand a word.

But also the things that Mamma didn't say. She wasn't using Italian words quite so much anymore and her mind seemed to be returning, more and more often, to her childhood, the Old Country.

Just yesterday, flicking through a magazine, she'd said, 'Oh, my aunt used to make this for me. This cake with honey and almonds and rosewater. It was my absolute favourite.' She'd said the name of the cake in the Old Language, sounding it out for Ella. She'd seemed genuinely pleased at the memory.

Another time she'd said, 'Do you know, Ella, that our family own a house in the mountains, north of Tehran? It is such a *beautiful* place. The air so fresh. The pomegranate trees ... I want to take you there one day.'

Ella found her mind drifting to this every time she swam. In the swimming pool, things cooled again. She could feel the blurred edges of her body being recast into firmer shapes.

She lay on her back under a lid of grey cloud, the rain prickling her face. She let herself hang there, in the pool's centre, and watch the steam rising from the water.

The surface was perfectly still.

The chestnut trees at the edge of the pool were thickening under the heavy air, drinking the stickiness into their green folds, growing darker, more brooding.

'Want to see something?'

Katrina looked up from the maths problem they were supposed to be solving and grinned conspiratorially.

'What sort of thing?' said Ella carefully. She had good reason to be wary of Katrina's show-and-tells.

'Something a bit creepy. Something I've never shown anyone else.'

She wiggled her eyebrows. 'So *do* you? Simple yes or no required.'

Ella sighed and laid down her pen. She knew that she wasn't going to get any more homework done.

'OK, but no funny business, all right?'

Katrina rolled her eyes and crossed her heart with fake solemnity. She grabbed Ella's hand and pulled her out of the chair.

'Come on. But we've got to be Quiet As The Grave,' she said in her stage whisper.

They stood on the large landing, Katrina straining for the slightest sound. The clattering of pans in the kitchen and the faint hum of Leonora's radio programme drifted up from far below them.

They crept past the door to Katrina's parents' bedroom, Katrina wincing as a floorboard creaked under Ella's feet. Mrs Cushworth usually took one of her naps at this time in the afternoon and didn't emerge from her bedroom until dinnertime.

They reached the far side of the staircase and Katrina slipped a key from the back pocket of her jeans and inserted it in a door that looked like all the other ones on the second floor.

She gestured for Ella to follow.

Ella realised that she was standing in a teenage boy's bedroom. It was a smaller room than Katrina's. There was a single bed with a duvet cover patterned with the Leeds United Football Club logo and a framed football strip on the wall above. Lined up on the windowsill at precise intervals were various bits of what looked like mechanical parts – cogs, pulleys, levers.

There was a large oak desk stacked with books and a shelf lined with more bits of machinery and large chunks of what looked like rock.

It was as if the occupant of the room had just stepped out for a moment – except that the bed was neatly made, the pillowcases smoothed.

Ella realised that Katrina was scrutinising her face for reactions.

'Whose room *is* this?' she whispered.

'My dead brother's,' said Katrina. 'Told you it was creepy. Weird, isn't it? Mum keeps it like this. She doesn't even let Leonora clean it. She spends hours in here on her own, dusting his bits of engine, his mouldy old books, his stupid fossil collection . . .'

Ella didn't know what to say. She remembered what Billy had told her about Katrina's brother.

'What was his name?' she said.

'Laurence. Poncey name or what? I called him Potato Head. Always had his head in a book. He was like my dad. You know, brainy but absolutely no common sense. Always inventing useless things.'

She picked up a piece of engine and fondled the outline of it with her thumb.

'Mum's never got over it. He was her favourite, you see. Her darling little boy. Her genius.'

'How did he die?' said Ella, softly.

'Kidney failure,' said Katrina. 'He was waiting for a transplant. Mum and Dad were just getting checked out to see if they could give him one of theirs, but then he got really sick . . .'

She shrugged her shoulders.

Ella pulled her cardigan closer around her body. The Signals were strong in here. It reminded her of the first day that she'd stepped into Katrina's hallway, of the colours she'd felt plucking at her throat, her elbows.

Here in this room, she could feel the air stirring around her, making little eddies of cold. It was like what happened when you dropped a pebble in a still pond and the ripples spread out endlessly across the surface of the water. It was as if, just by being here, she'd somehow disturbed the surfaces of the room and now concentric circles of silver and blue were spreading out all around her body.

'How long ago?' Her voice came out in a dry whisper.

Outside the room, there was a sudden noise of floorboards popping. They both jumped.

Katrina froze, her eyes wide, listening again.

Ella wondered if they were imagining it. The sound of footsteps receding, as if someone had been standing listening right outside the door, and was now walking softly away.

'C'mon,' she said, finally, 'Mum'll kill me if she finds us in here.'

She placed the piece of metal back on the shelf – gently, precisely – and then opened the door a crack.

'Quick. Now. Coast's clear.'

Later, when they were safely back in Katrina's bedroom, lolling on the white rug, their textbooks spread in front of them, Ella glanced up to meet Katrina's stare.

Her face was pale, serious, and she was watching her intently with those eyes of hers – one blue, one brown.

'To answer your question, Ella-Pella, it was six years ago when he died. The Potato Head. It happened when I was nine.'

She shut her copy of *New GCSE Maths Revision* with a snap.

'Katrina. I'm so sorry . . .' Ella said. 'Do you want to? I mean, would it help to . . .?'

'Talk about it?' said Katrina, pulling a face. 'Not really. I think I want to be on my own now, El. We're finished, anyway, aren't we? I'll see you on Friday for the party.'

21

Halterneck gown of foiled silver silk with an iridescent sheen. Made by Fabia Moreno to an original 1950s design.

Ella wishes that she were invisible.

She wants to slip silently past all the guests, kicking off her shoes, feeling the cool tiles against her bare feet.

No one would see her as she moved through the hallway, running her hand along the white wall, letting her fingers linger over the plaster border, its weave of vines and flowers.

At the foot of the staircase, she'd step out of the black dress, turning her body through the pools of light from the stained glass windows, letting red and yellow fall all over her, splashing her hair, her arms, her bare shoulders.

'Ella, Ella-issima, you're miles away, *tesora*.'

Mamma is looking at her, a smile hiding at the corners of her mouth.

'Come on, Dippy Day-Dream. I want to show off my beautiful daughter.'

Ella smiles and smiles until her lips are dry. She smiles at Katrina's mum and at Katrina's dad, who she meets for the first time. She smiles at Councillor Pike and at Mrs Cossington and at all her Mamma's customers. She even returns the smug smile on Katrina's face, Katrina poised on the stairs in her dress – a skin-tight, strapless, pale pink, sequinned sheath. There's a blotch of red light falling through the stained glass window and seeping over Katrina's shoulder. Like blood, thinks Ella.

She takes a glass flute from the silver tray and follows David's immaculately tailored back into the drawing room. She looks at the pattern in the Indian rug. She admires, when prompted by Mamma, the prints on the walls, someone's particularly lovely pair of earrings, a vase of white roses. She smiles and smiles again.

All the time, she feels The Signals, pressing at her throat and elbows, pushing up between her shoulder blades like tiny pairs of hands.

Run, they whisper. *Run*.

In the television room, in front of the vast TV, a group of men had sunk into the enormous leather sofas.

The window blinds inched their way silently down the windows.

'They're on very sophisticated motion sensors,' Katrina's father explained, to no one in particular. 'They pick up anyone entering the room.' He pointed to the door. 'Invisible, huh? All hidden behind the cornicing. And they adjust to the exact levels of light at any one time, to minimise reflection on the screen.'

He crossed to the window. 'Of course, you can adjust the settings to your own personal preferences. I like total darkness for film-viewing myself but my wife, well, she prefers a softly dimmed light.'

He gestured out of the window to the summer house and the expanse of perfectly manicured lawn. 'Got the same over there too. You can get the cinema experience there even on the brightest of days. And our entire irrigation system – sprinklers, hidden hoses, all that stuff – is linked up too. All works like a dream.'

'Well,' said David, 'that's very impressive. I've never seen anything quite like it.'

Mr Cushworth looked at them both with a suddenly self-conscious expression. Katrina saw that the collar of his carefully pressed shirt was limp with sweat. The bold blue checks hung crumpled and askew. As she watched, he undid the second button at his collar and began to unfasten his heavy silver cufflinks, folding his sleeves up over themselves as far as the elbow.

'It's going to revolutionise the way we live,' he said, a little defensively. 'DOMOHOME, we're calling it. Because, of course, the correct term for home automation is *domotics*. See what we've done there?' He gave a little nervous laugh.

He's not at all like Katrina or her mum, thought Ella. He actually cares what we think. He doesn't want David to think he's stupid.

'We've got Sony and a whole bunch of other people signed up,' Mr Cushworth went on. His voice was getting higher, faster, as if he sensed that David's attention might be waning. 'Been holding talks with Microsoft this past week, in fact. We've already got contracts with celebs and musicians and footballers. They can't get enough of us, those guys.'

'Is that so?' said David, stroking his chin. 'Incredible.'

'Yep. The world's going mad for home automation. It's the future. If you're interested, I might have a few tips for you.' He touched the side of his nose and winked at Ella.

David smiled. 'Ah. I'm not an investing man, myself,' he said. 'Never understood how it all works. No, I'll stick to medicine and leave the rest to the people that know what they're doing. Men of business, like your good self.'

'Well, don't say I didn't tip you off. You *do* have Blu-Ray though, I presume?'

'I'm afraid I'll have to disappoint you on that score too,' said David, good-naturedly. 'I hardly even have time to sit down most evenings. In fact, you'd probably think my TV set a bit of a museum piece, but it suits me just fine.'

Mr Cushworth looked genuinely perplexed. There was a moment of silence in which he ran his finger around the rim of his wine glass.

Then a loud voice broke in.

Mrs Cushworth swept through the door, balancing a tray of canapés in one hand and a champagne flute in the other. The fullness of her skirt rasped against the velvet sofas. The Marilyn Monroe inspired dress – the one that Mamma had made from the silver fabric brought specially from London – was stunning. Even Ella had to admit that. Mamma had said that the cut of the halterneck was designed to showcase Mrs Cushworth's favourite earrings – family heirlooms set with enormous diamonds – and now Ella watched them flash and bob as she leaned in, proffering the tray.

'Graham, I really hope you're not boring everyone to death,' she said in her harsh, bright voice, then turned to David with her fake smile. 'I do apologise for my husband, darling. He's getting to be an absolutely awful bore. I've told him. Haven't I, Graham? I've told you over and over again, if I hear another thing about sprinklers or automated HVAC –'

'That's heating, ventilation and air conditioning ...' Mr Cushworth chipped in hopefully, his voice dying away as his wife shot him a look.

'Yes, *dear*. Thank you for enlightening us. As I was saying, and I say it to him all the time, *all* the time, if I hear another darn thing about it, well, I might just slit my wrists. I certainly would have to think about leaving him for someone *a bit more interesting*, anyway ...'

Her laugh whinnied around the room, drifting over the heads of the guests on the sofa, some of whom now hoisted themselves to a standing position and drifted off, muttering excuses about getting another drink, or more of those delicious little snacks.

The familiar warm tide began at Ella's neck and crept over her face. She could feel The Signals leaping between Mr and Mrs Cushworth, scratched shapes with red spikes, hers firm and jagged, his wavering, curling back on themselves, already beginning to fade to orange.

David moved in swiftly. 'I find it quite fascinating,' he said. 'Quite, quite intriguing,' and he flashed Mrs Cushworth one of his friendliest smiles. 'Yes, I think your husband should feel awfully proud of what he's achieved here. As I understand it, and I don't really know what I'm talking about, but it's one thing building a purpose-designed modern home and quite another to update a house as old as ... erm, your very beautiful period property here, concealing everything, retaining all the lovely features and so on.'

His voice was slow, purposeful, smooth as the *crema* on Mamma's coffee. It was his reassuring-a-patient voice and it worked like a charm on Mrs Cushworth, bringing her back to herself, leaving her, for once, lost for words.

She put her hand to her throat and directed her icy blue eyes at David.

'Well, I can see that you two boys are already hitting it off,' she said. 'The doctor and the inventor. How charming! Now, if you'll excuse me, I'll leave you to play with your little toys.'

She stalked off.

'Cheers,' said David, raising his glass. 'Now, tell me about this sprinkler system.'

Mr Cushworth cleared his throat and jangled the loose change in his trousers. 'Sorry about my wife,' he said. 'She doesn't mean it. She's always been a bit . . . well, fiery. One might call it *passionate,* you know. So OK, what exactly would you like to know?'

'It's starting,' someone shouted in the hallway and people began to press into the room around them, balancing on the arms of the sofas, even crouching on the floor.

Ella noticed that Pike had placed himself at Mrs Cushworth's elbow, handing her another brimming flute of champagne. His hand strayed to the small of her back where her dress – the one that Mamma had cut so skilfully – left it almost naked. Pike, on the other hand, was wearing a very shiny grey suit, in a fabric that Mamma would have described as cheap. An anaemic red tie thrust itself from his button-down collar and every so often he smoothed at it nervously with those long white fingers. Ella could see that, despite the casual way that he was leaning against the marble fireplace, his eyes fixed on Mrs Cushworth, he was uncomfortable.

His eyes flickered over hers briefly, scanning the room and then returning to her once again. Did she imagine the tip of his tongue darting over his thin, dry lips as his eyes travelled up and down her body and then fixed her with a stare? Katrina was right. He really was a snake. There was something reptilian about him.

There was a general *shhhing*.

On the enormous TV screen, the Prince had just arrived at the Abbey. He was tugging at the tunic of his uniform.

'Oh, bless his heart,' a woman in a purple kaftan slurred, tipsily.

Mamma stood transfixed, alternately exclaiming and protesting at the procession of hats, handbags and dresses.

Finally the Princess-to-be arrived. She stepped from the silver car and Ella heard Mamma let out a long slow gasp.

'Alexander McQueen,' she breathed, admiringly. 'Oh, look at all the lace, the detail. It's just perfect.'

Later, they watched as the couple emerged and climbed into the state coach.

'Marvellous,' said Councillor Pike loudly, tugging at his tie as the camera zoomed in on the gold of the cherubs and the rich braid on the footmen's uniforms.

The rain held off and sunlight glinted on the guardsmen's plumed helmets, making little patches of intense white on the screen.

The sunlight flooded the room where people continued to linger, shifting their weight from one foot to another. It fell through the long conservatory windows.

Glasses were filled and chinked together. People began to speak at a normal volume again.

They watched as the Queen and the Royal Family stood on the Palace balcony, waving at the people gathered in The Mall.

'Every man, woman and child of Britain, her Commonwealth and Empire, must be rightfully proud, at this moment, of what we in Britain do best, of our rich heritage, our history . . .' said the commentator.

'And, of course, our *foreign* guests to these shores are most welcome in joining us in our celebrations,' announced Councillor Pike.

Ella felt his gaze settle over her. He made a deep mock bow from his position on the other side of the room. She felt her face tingle as the other guests turned to look at them.

Mamma's face tightened with anger. Ella watched as she opened her mouth to say something, then shut it again. David stepped closer and squeezed her hand.

'Damned tricky business, that,' someone said, nodding towards the screen where the cameras were focusing in on the Red Arrows, their formations gathering and scattering. 'One false move and you're done for.'

Ella would have liked to dance. She stood for a while, watching the other people, their bodies twisting and writhing, loosened by wine and laughter. She saw the way that some of the women kicked off their shoes, sighing with relief as they spread their pinched toes.

She thought of Billy, found herself wondering if he was dancing. Probably not. But whatever he was doing, he was probably having much more fun than she was.

She checked her phone constantly, unsnapping the little clutch bag sewn all over with yellow satin petals, her one concession to Mamma.

Finally, she wandered through rooms and corridors, looking for Katrina. She hadn't seen her much since they'd arrived. Even Katrina would be better company than the men who kept trying to catch her eye over the rims of their half-filled pint glasses.

She passed the inner hallway, the small space that Leonora used to hang up her coat and change into her pinafore and carpet slippers. Leonora wasn't at the party, of course. Katrina had said that she was in an awful huff about being given the day off. She didn't think it was right to find herself temporarily replaced by a team of hired caterers in stupid frilly outfits.

Now Ella heard a noise coming from the unlit vestibule. A giggle and a sound like scratching in the walls. She stopped in the corridor. The sound stopped. She walked again and the sound began again.

Suddenly, from out of the gloom, stepped Katrina, smoothing her pink dress over her hips, patting her hair into place.

'There you are,' she said, as if she'd been the one looking.

Ella allowed herself to be led away down the corridor. She let Katrina's arm slip through hers. She half-closed her eyes and listened to her chatter.

It was only as they turned into the drawing room again that she saw it for a moment. A dark shape at the edge of her vision, moving from the shadowy corner, crossing the corridor that they'd left behind. It was so quick that she might have imagined it. The creak of a polished shoe. A flash of striped shirt.

'What?' said Katrina, catching Ella's eye, sticking out her chin. 'What's the matter?'

'Nothing.' Ella's mouth moved easily, as if of its own accord. So Katrina had secrets too, it seemed. 'I thought I saw something, that's all.'

'These waiters seem to get everywhere.' Katrina couldn't resist a stagey wink. Her hands went to her dress again, tugging it down. She snapped open her handbag, fishing for her lipstick, and started to dab at her lips. 'There. Do I look all right?'

Ella nodded. 'Katrina –'

She put her hand on Katrina's arm but Katrina shook it off, pouting.

'Oh, get over yourself. You're so boring sometimes.'

22

Handkerchief with embroidered initial, 'F'. Lace edging. 1930s.

Fabia swirled the champagne around her glass. She felt the warmth of it spreading through her arms and shoulders, flushing her cheeks.

Despite that awful man Pike and his little speech, she was enjoying herself. She'd always liked parties. And in fact, since Pike's badly judged words, several people had made a point of coming up to her, complimenting her on the success of her business and asking her how she was settling in. They seemed at pains to be genuinely welcoming and friendly, to cancel out any lingering air of unpleasantness, and she began to feel her shoulders relax, to enjoy the music and chatter as it swept through her in waves of green and gold.

She was also enjoying, with a sense of satisfaction, watching several of her dresses move around the room. There was Ali Braithwaite in a simple dress of navy crepe, draped at the neck with a tulip skirt, and accessorised with one of Fabia's favourite finds – an enormous Trifari brooch of clustered flowers in crystal and gilt. She'd risked the leopard-print courts, too. They looked perfect.

'Who'd have thought it?' Ali had said, giggling in front of the mirror. 'I'd never have dared try them on if you hadn't suggested it. I *love* them. But are you sure they're not, well, a bit *tarty*?'

'On the right person, worn in the right way, absolutely not,' Fabia had said. 'The trick is to keep things simple.' Ali had followed her advice, the shoes and the brooch her only accessories except for a tiny pair of diamond stud earrings. Ali glanced across at Fabia and smiled, raising her glass. She looked radiant.

Then there was that nice young woman who worked in the Braithwaites' shop. Fabia could never remember her name. But here she was in such a lovely outfit, the 1950s dress in daffodil silk, with a prettily ruched sweetheart neckline and a lovely full skirt with six net petticoats. With a few alterations, it looked as if it had been made for her. And Fabia had found her just the right handbag too – a basket bag of the same era, with a base of natural-coloured woven raffia, the lid covered in imitation seed pearls and embellished with a cornucopia of fruit made of appliqued and beaded velvet. Strawberries, oranges, a bunch of grapes – it was such a fun piece. Fabia watched her now, flirting with one of David's colleagues. Yes, she could really carry it off.

'Mrs Moreno? My dear . . .'

Fabia felt a firm hand on her shoulder and turned to see Audrey Cossington, Ella's teacher, beaming at her.

'Fabia. Do call me, Fabia. Please . . .'

Audrey nodded, tilting a bottle of champagne, wrapped in a starched white napkin in the direction of Fabia's glass.

'Thank you. But I have to be careful. It goes straight to my head . . .'

'I'll drink yours then, shall I?' Audrey emptied the remains of the bottle into her own glass and placed it on a table. She made a little grimace. 'Quite a gathering, isn't it? Jean certainly knows how to do these things. I usually find them a dreadful ordeal but I've been rather enjoying spotting your creations. You've been busy transforming the entire town . . .'

Fabia felt her cheeks grow hotter. 'Oh, I don't think I can claim –'

'*Certainly* you can, my dear. Like I said, a breath of fresh air. Just what we all needed.' She looked down at her own dress. 'Look at me, for example. You've got me in red. *Red*, for goodness' sake! I've had so many compliments.'

Fabia smiled. 'You look wonderful. Really, you do. I love your hair. And your shoes . . .'

Audrey extended a foot in front of her, turning it this way and that, admiring again the elegant gold kitten heels.

'So, my dear, I just wanted to say that you mustn't bother about *him.*' She gestured to where Pike was standing stiffly at Jean Cushworth's elbow, fidgeting with the sleeve of his shiny grey suit jacket. 'He's not well liked, you know, despite what he'd have you believe. My betting is that he won't get re-elected. Some of his policies . . .' She gave a little shudder. 'Well, they're much too right-wing for this town. Goodness knows what Jean's doing getting mixed-up with him.' She looked Fabia directly in the eye. 'I've said that to her face too, you know.'

Fabia felt the tension return to her shoulders. She angled her body away from Jean Cushworth so that she wouldn't guess that she was being discussed.

'Oh, don't mind me, dear. I don't want to embarrass you. I just *desperately* wanted you to know . . .' She laid a hand on Fabia's arm. 'Well, I think you know what I'm trying to say . . . And Jean. Just look at her. She looks amazing too. A-*mazing*. I'm guessing the dress is one of yours?'

Fabia nodded, grateful to find herself on safer ground. 'I designed it for her, especially. It's inspired by a dress I found in an old *Cinemascope* magazine.'

'Well, she certainly looks the part.' Audrey winked. 'She must be very pleased. Yes, she looks really quite triumphant.'

With his usual perfect sense of timing, David appeared at Fabia's side.

'Mrs Cossington,' he said, his eyes crinkling at the corners, 'May I just say that you're looking positively ravishing?'

Audrey poked him playfully in the ribs. 'Oh, go on, you old smoothie,' she laughed. 'It's all down to Fabia, here. Well, I'll leave you two lovebirds to it.'

And with that she turned, waving her champagne glass at them, a gold bangle glittering on her wrist.

'Wonderful,' David said, grinning. 'Just wonderful. Speaks her mind. Tells things how they are. Always has done . . .'

The party continued. A marquee had been erected on the lawn and now it glimmered softly in the fading evening, lit from within by strings of lanterns.

The guests drifted over the lawn. From the conservatory, Ella watched them grouping and regrouping like clouds of moths.

'What's the matter with you, then?' said Katrina, 'Missing Lover-Boy?'

Ella scowled and trailed after her over the wet lawn. The canvas marquee had begun to steam gently. It seemed as if it was floating a few inches above the grass.

She found Mamma and David at one of the many circular tables flanked by gold-painted chairs and sat down next to them, fanning herself with a napkin.

Mother's face was flushed. She gripped Ella's hand in hers and turned it over, examining the shapes of her fingers.

'Your father's hands,' she said. 'You look so like him tonight, *tesora*.'

Ella pulled her hand away in annoyance. Mamma had drunk far too much wine.

'She's certainly turning out to be a beauty,' said David, beaming at her across the tablecloth. 'That young man over there hasn't been able to take his eyes off her all evening.'

He nodded towards the bar. A dopey-looking boy from the fifth-form, who was obviously working for the catering company, stood dabbing at a glass with a limp tea towel. As Ella met his eyes, he looked away quickly.

'Yes, I can see we're going to have to keep a closer eye on her,' David said, winking. 'She's going to be breaking hearts all over the place before too long. But,' he said, lifting Mamma's hand and kissing it, 'I think she takes after her mother in that regard.'

Nice, kind-hearted, handsome David, his blue eyes shining, his tie loosened, his hair flopping over his forehead like a schoolboy's.

Ella felt sulky, rude. She was sick of herself. What was wrong with her? Why couldn't she be happy?

She looked down and straightened her place setting, lining up the knife with the fork, the spoon at perfect right-angles to the glass.

'Can I have some wine, please?' she asked and watched them, full of the sense of occasion, humouring her, making a ceremony of splashing champagne into her glass, following it with the plink of an ice cube from the bucket.

It made Ella think of the snow globe that Mamma had given her one Christmas, of watching the snowflakes whirl and all the bright little figures get blurry, sealed tightly in their miniature storm, while she watched from the outside and the reflection of her own face loomed at her in the curve of the glass.

Shhhhh . . . Don't tell. Shhhh . . .

This house is full of secrets. It keeps them close, behind the thick white plaster of the walls and in the heavy folds of the curtains.

But when you're invisible, when you don't belong anywhere, you're free to move through the rooms and corridors. The house opens itself to you. You hear everything, see everything.

Ella walked down the hallway to the cloakroom. Mamma had asked her to fetch her handkerchief, which she'd left in her raincoat pocket and Ella had been only too glad of the excuse to leave all the whirl and blur behind her.

Later, she didn't remember how it happened. She must have opened the wrong door. One minute, she was standing in the hallway, her hand pressing the brass finger plate with its beaded edge. The next minute, the door swung open and she was standing there, her feet rooted to the spot. She was looking at the inside of Katrina's dad's study, but it was as if another part of her, the hidden part inside her, was not really seeing at all.

Shhhh, this other part of her said. *Shhhh.*

That was when, silently, she closed the door. She slipped off her shoes and held them in her hand. She made her way, as quickly as she could, down the corridor.

But on the insides of her eyelids the image still burned. Jean Cushworth lying across an antique writing-desk, the V-shape of her splayed legs and her bare white feet crossed at the ankles, clasped around the moving back of Councillor Pike.

Ella kept walking. The air bunched up around her, compressing itself into hard ridges. The Signals leapt around her like flames. *Run,* they whispered. *Run.* But she felt too hot and faintly sick. She put her hand against the wall and forced herself to breathe deeply.

She found the right door. She slipped the handkerchief from Mamma's coat pocket, and folded it into her palm.

And then she stopped. A crackle of red – of danger – flickered through her body. Someone had followed her into the cloakroom. She could feel their eyes prickling the back of her neck. She turned slowly.

Councillor Pike, his shirtsleeves pushed up his thin, white forearms, stood in the doorway, wiping his forehead with the back of his hand. He pushed his hair out of his eyes and his breath made a hissing sound between his teeth.

'What are you doing?' he said, his voice slurred with drink. 'What do you think you're doing, sneaking around, spying on people?'

Ella looked at him. She felt the other part of her, the hidden girl inside her, looking and looking. It was as if she was staring down a long tunnel with Councillor Pike at the end of it, his face slick with sweat, those eyes boring their way into her.

'I said, what are you doing in here, hmm? Going through people's pockets? Pinching things?'

He grabbed her wrist and wrenched her hand upwards so that a gasp escaped from her mouth. He forced her fingers open.

'It's my m-mother's.' She used her free hand to unfold the handkerchief and show him the embroidered initial: *F.* 'She asked me to get it.'

He dropped her hand then, as if even the touch of her disgusted him. He shook his head, opening the door just enough to let her pass through.

She angled her body so that she wouldn't have to brush against him. She could hear his breath coming quick and hot. The sweet stench of alcohol made her want to vomit.

Then his foot came out to trip her. She heard him laughing – a harsh, jagged sound – as she stumbled against him, putting out her hand to save herself. As she fell against his shoulder, he grabbed her arm with one hand, his other hand sliding easily up the skirt of her dress, finding the elastic of her knickers, pinching the soft flesh of her buttock between his finger and thumb.

'Little tart,' he said, laughing softly to himself. 'Not so full of ourselves now, are we?'

He pulled her closer towards him and she struggled to get free. A wave of nausea rushed into her throat as she realised that his fingers were working their way around inside her knickers.

'Bet you like that, don't you,' he sneered, the stench of his breath now full in her face. 'Bet you can't get enough of it. But I really don't like *you* very much. You and that stuck-up mother of yours. You think you're something special, don't you? *Don't you*? Well, you're nothing. Nothing at all.'

He pushed her away then, wiping his hand on the handkerchief, tossing it to the floor. The door closed softly, quietly, behind him.

She leaned on the wall, her face burning, feeling the cool of the plaster between her shoulder blades. She didn't know how long she stood there staring, staring at the back of the closed door.

'Where did you go, *tesora*?' Mamma smiled.

'We were about to send out a search party for you,' said David, grinning, offering her more wine.

'I couldn't find your handkerchief,' Ella heard herself saying. 'It wasn't in your pocket. It wasn't there . . .'

Ella couldn't remember very clearly what happened next.

She felt her phone in the petalled clutch bag buzzing against her thigh and she checked it under the cover of the tablecloth.

It was Billy.

Meet me in 10 min outside K's house?

She texted back, feeling a wave of relief flood through her.

It was easy to slip away again. This time, she avoided the house, skirting around the side, sticking to the pathways strung with party lanterns. Groups of smokers congregated in little clusters at various points along the terraces. One of them waved to her.

'Oi, Ella. Want a smoke?'

She caught the faint whiff of a joint hanging in the air above the scents of roses and newly cut lawn. She didn't stop, just shook her head and heard the sound of laughter drifting.

Billy was leaning against one of the ridiculous mock-Victorian lampposts at the top of the driveway. When she saw his face in the circle of orange light, Ella had to stop herself from running towards him, hurling herself against him.

'Wow,' he said, looking her up and down. 'You look fantastic.'

She could feel herself reaching for the right words, some-where out on the edge of her awareness.

'It's awful . . .' she said and heard her voice float into the great expanse of darkness, thin and flat.

'Really? That bad?' Billy grinned. 'Well, madam, your car-riage awaits you . . .' He made a little bow towards the empty driveway. 'Where shall we go? The river?'

Ella nodded and shivered.

'Where's your coat? Want to go back and get it?'

She shook her head and shivered again.

'OK.' Billy took off his big, black waterproof jacket and wrapped it around her shoulders. He pulled her arm all the way through the loop of his and rubbed her hand to warm it.

They walked as far as the Millennium Bridge and sat right out in the middle. The river spread out on either side of them, smooth as glass.

Ella remembered feeling then as if all the life-force had left her body. She was so tired that she thought about lying down, right there, on the bridge. She ran her hand over the warm planks. She looked down at her outstretched fingers and it was as if they weren't her fingers anymore, even when she saw Billy's bigger hand moving to cover them. She breathed.

'Hypnotic, isn't it?' she could hear him saying. 'Up here, you feel as if you could just let go, fall backwards into the water and you wouldn't make a sound. The river would just take you. You could float forever . . .'

Ella's dream drifted back to her, the trees reaching down to brush her face, the boat, Mamma, David. She blinked.

She could feel Billy's eyes on her, his face leaning in close and then his hand coming up to cradle her head, his lips gently brushing against hers.

That's when the panic started to rise in her again. Something crushed against her chest. Her mouth felt as if it was filling with river water.

She stood up, shoving him hard, sending him flying backwards against the curved railings.

'What did you do that for?' She was shouting now, the words tumbling over one another, thick and fast. 'What the hell did you do that for?'

Billy's face was white in all the blackness. 'I thought . . . Ella, I'm sorry, I thought . . .'

'Well, you thought wrong, didn't you, you *idiot*!' She heard her voice bouncing back at her from the water. Why was she yelling? Her heart was banging hard enough to burst and she couldn't even see properly anymore, just lines of wavy red that sent the blackness bobbing and rocking around her, so that she couldn't tell where anything began or ended anymore, just a feeling that everything was spinning, faster and faster, away from her.

She heard her feet in the stupid silver ballet flats slapping the tarmac path, her mouth making gasping noises and Billy panting close behind her. His voice, 'Ella, *ELLA!* Wait. I'm sorry. *Please, Ella. Ella, WAIT . . .*'

But she kept running until all the breath had been squeezed out of her. She kept going until she couldn't go any further, bending over the handrail at the top of the steps on the other side of the river, sweating, heaving, waiting for her breathing to slow.

As she began to see properly again, she could just make out a thin shape in the darkness at the foot of the steps.

'Ella,' he was saying. 'I'm so, so sorry. I got it all wrong. You know I'd never . . . well, I'd never do anything to make you feel bad. Please, just let me keep you safe. Let me walk you back home.'

Keep her safe? *Safe*?

Ella felt the tiny bubbles of red begin to gather again at the edge of her vision. She narrowed her eyes.

'You must be joking.' Her voice was quiet now, calm, as glassy as the river. 'Don't come anywhere near me, ever again, Billy Vickers. I don't ever even want to look at you.'

Then she pulled herself upright and walked carefully through the quiet streets, holding her body very straight, keeping her arms perfectly still at her sides.

At the corner of Alma Terrace and the Fulford Road she turned right and kept walking until she could see the lights glimmering through the chestnut trees at the top of Katrina's driveway. She walked on, her feet crunching across the gravel now, smoothing her hair out of her eyes.

Mamma and David were on the front steps. Ella saw that Mamma had her coat folded over one arm. She gave Ella a little wave.

'*Carina*. We were just looking for you. Where've you been?'

23

Full-length slip dress. Oyster-coloured silk. Bespoke Chanel. Date unknown.

What *was* Jean Cushworth thinking?

Fabia turned the question over in her mind as her needle dipped in and out of the seamed panel. She liked the feel of the cotton jersey in her fingers and the way that her mind stilled to the rhythm of the needle. In and out, in and out.

Since the party, everyone had been so kind. So many nice words. So many new customers.

Perhaps she'd been wrong about Jean Cushworth. She certainly knew how to throw a party, and it seemed that, if she decided that she liked you, that was that. You were in.

'A monstrous woman,' David had said. 'That poor husband of hers. I don't know how he puts up with it.'

But Fabia didn't like to be cynical about people. She could see Jean Cushworth now in her mind's eye, silhouetted against her enormous French windows, her hair perfectly coloured and coiffed, her perfect nails, her perfect make-up. Everything always so perfect on the outside. Who knows what she felt on the inside?

Loneliness, maybe? Wanting to be good enough? Wanting to be loved? Fabia knew how all those things could change a person.

But now there was the problem of this dress.

Yesterday evening, after school, the girl Katrina, such a strange young girl, always looking so unhappy, had arrived at the shop door with a parcel.

'My mum's been going through a few old things and thought you might be able to use these,' she said.

She'd turned away then, sweeping out of the shop as quickly as she'd come in. Hardly time to thank her.

'Give your mother my regards,' she'd called, but the girl was already across the courtyard, turning the corner, that funny half-smile on her face. So rude, thought Fabia. But then, that girl's eyes never seem to smile. Hadn't Ella said something about a brother who'd died? Maybe she too is suffering.

When she cut carefully through the brown paper and separated the layers of tissue, she couldn't help exclaiming to herself.

Dio mio. A headpiece, such a thing, a confection of white feathers, diamante and crystal-studded veil. So theatrical, so dramatic. So Jean Cushworth, really.

A silk clutch sewn with what must be thousands of crystals. Swarovski, thought Fabia, nodding her head, approvingly.

A silk kaftan in toffee-coloured silk. A signature piece. Fabia didn't even need to check the label to know that this was Donna Karan, circa 1995.

And, finally, the dress.

As she lifted the layers of tissue, it slithered into her hands and spread itself across the counter.

Fabia looked and looked. As with any new garment she encountered, she began to explore with the tips of her fingers, examining the spill of oyster-coloured silk, each seam fine, supple, creating such fluid lines, the hem perfectly hand-rolled, the body cut on the bias to dip deep between the breasts and drape just so.

Ferretti? Balmain? No, here – *dio mio* – was the label. Chanel. She ran her fingers over the tiny embroidered letters.

She had to try it on.

Of course, she thought, in the privacy of the fitting room, it was a little too small for her, a little too long. She'd known that. Jean Cushworth was taller, thinner, her body angular, exercised, kept in perfect trim by a personal trainer and private yoga classes. The silk rucked a little across Fabia's softly rounded stomach, straining just a touch over her hips. Her breasts pushed against the silk, giving it the wrong line altogether. She'd had to balance on her toes to prevent the silk from puddling around her feet. But yes, on the right person . . . well, this dress would be nothing short of magical.

Fabia wondered when it had last been worn and how Jean could possibly bear to part with it. Unless it no longer fitted her either, she thought, with a flash of spite for which she quickly chastised herself.

This was very kind of Jean. Really, very kind. Wasn't it?

Because as she unzipped the dress, stepped carefully out of it, and searched for a suitably padded hanger, she wasn't sure.

'My mum's been going through a few old things . . .' Katrina had said.

Was Jean trying to make a point? Was this her way of saying that she, Jean Cushworth, could afford to send her unwanted clothes in the direction of someone like Fabia, someone who made her living selling other people's cast-offs?

Fabia could imagine her loud laughter.

'This old thing? Oh, you're welcome to it, darling. Plenty more where that came from.'

She could hear the whispers behind the manicured hands.

'Oh, yes, I sent her my old Ferretti, my Missoni. Well, I didn't need them anymore. She may as well make something of them.'

Fabia didn't like this possibility at all.

But then, she thought, if it really was a . . . how would David say it? Yes, that's right. A *dig*. If Jean Cushworth really did want to humiliate her, would she have asked Fabia to make a dress for her? Would she have recommended Fabia to all her friends?

Fabia hated how suspicious she'd become. She just wasn't herself since, well, since everything that had happened before, that great black rent in the fabric of her life, that part of her that she still couldn't really let herself think about. Such a long time now. Thirteen years since Eastbourne and Enzo's death, and everything that came after. Time to move on, she kept telling herself.

Because the past itself was like a dress – you could keep it very close like a second skin. It might shield you in some way, from the cold, from whispers and bad words, from memories of other people's kitchen floors. You could use a dress to make you look stronger, more beautiful in other people's eyes, to help you to stand out or fit in.

Or you could simply ease down the zip, undo the buttons and step out of it, any time you chose.

Maybe this dress was like that for Jean Cushworth, something she'd like to unfasten and step out of, something she'd rather not wear any longer.

Now, with her head bent over her work, following this seam with her needle, an idea began to form itself in Fabia's mind.

She felt it take shape, like the curve of a sleeve or the soft drape of a neckline and, once it was there, it seemed perfect.

She smiled to herself as she sewed, forming the bold descending stroke of the final letter 'a', tying off the work, clipping the thread and dropping the end into the jar on the counter.

Sunlight slipped through the window and across the backs of her hands, soft as butter. It glistened on the silk panel, highlighting the word she'd just embroidered: *Aurora*.

She stroked the letters with her fingers, the sharpness of the 'A', the roundness of the 'o'.

Aur-or-a.

Goddess of Sunrise. Coloured lights in the northern sky.

There were so many beautiful words in the world. Words with such power, to enhance, to protect, to transform. She thought of them softly caressing the delicate skin of their wearers, a long curved 'l' on the inside of an elbow, a hidden 'm' kissing the nape of a neck. Her secret words were like charms or promises – and perhaps a little of their magic would rub off, making her customers bolder or lighter or stronger.

So many words to choose from and yet, by the time her work was finished, one word always made itself known. *Calypso. Plume. Shimmy. Petal. Arrive. Open. Sparkle. Resound.* They each held their own particular kind of future.

And now this word.

Aurora.

She savoured the taste of it on her tongue. The perfect word for this customer, a brave and lovely woman who was beginning her life all over again, in this dress that would now fit her perfectly.

And she, Fabia, was beginning again too. Shedding the darkness. Stepping into the light.

As she laid the finished piece carefully aside and stretched herself, she realised that she had a plan. An idea for her own little celebration. Yes, that was it. That was what she'd do.

'Going to pass me the scissors, then?'

Billy stood in the doorway. He looked uncertainly at the pile of invitations on the kitchen table, at the saucer of silver sequins, the pot of glue.

'Who let you in?' Ella heard her voice come out all ugly and misshapen. She hated herself like this but it was as if she couldn't stop, couldn't push her way out of the blackness that kept ravelling up all around her.

He winced, visibly, as if she'd slapped him in the face. 'Your mum let me in,' he said. 'I just wanted to –' His eyes met hers. She felt her hands curl into fists. 'OK.' He was already turning away.

'I'm sorry. I guess I'll go then.'

Ella sighed. No doubt her mum was overjoyed to see Billy. She'd been going on about it for the last two weeks, trying to get it out of her, what had happened, why Billy wasn't coming round anymore.

'Everyone has their little fights, *carina*. It's usually all about nothing,' she'd said. 'Everyone deserves a second chance.'

'Anyone would think he was *your* friend, Mamma,' Ella had said, but she'd felt something pulling at her insides. She had no words for what had happened. It felt like a black gap that got wider and wider with every day that passed.

That first day he'd called for her to walk to school, she'd made him stand in the courtyard, feeling the rage pushing its way up in her. How dare he? Who did he think he was?

'I'm sorry, Billy. She's not coming,' she'd heard Mamma say from the doorway and she'd seen him glance up then from her look-out place at the bedroom window, that silly expression on his face.

'Like a little lap dog,' Katrina had always said.

'Don't expect me to do your dirty work for you,' Mamma had said to her crossly as she came down the stairs.

'I don't. Just ignore him, Mum. It's none of your business . . .'

Mamma had sighed and begun to fold a basket of silk scarves, shaking her head sadly and it was her quiet disapproval, the purposeful movements of her hands, that had been harder for Ella to bear than anything.

Now Ella listened to his tread on the stairs, heard the murmur of his voice mingling with Mamma's. That cold, black feeling opened up again in her chest and tears prickled in her eyes.

She took one of the invitations, one she'd just glued with a sequin, and held it up:

> Fabia Moreno invites you to a special Charity
> Auction of finest designer dresses.
> 21 June, 2011.
> In aid of *Médecins Sans Frontières*.
> Champagne and cupcakes.
> *RSVP*

Then she ripped it into two pieces.

She stood up, swiping at the stupid tears with the back of her hand and began tapping old coffee grounds into the sink, running the filter under the tap.

All the time, she kept up an angry conversation inside her mind: Keep your head down, *tesora*. Work hard. Don't draw too much attention to yourself. Don't get yourself, heaven forbid, a *reputation*.

She held down the coffee grinder for a few seconds, enjoying the angry buzz of it under her palm. But now Mamma was busy spraying posters and flyers all over the place and inviting everyone and his dog to this stupid auction. She reached for one of the white saucers, banging it down hard on the tabletop, scattering sequins.

Why couldn't Mamma understand? Why was Billy always so calm and reasonable? It wasn't as if she could tell him what had happened or what she really felt: that she had this feeling, something she knew in a way that she couldn't explain, something black with jagged, crimson edges. That every night, when she closed her eyes, the feeling grew stronger, moving in a wave from her stomach up into her chest and spreading out all around her in ripples.

Now she let the coffee run through the machine, watched it pool in the cup, set the cup down, gently this time, on the saucer. She sipped and felt the heat flow through her.

'OK,' she muttered to herself, spearing a sequin with a cocktail stick. 'It's just your imagination. Everything's going to be OK.'

24

A silver sandal with a red sole. Christian Louboutin. 2010.

Fabia loved the shop at this time of day. The courtyard filled with evening sunlight and each leaded pane in the shop windows cast an oblong of light onto the wooden floor. Everything glowed or sparkled and, at such moments, Fabia could almost believe that she really had made something magical.

The floorboards were freshly washed with a special solution of cinnamon and brown sugar, dissolved in white wine vinegar. Now the floor seemed to shine with more than just reflected sunlight.

The effect was intensified by a small table that she'd draped with a white cloth and stacked with a pyramid of champagne glasses. David had assured her that he knew how to pour the champagne into the first glass and let it fizz down, not too slowly, not too quickly, in a cascade of bubbles, until each glass brimmed.

Where did he learn such a thing? She remembered the first time she'd ever tasted champagne, Enzo passing her the glass with a little flourish: 'For you, darling, only the best.'

Twenty years ago now.

A lifetime.

Outside, a marmalade-coloured cat stretched herself on the cobbles and played with the light between her paws.

Fabia checked the final details, adding a vase of peonies, her favourites, the tight pink fists just beginning to burst into bloom. She shifted one of the dressmaker's dummies, a little to the left then back to the right. This is how she'd chosen to display the various outfits to be auctioned, the Donna Karan kaftan now accessorised with gold wedge sandals and enormous sunglasses, the two dresses she'd made especially as her own contribution and, of course, the centrepiece in the window, Jean Cushworth's oyster silk dress.

She opened the cash register. Yes, her newly charged piece of green malachite was safely in the change drawer, hidden beneath a pile of copper coins. She wondered if she had time for just a little extra touch. She knew that she shouldn't. But, really, there was no one around and what harm could it possibly do?

She took a small silver hand mirror from under the counter and held it up to the sunlight. It sent a wobbly disc of light dancing over the white ceiling.

'Hellooo! Sorry I'm a bit late!' Mandy was making her way expertly across the cobbles in her blue velvet sandals, her handbag swinging from the crook of her elbow as she balanced two precarious trays.

'Sorry, Fabia. Only just got them finished!' She whipped off the tea cloth covers to reveal rows of miniature cupcakes iced in pink and white, each topped with the tiniest flake of gold leaf. 'What do you think?'

'Perfect!' Fabia breathed, tucking the mirror back under the counter, clasping Mandy's hands in hers. 'Exquisite. Thank you so much, Mandy. And, by the way, you look absolutely . . . well, *delicious!* Just like a cupcake yourself!'

Mandy's face dimpled. 'You don't think it's too much? I was worried I'd be a bit too, well *warm*, actually, but it's surprisingly comfortable.'

She smoothed her vigorously back-combed hair and ran her hands over the mustard wool dress, now minus its convertible sleeves.

'Not at all. I told you that dress was just meant for you. As soon as I saw you, I just knew.' Mamma rubbed the nap of it between her finger and thumb and sighed. 'It has something very special in it, this fabric. All through it. Like . . . like a special ingredient in one of your concoctions . . .' She smiled. 'But I love what you've done with the shoes too. The peacock blue. It's just the right contrast.'

Then she narrowed her eyes teasingly, in mock disapproval. 'But wait a minute now. This handbag, I recognise. But those shoes are not mine, I don't think?' She raised an eyebrow.

Mandy blushed. 'I found them in a car boot sale. Couldn't resist them . . .'

'*Brava*,' Fabia laughed. 'A woman after my own heart.' She gave Mandy's arm a squeeze and then, to distract herself from the nervous feeling that had begun to flutter inside her, she busied herself plucking the cakes from the trays, arranging them on the coloured pressed-glass stands.

'Erm, Fabia . . .' Mandy blushed, twisting her hands together nervously. 'I've got something to show you. I've been meaning to do it for ages but . . .'

She fumbled in her handbag and drew out a thick wad of envelopes bound with a thin black ribbon.

Fabia wiped her hands and opened the first one. The paper was thick and creamy. The handwriting was firm, a perfectly formed pen-and-ink copperplate that swept boldly across the page. She thumbed through the pages. There must be a dozen letters or more.

'I found them in the pocket of the dress,' Mandy said. A red stain spread over her neck. 'I feel bad. I should have told you earlier. But I wanted to read them. I couldn't help myself . . . You know, you told me that the woman who owned the dress before me was an incredible person and I was so curious to know more, but now I feel terrible.'

Fabia took the letters and stroked the paper.

'You mustn't worry,' she said. 'I'd have done exactly the same.' She noticed that the top envelope was postmarked 1949. Wasn't that the same date as the careful entry in Eustacia's journal: *Day dress. Bought in Selfridges, London, for lunch with R?*

She slipped a single folded sheet out of the envelope.

'*My darling,*' it began.

'*It was so good to see you, if only for that snatched hour together. You looked radiant, as always, dearest Eu. Quite the loveliest I've ever seen you. I cannot get that image of you out of my mind. You sitting there, among all the china and paraphernalia and those vile souffles and the dreadful women chatting about nothing at all. You were like something from another world, another time, and I felt like the luckiest chap alive to be sitting there with you.*

And that's why I simply can't accept your decision, my darling. Now that you're a part of my life – a part of me – I don't know how to be without you. We have to be together, Eu. We simply have to.

I don't care about your father. You may think me callous, but I really don't care what Mitzi thinks either. She doesn't love me. She never did. To be frank, I think she'd be happier if I was off the scene.

And you and I, we'd be free to start again. I don't care if we have to elope somewhere, live as exiles in some godforsaken place – and anyway, wouldn't you like that, darling? An adventure, a chance to see something of the world, like you're always saying.

Forgive me, please forgive me for this outburst. I've thought long and hard about writing to you. But I can't have any peace until I'm sure that you don't feel the same. And you do, don't you, Eu? I know in my heart that you do.

Please, my darling, just say the word and I'll –'

'Buongiorno, signorinas!'

Fabia looked up from the page to see David striding across the courtyard in his rented tuxedo and perfectly shined shoes, swinging an auctioneer's hammer that he'd borrowed specially for the occasion. In the golden light, he looked like a picture from a catalogue.

She waved and then her eyes darted back to the bottom of the letter, signed with a final bold flourish, '*Your* Robert.'

She smiled again at Mandy.

'Thank you,' she said. 'And please don't worry. But I'll need to return them to Eustacia's nieces. I'm sure they'll want to have them.'

She put the letters in the shoebox under the counter where she kept old receipts and bits of ribbon.

'Let's get this party started,' David said, kissing her on the cheek, crossing to the shop stereo and selecting a CD, then whirling her around the floor, ballroom-style.

He paused, mid-waltz, to put a cupcake into his mouth, winking.

'Delicious. Now where's Ella?'

'I don't know,' said Fabia. 'Upstairs, I think . . . She's taking her time.'

Fabia forgot to think about Ella and about Eustacia and Robert and the mysterious love letter as the guests began to arrive and David expertly popped the cork on the first bottle of pink champagne.

Whenever she looked back on this moment, Ella realised that she should have trusted The Signals – the black and red that kept washing over her in waves.

She hadn't slept properly for weeks, Mamma scrutinising the dark circles under her eyes: A*re you really all right, darling?* And every time Billy tried to catch her eye – in the classroom or in the dinner queue – she'd look away.

She really couldn't let herself think about that night. Inside her mind, she saw a high ivy-covered wall and behind it, there was a part of herself, the secret hidden part, still sleeping the enchanted sleep of fairy tales, while first the ivy, then the twisted branches of trees and then an entire forest grew up all around her.

Sometimes she found herself longing for Billy to scale the wall, to find the first footholds, to hack back the thorns and branches, haul himself up, arm over arm, wake her from herself. But how could he do that now?

Not with a kiss. She'd blown that completely. He wasn't exactly going to risk trying that again.

Did she even want him to? This was the question that she turned over in her mind. Each time, the dark gap inside her seemed to get bigger. Sometimes, as she walked down the stairs to the shop, she'd imagine she could hear Billy's easy laughter as he cracked a joke with Mamma, but he was never there. He's stopped trying to talk to her. Something had shifted between them, something she couldn't even name. His Signals when she moved past him in the school corridor were wobbly lines of grey and palest yellow, like cobwebs that she had to brush away. Billy was scrupulously polite, carefully considerate. She hated it.

Night after night, on her side of the embroidered curtain, the hidden Ella, the secret part of her, went on sleeping and the wild birds wove a coverlet of leaves for her white body as she dreamed the dreams of the dead.

Meanwhile, the rest of her was very much awake, tossing and turning, alive to her own Signals, which seemed stronger now than ever. Her pillows crackled with static. There were the lines of red that licked at her like flames.

The wrought-iron woman from above the doorway with her seaweedy hair had long ago stopped smiling at her. Instead, she held out her thin, pale arms. Her mouth moved, forming stale words – *sink or swim, sink or swim* – while the river mist rose around her. A foul-smelling flotsam swirled over her bare feet – scraps of old fabric, broken bottles, beer cans, animal bones, a tattered white handkerchief with a monogrammed corner.

Now the day had finally arrived.

Ella was waiting. She watched from the bedroom window. She knew that he was coming. She could feel his breath on the back of her neck, the touch of his clammy, white fingers.

As he stepped into the courtyard, the hem of his black over-coat caught by a sudden flurry of wind, she was ready. She stood back a little, half-shielded by the curtains.

So she had the perfect view of Mrs Cushworth's face as she balanced on his arm, tripping lightly across the cobbles in her strappy silver sandals.

She watched Jean Cushworth's mouth contort, heard her shriek, saw her stumble and hurl herself blindly through the shop door.

The hum of voices subsided. There were only the faint chords of the French accordion music playing on the shop stereo.

And then a voice, a hard, bright voice shrilling, 'My dress! How *dare* you? Could you be so kind as to explain to me, please, what *my dress* is doing in the middle of your window?'

As Ella reached the bottom of the stairs, the first thing she saw was a silver sandal, lying in the middle of the shop floor. A silver sandal with a red sole. The red sole looked obscene. It made her think of a cut-off tongue.

She stooped and slipped her finger through the loop of the ankle strap and handed it to Mrs Cushworth, who stamped her bare foot like a child having a tantrum and threw it to the floor again.

The shop was full of people. Mamma was white-faced, one hand gripping the counter. The accordion player continued his inevitable easy crescendo until David crossed to the stereo and switched him off.

'Well?' Jean Cushworth's voice was like rusty razorblades. Her eyes were narrowed. 'I demand an explanation. How did you get hold of my dress? You *must have stolen it*. And how did you . . ? How in God's name did you? Oh, *now* I see! *Now* I get it. Yes, you must have taken it from my wardrobe on the day of the party!'

Ella watched Mamma, saw how she kept her face very still. Mamma looked around the room at all the people looking at her and then she sighed and raised her glass in Jean's direction.

'Brava,' she said. 'I salute you. Brilliantly done.'

Ella saw how people looked at the floor, shifted from one foot to another, exchanged glances. The girl from Braithwaites stared at Fabia, her face flushed pink. The woman from the shoe shop in Petergate was already making for the open door.

'What do you mean?' Jean Cushworth was shouting now, her face reddening, her hair escaping from its careful chignon as she gave up any pretence of control.

She turned to Pike. 'John, what does she mean? Is she making fun of me? Is that what she's doing, this . . . this *floozy*, this cheap *tart* . . .'

'Now, excuse me, that's quite enough.' David held up a hand, stepping into the centre of the shop floor.

'Ladies and gentleman,' he bowed in Pike's direction. 'If you would be so good as to bear with us, I'm sure we'll have this little misunderstanding sorted out in no time at all. But, really, Mrs Cushworth, I don't think we need to resort to –'

'Resort to what, exactly, Doctor?' said Pike, his eyes glinting. 'A few home truths? Finally telling it like it is?'

'Like it is?' repeated David, incredulous, and Ella could see now that his nostrils were flaring, his starched white tie bobbing up and down with the effort he was making to calm his breathing.

'David, please. Really. There's no point,' Mamma was saying now. 'Mrs Cushworth has already made up her mind.'

But now it was Billy's voice that cut across Mamma. Ella hadn't even noticed him standing next to Mandy, over by the foot of the stairs.

'Mrs Moreno,' he said. 'May I just ask you how you came by the dress in question?'

That's how he said it, calmly, confidently, like a TV detective. Ella almost laughed out loud. And Mamma smiled at him, indulgently.

'Billy,' she said. 'These people really don't have the slightest interest –'

'Just answer the question, Mrs Moreno,' said Billy. 'That is, what I mean is, could you, please?'

'Well,' said Mamma. 'You *know* how I got it, Billy. Katrina brought it to me. It was in a parcel, with a lot of other things. Of course, I had no idea that the dress was . . .' She stopped herself.

There was a gasp and a little flurry of activity that travelled around the room as people took this information in.

'Katrina, you say,' said Billy, getting into his stride, raising an eyebrow, looking theatrically around the room. 'And is she here?'

'My daughter is at home with a cold,' said Jean Cushworth. 'This is outrageous. I hope you're not implying . . . Wait a minute . . .' She looked wildly around the room again. 'Yes, I'm right aren't I? This is my Donna Karan, isn't it? And the headpiece from my *wedding*, for goodness' sake and . . . My God! At least half of this damn auction is something from my wardrobe. This is ridiculous! You want to make a laughing stock of me, obviously.'

Mamma looked at Billy and lifted her hands, palms upwards, in a little gesture of I-told-you-so. But Billy pushed on.

'I'm sorry, Mrs Cushworth, but why would Mrs Moreno lie about this? I'm afraid that I really don't see her motive. Perhaps you can explain?'

Here it comes, thought Ella. Her mind was already running ahead. She knew exactly what Pike would do next.

She watched almost as if she were watching a slowed-down film, as Pike wheeled around on his heel and pointed at her, his jowls wobbling, his long finger shaking in a perfect imitation of righteous anger.

'Oh, I can explain it all perfectly,' he said, with obvious relish. 'It's *her*. This girl here, looking like butter wouldn't melt. *This* is the girl who stole your dress. I caught her going through everyone's pockets in the cloakroom at the party. I tried to be understanding. I told her I'd let her off, just this one time, but clearly she sneaked upstairs and went through the wardrobes too.'

Billy fixed Pike with a cold stare. He looked down at the floor, gathering his thoughts. When he looked up his face was like a mask.

'That's a very serious accusation you're making, Councillor,' he said, quietly. 'And so I assume you have evidence that Ella actually stole things? I mean, I beg your pardon, but why should we believe you? And I can't help thinking that this is all a bit illogical. Why would Ella steal dresses and then give them to Katrina? You're not making any sense.'

'Oh, use your brain, lad.' Pike was hissing through his teeth now. Ella watched a delicate spray of spittle fly from his lips. 'Katrina doesn't have anything to do with this. They've got the wool pulled over *your* eyes, good and proper. I knew you were simple, lad, but I didn't think you were such a *moron*.'

Now it was Ella's turn. She had felt it rising and rising in her, the hot red shape of her anger, but now, with that one word 'moron', it was finally released. It broke the surface and spilled over. She felt it surge through her entire body.

She heard herself saying, very calmly, very clearly, 'He's lying. I didn't steal anything. I was fetching my mum's handkerchief from her coat. This man assaulted me. He put his hand up my skirt and . . . and tried to . . . well, things I don't want to say here . . . And all because I caught *them* . . .'

She let her eyes meet Jean Cushworth's then, saw the look of undisguised horror beginning to creep across her face.

'I caught them together,' she went on. 'These two. Councillor Pike and Mrs Cushworth. I saw them together doing things that were . . . things that they shouldn't have done . . . And *he* knew that I'd seen them and so he came after me.'

There was a shocked silence.

The silver sandal with its stilled red tongue leered at her from the middle of the floor.

Ella didn't wait to hear what Pike would say next. She ran out of the shop and kept running.

Fabia followed Billy, weaving through the streets, through the stream of people making their way to the station or back home to their families for the glass of wine, the evening meal.

My daughter, Fabia thought, my poor daughter. How I've failed you. She felt a terrible straining and tugging at her insides.

'We must find her, Billy,' she said. 'She mustn't be on her own.'

Billy's mouth was set, his shoulders thrust forward in grim determination. Fabia let him take her hand and pull her along after him. She could feel his fury in the tight grip of his fingers.

They arrived at the river and Billy turned sharp left, kicking out impatiently at the geese that wandered in their way, heading upriver, faster, faster, towards the taller trees and the new bridge.

SOPHIE NICHOLLS

People here walked lazily along, making their way into town. Cyclists in fluorescent jackets swerved as they strayed onto the cycle path. Billy shoved past them all and headed on.

There she was, sitting out there, half-hidden in the long grass, her legs tucked up, her arms wrapped tightly around her shins, her chin resting on her knees, staring out at the river.

Fabia began to run towards her, her feet in their high heels slithering over the damp paths trodden in the grass.

Ella heard her coming. She turned her face and Fabia could see that it was pinched and red and streaky with tears. She crouched in the muddy grass and held her daughter, stroking her hair.

'*Tesora*. My Ella-issima. I am so sorry, so sorry.'

She felt Ella break against her then, her breath wrenched out of her in gasps and sobs. She knelt and held on as tightly as she could.

'Ella. Mrs Moreno. Could I . . .?'

Billy had been hanging back, waiting under the trees. Now Ella saw him come forward, running his finger around the inside of his collar, his face uncertain.

She nodded to him, tried to twist her face into a smile.

'Billy . . . I'm sorry I . . . I didn't want to tell you before. I –' She looked at Fabia. 'Mum. Do you think you could –? Billy and I. I need to talk to him.'

'Of course.' Fabia got to her feet. 'Billy,' she said, trying to blink away her tears. 'You make sure you bring her home safely. Don't be too long now, *carina*.'

Billy nodded. He squatted next to her on the riverbank. He tore at the grass, pulling it out in handfuls. She could see that his hands were shaking.

'Billy,' she tried again. 'I'm so sorry. I –'

'That bastard,' said Billy, turning to her. 'I'll . . . I'll kill him, I will. I swear. I'll . . . That complete *bastard.'*

That's when his eyes met hers and she felt a trace of the old laughter begin to creep around the edges of her mouth.

'Piece of work . . .' she said. 'Remember? *Piece of work*?'

The laughter began to escape from her. It took hold of her insides and burst from her lips and went echoing and juddering over the riverbanks.

Billy was looking at her as if she'd gone mad. But she couldn't stop. She couldn't hold it back.

'It's OK, Billy,' she said, between gasps. 'Really. It's OK.'

And she put up her hand and stroked his cheek.

He flinched. His eyes closed.

'Don't, El,' he said. 'Please. Don't.'

'But I want to,' she heard herself saying. 'You see. I always did . . .'

He looked at her again, then, a long, searching look and then he took her hand in his, turning it over, carefully, hesitantly. She felt the warmth spread through her as he lifted her hand and pressed her open palm to his lips and then his arms came around her, and he pulled her into him. She could feel his heart hammering against her chest.

She could feel the river all around them, The Signals jumping, as he tilted her face up to his and kissed and kissed.

Fabia leaned against the huge gnarled trunk of a chestnut tree. She watched the river, wide and faster-flowing here, brown with peaty water. She thought of the rain falling on the hills and making its way, slowly, persistently, overground and underground, seeping through the fields and the layers of rock, burbling over channels of flat stones, swirling around the bulging tree trunks and then disappearing again, far beneath the surface, to emerge here in this one current pressing onwards, always onwards, sweeping everything with it, soil and twigs and branches and the small bones of animals and birds, gathering force, moving relentlessly on through the next towns, on towards the sea.

Fabia thought that she understood how it would feel to be part of this river. She knew why Ella loved to swim and could lose herself in the water for hours at a time.

The surge inside her, the long, dark pulling feeling that had brought her out of the shop at a half-run, following in Ella's wake, leaving everything, even David, behind her, had not subsided. It was urging her on now, like many voices all speaking at the same time. And even as she tried not to listen, the voices grew louder, more insistent, and she could hear them speaking to her in the tiny rustlings in the grass and the wind moving through the leaves above her head and the sound of the river, pressing its smooth sides against the banks.

It was firm, muscular, so much bigger than her. She felt her body already surrendering to it.

She thought of David, his horrified expression as the words, those terrible words, had fallen out of Ella's mouth and into the silence.

She thought of those words – *floozy, tart, thief, he touched me* – lying all around the shop where she'd left them. How in the weeks and months to come, they'd crouch in the shadows, covering the bright fabrics, the embroidered shawls, the glitter of crystals and sequins, covering them all with a fine layer of dust, making everything look suddenly cheap, tawdry, worthless.

Perhaps no one else would see it or know that the words were there. But she would. She, Farah Jobrani – her real name, the name given to her by her own mother. She thought of all the other beautiful and powerful words that she'd stitched into seams and fastenings and that, right now, were being carried by women all over this city in the silk linings of pockets, in the turn of a sleeve and the flick of a hem.

She had failed. She was useless. She'd allowed her daughter to be touched by something so awful that there were no words in the universe that could speak it. She'd betrayed Enzo and her promise to him.

There's another way, another way, the wind whispered.

But she shook her head stubbornly. No, she wouldn't give in.

She watched Billy and Ella now, their heads tilted towards one another, seeing only each other, and she put her hand to her heart. Somewhere under there, beneath the layers of satin, the shaping and sparkle, was the real heart of Farah Jobrani. She thought of it like a peony, a flower that over the last few months had slowly begun to burst open and now – yes, she could feel it – was already furling each layer of petals around itself again, closing like a fist.

Billy was a good boy and he'd soon, very soon now, be a nice man, a kind man. Just like Enzo. Just like David. And that was just one more reason why they couldn't stay here.

She turned and began to walk downriver again, retracing her steps, seeing the city come into view, the walls and spires shaped so long ago and that would still be here tomorrow and the day after that and the day after that and long after Fabia and Ella and David and Billy and Jean Cushworth and Pike were gone. Because one day they'd all be gone. Sinking back into the brown earth, tangling once more with the tree roots and the river.

SOPHIE NICHOLLS

She knew what she had to do. She'd go back to the shop and climb the stairs to the little flat where David would be patiently waiting for her, back to what she now knew she had to tell him, and she'd take the suitcases from under the beds and begin, once again, to pack their belongings.

25

Navy blue blouse, silk chiffon with hand-stitched embellishment. Late 1940s.

Although the boy was quite out of his mind, Jean Cushworth decided that she really quite liked him.

Pike had told her to beware of him, that he was trouble, a boy from the wrong side of the river, brought up – *dragged up*, he'd said – with half a dozen brothers in one of those poky little terraces with the bathroom downstairs. His dad was a foreman at the Nestlé factory, a union man who liked his beer and his football and thought he might stand in the next local elections. Fat chance, Pike had said.

And now the boy was here, right here, in the middle of her living room floor. Really quite presentable, she thought, with clean jeans and a pressed shirt and those intense blue-green eyes. His face was chiselled, with high cheekbones. His mouth was moving very quickly. She found herself strangely fascinated by his mouth, the sounds that were coming out of him. His hands were cutting the air in quick gestures that she couldn't make any sense of.

It was as if he was ablaze with something from the inside. Which was a shame, really, Jean thought. What a waste. Because the Moreno girl really wasn't worth all this bother.

She'd be gone soon, she and her mother. That much was clear. You couldn't go around making those kinds of accusations, casting aspersions, using that kind of language. And about the leader of the council, no less. It was bound to backfire. Yes, she had it coming to her, that Moreno woman and the strange girl, so silent, always looking at you, as if she could see inside you, see what you were thinking.

What really gets to me, she'd said to Pike, is that she's been here, in my house, so many times. Katrina was so kind to her when none of the other girls wanted anything to do with her. To turn on us like this just isn't fair. It really isn't good enough.

Back there in the shop, she'd been caught out for a moment, when the girl had said that thing about seeing her with Pike. Her mind had whirred like a faulty clock, trying to remember what exactly had happened that night of the party. To be honest, it was all a bit of a blur. The champagne, the whisky, her tablets which, she had to admit, were making her forget things. But she was sure, quite sure, that they couldn't possibly have been seen. She'd locked the door. Surely she had? She was always so careful.

Even if the girl *had* seen something, or guessed something, well, it was her word against theirs, wasn't it? And, quite frankly, who was going to listen to a common thief?

She forced herself to concentrate now on what the boy – Billy, yes, she remembered now, that was his name – what it was that he was saying. He seemed very worked up about it. On and on he went, that rosebud mouth moving endlessly, that nice clean jaw opening and closing. She really should tell him not to waste his breath. Plenty more fish in the sea, that's what she'd say. Especially at his age. His whole life ahead of him. He could really make something of himself, a handsome boy like him.

She lifted her hand and he paused for a moment. She tried to say something, but the words wouldn't come. She swallowed, made herself focus on setting down her wine glass, watching her hand move slowly towards the little mahogany side table.

She felt as if she were moving underwater, as if her bare arm in its silver bracelets was floating out from her shoulder and her hand wasn't her own anymore.

'Oh, for goodness' sake,' the boy was saying. 'You haven't made sense of a word, have you?'

She smiled, nodding at him. He reminded her a bit of a naughty Yorkshire terrier with his fiery eyes, his thatch of black sticky-outy hair.

'Where's Katrina? I want to speak to her.'

His voice reached her from a long way off. She felt herself sinking backwards into the cushions, which were soft and deep and welcoming, the waves coming faster now, her arm buoyed upwards again, drifting of its own accord, floating out on the surface of the water, her finger pointing up, up through the white ceiling before it burst open and the sky closed over her.

Ella saw them from the bedroom window.

She was watching Mamma spread her silk blouses on the bed, folding their limp arms across themselves, straightening their collars, smoothing them between layers of tissue paper.

'Mum, please,' she pleaded and then, feeling the fluttery feeling under her ribs, 'Well, if you go, I'm not coming with you.'

Mamma turned then to look at her, making that clicking sound with her tongue.

'Tsk. Really? And where will you go, *tesora*? Where will you live? With Billy and his family? You think they'll take you in? You think you'll want to be here tomorrow, the week after, the week after that? When the name-calling gets worse and every small thing that goes wrong in this town gets blamed on you? Do you think Billy will be able to protect you, all day, every day, forever?'

'Yes,' said Ella, 'Actually, I do. Everyone hates Pike. Well, everyone who really matters. And David. He's already said that we can go and live with him. You and I. He wants to *marry* you, Mum, for goodness' sake. You *love* him, I know you do. This is all just because you're scared.'

'Ella, you don't understand what you're saying. You don't even know my reasons –'

'Then explain them to me, Mum. Explain why you're so frightened, why you think we have to run away. Because I just don't get it.'

'I've told you, there are some things I can't explain. Things you don't need to know about . . .'

'Oh, Mum. I don't know what you're talking about!' Ella punched the pillow. She felt hot, tired, frustrated. 'Don't you understand? You can't ruin my life just because you haven't got the guts to stay here!'

'Ruin your life? *Tsk.* Six months ago, you didn't even know these people, Ella. You didn't want to come here. I had to drag you, kicking and screaming –'

'Yes, I know. But I'm just starting to get used to it, and now you want to do it all over again. Who cares what people say about me? They've been saying it all along, anyway. They'll believe whatever they want to believe. I don't care anymore, and neither should you, Mum.'

She launched herself from the edge of the bed to the window and stood, looking out over the little courtyard, the rooftops where the pigeons jostled one another.

She tried to relax her mind. It was worth a try. If she could just, for a few moments, feel her way into Mamma's thoughts, tune in, find out what she was thinking . . . But there seemed to be something in the way. It was as if something was blocking her.

'Ella.'

'Yes, Mum?'

'Don't even think about it. I can feel what you're doing, and I have to warn you. You won't get anywhere. Some things are none of your business. So just be very careful, OK?'

Outside in Grape Lane, there was a scuffle and the sound of voices and then Billy appeared in the courtyard below, gripping Katrina by the arm. She was trying to wriggle her arm free, digging her elbow into his ribs, but he held on tight.

'El,' Billy shouted. 'Let us in. Katrina has something she wants to say to you.'

Ella felt Mamma's hand on her shoulder, gently pushing her aside. She leaned out of the window.

'Billy. Please. It's no use. Go home. You'll only make things worse!'

But Ella was already running down the stairs, unlocking the door. Billy shoved Katrina roughly through the doorway, standing behind her, barring the door.

'Go on, then,' he said. 'Say what you're here to say.'

Katrina scowled. She stuck her chin out and rolled her eyes heavenwards.

'It was only meant to be a bit of a joke,' she said. 'For God's sake. I didn't mean for all this to happen.'

Billy jabbed his finger between her shoulder blades. 'No, that's not it. That's not why we came here. Go on. *Say it.*'

'Chill out, OK?' Katrina hissed. She folded her arms in front of her and glared at Ella.

'I'm sorry,' she said. 'I was angry. I didn't mean for you or your mum to get into trouble. I just wanted to get back at *her* for never being there. You're lucky, Ella, to have a mum like yours. Mine doesn't give a damn about anyone except herself. I just wanted to hurt her. So I took her stupid dresses.'

Ella watched her carefully. She could feel and hear The Signals. They crackled around her, the colour of flame. *She's lying. Don't believe her.*

Katrina sighed and unfolded her arms, as if she could hear them too.

'Look, it's The Truth, Ella,' she said. 'Honestly, it is. I'm sorry. I really am.'

She turned to Billy, her hands on her hips. 'See? I told you this was a stupid idea. That she'd never believe me. She doesn't want to listen.'

Inside her, Ella felt a certainty that she hadn't had before. She was learning to trust what The Signals told her.

'I know that you're lying, Katrina,' she said, slowly. 'You've never liked me. Not really. And, anyway, it doesn't make sense, your story. If you wanted to take your mum's dresses – just to get at her – well, you could have thrown them in the bin, cut them up into little pieces, taken them to the charity shop. You didn't have to bring them here.'

'Yes,' said Billy. 'I don't get it, either. *Why* did you do it? To Ella? To Mrs Moreno? What've they ever done to you?'

Katrina looked away then, out of the window. She seemed to be asking herself the same question.

Suddenly her face crumpled. Her mouth twisted up on itself and she hid her face in her hands.

Ella saw that Katrina wasn't pretending. These were real tears. But Billy sighed impatiently.

'Oh, spare us the waterworks, Katrina. You'll have to do better than that. You'd better tell us *exactly* what's been going on.'

Fabia finished folding the last of her blouses. It was her favourite one, navy blue, which was always an easy colour to wear, and she smiled to herself now to think that even Ella, with her sober tastes, would approve of it. Fabia loved the collar and the wide buttoned cuffs; and she loved the way that someone had edged these, patiently, carefully, with tiny hand-sewn criss-cross stitches in cream. But most of all, Fabia loved the way that the fabric felt in her hands and the memory of it, so soft and supple, against her bare skin.

She'd last worn it on the trip to London with David. They'd sat in the first-class restaurant car and she'd been slightly tipsy already, at nine o' clock in the morning, on two glasses of bucks fizz. She'd watched the fields slip by and she'd felt lighter and lighter, as if she were finally leaving the past behind. She'd imagined that she was in one of her favourite films – as Marilyn or Audrey or perhaps Jane – travelling into another life, a new life in which nothing else would ever matter again except this moment. She smiled at David and, as she did, she caught her reflection in the train window. It was almost as if she could continue travelling forwards, smiling, while this ghost of herself, the sad part, the pale part, fell further and further behind until it disappeared completely, fading away like the trees and the fields in a green haze.

Fabia sighed. She could hear, from the shop below, the sound of Katrina sobbing and she felt her skin prickle all over with irritation.

Why had the girl done this to them? Fabia couldn't understand. She knew that Katrina was unhappy. She had known this for a long time and had even felt sorry for her. But to do such a spiteful thing. It was unforgivable.

And why was she here now in the shop? Billy was a nice boy. He was trying to help. But it couldn't possibly achieve anything. Things had gone too far.

Tart, ridiculous, floozy. Fabia heard those words, over and over, as she lined-up the cuffs with the hem and smoothed the sleeves and laid the blue blouse in her suitcase. She felt the words enter her body, again and again, the little sharp points of them.

Her mind drifted back to Eustacia's parcel of letters.

'That's why I simply can't accept your decision, my darling . . . We have to be together, Eu. We simply have to . . .'

But they hadn't been together in the end, had they? Some things were just not possible. Eustacia Beddowes had made her choice. She'd remained single all her life. Fabia didn't know the whole story, but she could guess. That was the choice you had to make sometimes, if you wanted to stay true to your principles. Falling in love with someone was the easy part. It was what happened afterwards that counted. And if Eustacia could make a hard decision, so could she.

Besides, she hadn't known David long enough. What had it been? Five months at the most. And as she'd always told Ella, you shouldn't give away your sealskin, your selkie skin, to just anyone.

She began to layer scarves over the top of the case – her Hermés, her Chanel, wisps of delicate silk and squares of brightly patterned cotton.

Through the floorboards, the sobbing had become a kind of wailing. Fabia's tongue made the *tsk*-ing noise. It was too much, just too much. She should go down and put an end to it, right now.

She crossed to the top of the stairs and paused for a moment with her hand on the rail, straining to hear.

'She asked me to do it,' Katrina was gasping now, her voice breaking between sobs. 'She *asked me herself* to drop off the parcel. Just a few old things, she said. I've been having a clear-out. Perhaps Mrs Moreno can use them . . . I didn't know. Honestly, Ella, I didn't know anything. I didn't know that you'd seen her with Pike. I knew they were seeing one another behind Dad's back, of course. But there was always someone she had on the go, lots of men . . .'

'But why did you lie when I asked you before? Why didn't you tell me that it was all your mum's fault?' Billy's voice sounded hard, unmoved, disbelieving.

'Because I didn't want people to know what a mess she is. I was ashamed to think she could plan such a horrible thing. I didn't want to admit it, even to myself. And she *is* my mum, after all. She doesn't know what she's doing, half the time. She's drugged up to the eyeballs and drinking when she shouldn't. I thought she might be grateful if I covered up for her, took the blame. I thought she might be nicer to me, more interested. But she isn't. I can see that now. I think she's lost the plot. You know, ever since my brother . . . She's never been the same. I think she needs some kind of help.'

Fabia pressed her hand against the wall to steady herself. She made herself walk down the stairs very slowly.

She saw Katrina put her face in her hands, saw her whole body begin to shake uncontrollably.

'Katrina,' she said and the girl stopped and looked at her from between her fingers and then the sobs and the shaking began all over again.

Fabia crossed the floor. She laid her hands on Katrina's shoulders. For the second time that day, she dropped to her knees.

'Don't now,' she said. 'Please. No more tears, *carina*,' and she smoothed a wisp of hair from Katrina's damp forehead.

26

A pair of ballet shoes. Red silk. Not for sale.

'But I still don't understand,' David was saying. 'The girl's told us everything. So why do you still want to leave? I don't get it.'

Ella clattered the coffee filter against the side of the sink.

'That makes two of us, then,' she said.

Fabia sighed. Her hand hovered over a cardboard box that she'd set on the draining board, ready to pack with kitchen equipment.

'It's really very simple. There are things that neither of you know, or would understand and I'm not going to start explaining them. But it's even clearer to me now that we're not welcome here and we never will be. Jean Cushworth, Pike, they've got it in for us, they don't want us here. And where they lead, hundreds of others will follow. So we have to leave before things get any more complicated.'

'No, you don't,' David said. 'Fabia, please. You don't have to leave. You don't have to go anywhere. Just stop for a minute. Slow down. Listen to me.'

He took her gently by the wrist. He prised a coffee cup wrapped in newspaper from her hand and laid it carefully on the table.

'Please, Fabia. I've told you. I want you and Ella to come and live with me. Please let me take care of you.'

Ella watched as Mamma pulled her hand away. She saw Mamma's eyes flash in that way that always meant danger. She watched her draw herself up straighter, tighten her lips in that thin, hard line. Her words were precise and carefully pronounced.

'David, I think I've been very clear. That's not what I want. Now, please, I must ask you to leave and let me get on with what I have to do.'

David's body went limp. It was as if she'd hit him, right there, wallop, in the middle of his chest, thought Ella.

She followed him down the stairs.

'David,' she whispered and, when he turned, 'please don't give up on her. Please. I don't want us to leave either.'

David shrugged and held up his hands in a small gesture of helplessness. 'I don't know what else I can do, Ella. I just don't know . . .'

As she watched him cross the courtyard, she felt hollowed out, emptier than she ever had before.

She could feel the air thickening around her, the gathering of The Signals in swirls of yellow static, around her neck and the back of her head. She could hardly breathe.

The story of the red shoes

To understand my mother, Fabia Moreno, there are two more stories that I need to tell you. The second of these stories is the story of the red shoes.

As a young girl in Tehran, Mamma was taken to see *The Red Shoes* one Saturday after school. It was the first film she'd ever seen. She remembers sitting in the darkened cinema with Madaar-Bozorg and looking up to see the motes of dust drifting in the beam from the projector and how the woman sitting next to her paused, her handful of pistachio nuts halfway to her mouth, as the curtains swished apart and the film appeared on the screen.

There in the dark, Mamma fell in love with Moira Shearer, the ballerina with the long, red hair. She was already taking ballet lessons at the *Lycée*.

She told me that she would stand in front of her dressing-table mirror, practising *plié* and *port de bras*, while whispering lines from the film out loud:

Why do you want to dance?
Why do you want to live?

She was too young to understand the irony. All she wanted was red shoes with red ribbons.

That long, hot summer, she begged her grandmother. There was a shop in their neighbourhood, on the corner by the café that would dye your shoes for you in any colour.

Madaar-Bozorg would not give in.

'Child, don't you remember how the film ends? Don't you know what happens when you want something too much? It eats you up from the inside. You'll never be free of it. You'll never be able to rest.'

When Mamma turned eighteen, she couldn't wait to leave. She packed her small blue suitcase with the essentials that she imagined she might need for her new life in Paris. She kissed her grandmother and took a taxi to the airport.

'Go. Yes, you must go,' Madaar-Bozorg had agreed. The city was already changing around them and it wouldn't be long before little girls could no longer take ballet lessons, before women couldn't even go out into the street without a headscarf covering their hair.

On the way to the airport, the taxi passed through streets Mamma had never even seen before, neglected shop-fronts, dusty squares where the café windows were half-boarded over.

The taxi driver slammed on the brakes.

A woman had run out into the middle of the street. Mamma could see that her face was bleeding. There were deep gouges down her face, her dress was ripped and her feet were bare.

For a moment, the woman was caught there, framed in the windscreen, her eyes too wide and all that blood on her face, before a man appeared and dragged her backwards by her hair onto the pavement.

Mamma could see now that there was a small knot of people around them and still more gathering. One of them, an old woman wrapped in a black *chador*, spat at the woman and muttered something. Another man picked up a stone from the street and flung it at her. The woman cowered, trying to shield her face with her bare arms. She crouched in the dirty street and Mamma could hear her voice: 'Please, please, Safiq. Listen to me. I haven't done anything!'

'What's happening?' Mamma asked.

'She has brought shame on her family,' said the taxi driver, scratching his chin. 'What's to be done? They will probably kill her.'

Sitting there in the back of the taxi, with the taxi driver's prayer beads swinging from the rearview mirror and the woman's voice in her ears, Mamma remembered the ending from her favourite film, the part where Vicky, the ballerina, has jumped from the balcony and is lying broken on the stretcher, begging her husband to take off her red shoes.

As she sat there in the back of the taxi, Mamma said, she realised that perhaps she might have to choose.

For so many years after, she wouldn't talk about the Old Country, the one that she'd lost.

'It's a different place now,' she used to say. 'The place that I'm from doesn't exist anymore.'

This was why she refused to teach me any Farsi. Because she believed that people in the West associated it with ignorance and lack of education, with young girls swathed in black from head to toe and women stoned to death in their own streets. They think we're all terrorists, she said.

But she did tell me my great-grandmother's stories, the stories from that lost country, the one that came before.

Yes, to understand the woman I learned to call not *Madaar*, in her own language, but *Mamma* in her husband's language and then eventually Mum, you have to understand how much she wanted to leave the past behind.

In the end, it wasn't so much that she wanted something else, something more. It was the thing that she didn't want, the thing that she was afraid of, that ate away at her from the inside. That was the reason she couldn't be still. That was what made it so hard for her to stop moving.

It took me a while to work it out. She was so good at pretending. She'd put on a dress, line her eyes with kohl, outline her smile with red lipstick and no one would ever know.

But despite all this and the beautiful shoes in her suitcase – leopard-print and gold and, of course, glossy red – she wasn't dancing. She was running.

'So where will we go, Mum? What's the plan? What about school, my exams?'

Mamma refused to meet Ella's eye.

'I'm not exactly sure,' she said 'I haven't quite got it all worked out yet. But I will. You know me. By the end of the week, I'll know what's happening.'

Ella picked up a magazine from the clutter on the kitchen table. It was folded back at a page from the classifieds:

Wanted: Live-in housekeeper for private home in beautiful setting in rural Scottish Highlands. Own accommodation provided to very high standard in separate coach house, plus use of car. To provide meals for Italian family of four, supervise cleaning and general maintenance. Fluent Italian a definite advantage.

Ella didn't finish reading.

'Is this what you've got in mind? *THIS?*' She didn't even try to keep the anger out of her voice. 'Rural bloody Scotland?'

'Please don't swear, *tesora*,' said Mamma, automatically.

'But what about the shop, your business, everything you've worked for? What about me? I don't want to live in some big, old house in the middle of nowhere. For God's sake, Mum. I'll end up like Katrina!'

'Don't be ridiculous,' said Mamma, quietly.

But Ella could see that Mamma still hadn't quite made up her mind. There was a little chink of doubt, a little gap in Mamma's usually cast-iron determination.

Ella took a deep breath.

'What about David?' she said.

Mamma waved her hand in irritation, as if she were swatting away a fly.

'*Tsk*, Ella. Let me get on.'

Ella had only been to David's house a couple of times before. The houses in his street all looked the same. Large stone terraces of three stories, small front gardens behind iron railings, front doors painted in elegant shades of green or grey, flanked by carefully manicured bay trees.

But David's house, Ella remembered now, had roses growing around the doorway. Mamma had remarked at how beautiful they were, the flowers big and pink and wind-blown. Ella breathed their fragrance in as she took the knocker in her hand. It sounded too loud in the quiet street. She waited.

No answer. Perhaps he'd been called to the surgery.

A woman came out of the house next door, negotiating the steps with a pram. She smiled at Ella.

'If you're after Dr Carter, you've just missed him. He went out ten minutes ago.' She nodded to the gap where David must usually park his car.

'Thanks,' said Ella. She wondered what to do next. Perhaps she should leave a note. She fished in her bag for a piece of paper.

The neighbour was already halfway up the road. Ella could hear her, cooing to the baby in the pram. She tried not to think about what it would be like to live here, in this nice neat house, on this nice, quiet, friendly street with Mamma and David.

She decided to walk to the surgery. Perhaps she'd find him there.

She turned left through the park at the end of the street and kept going, over the bridge where she'd sat with Billy that night, up the steps, hitting the main road now, with its steady flow of traffic.

Only a couple of weeks, but it already seemed such a long time ago. She thought of Billy and felt that familiar fluttery feeling in her stomach. She hadn't told him that they were leaving, after all. Not yet.

As if on cue, her phone buzzed in her jacket pocket. A text message from Billy: *El? Where are you? XXX*

She swallowed. She wouldn't cry. She wouldn't let herself.

She was so lost in her own thoughts, walking towards the surgery, that she almost didn't see it. Up there, on the left, outside Katrina's house, a flash of yellow between the trees. She got closer.

Yes, it was what she'd thought. An ambulance parked in the driveway, its doors open. She started to run towards it, the gravel getting into her sandals, slowing her down.

Then out of Katrina's front door, ahead of the stretcher, came David, bending to help lever the wheels of the trolley down the steps.

'David!'

He turned.

'Ella,' he said, and a wave of concern crossed his face, 'Is everything all right? Your mum?'

'Oh, yes. Yes. She's . . . well, she's OK, I suppose. I was just looking for you. But what's happened?'

From the stretcher there came a low moaning sound. Ella made out a limp figure under the red blanket, a face with a plastic mask over it, before the ambulance people – a man and a woman – began trundling the stretcher towards the ambulance, the man holding a drip full of some clear fluid high above his head.

David took her arm, manoevering her off to one side. 'It's Katrina's mum,' he said. 'I got the call fifteen minutes ago. I told Graham to call an ambulance, right away. They were very fast. I got here at roughly the same time.'

'But what happened?'

'I don't know yet. I shouldn't even be talking to you about this, you understand? Overdose, we think. Graham found her collapsed on the living room floor. She'd been drinking a lot. She was on some medication.'

Katrina appeared in the doorway now, with Graham behind her, his hand on her shoulder. Katrina looked dazed and white-faced. She looked over at Ella and smiled weakly. Ella waved her hand.

'Will Mrs Cushworth be OK?'

'She should be,' said David. 'Graham heard her fall, so it was all very immediate. She's just about conscious now and her breathing's not too bad. They're pretty efficient with this kind of thing. I hope they'll soon get her stabilised.'

Katrina and her dad disappeared into the ambulance.

'Are you going with them?'

'No. Nothing I can do. I'll phone in a bit and find out how she is.'

They watched the ambulance pull out of the driveway, its lights flashing. David took his car keys out of his pocket.

'So, you say you were looking for me? Want a lift?'

27

Sundress, white cotton with giant sunflower print.

When Fabia saw them getting out of the car, she knew that something had happened. Ella's face looked serious and drawn. David looked nervous, as if he didn't really want to be there.

Her fingers felt clumsy as she undid the locks and threw open the door.

'What is it? What's the matter?'

David cleared his throat. 'I'm just dropping Ella off,' he said, jingling his car keys. 'Don't worry. I'm not going to get in your way.'

'It's Mrs Cushworth,' Ella blurted, her voice breaking. 'She's tried to kill herself, Mum. She's been rushed to hospital. You see? No one's going to pay any attention to her. She's lost the plot completely.'

Fabia felt as if she were watching them from a long way off. She saw the alarm on David's face.

'Well, Ella, we don't exactly know that she tried to kill herself,' he said slowly. 'You really mustn't go round saying that.'

Fabia saw Ella look at him then with those big, clear eyes. Her father's eyes, Fabia thought. She looked again at David. His hand was resting on Ella's shoulder. She saw something pass between them. In the look that they exchanged, there was something so tender, so full of understanding that Fabia felt herself begin to give way.

'Oh, come in, both of you,' she said, and then to David, 'Please? Please will you?'

That was when the tears finally came. They broke over her in a wave so that she couldn't see anything.

The story of Enzo

'You have to understand,' said Mamma, sitting at the kitchen table, 'that I have never told anyone else about this. It's very hard for me, Ella, to tell you this story. I still don't know if I'm doing the right thing.'

David took her hand. We looked at her. We didn't dare say anything. We were making the space for her to find the right words.

'Ella, when your father, Enzo, was a little boy,' Mamma began, 'he dreamed of travelling to far-off countries. He told me that he used to pretend that the hearth rug was a kind of magic carpet. He'd sit cross-legged in the middle of it and command it to take him to Spain, India, China, Turkey. But he was always especially curious about France.

His father had an album of postcards that his parents had exchanged during the war. His grandfather had fought in France, had spent some time posted in Paris, and there were pictures of the Eiffel Tower, and a couple walking along the Seine. He liked that one, especially. The sky had been hand-tinted a rose pink. He once told me that he'd thought the sky in Paris was always that colour.

So as soon as he was old enough, Enzo – your father – left for Paris. His parents didn't want him to go, of course. He was supposed to stay behind and help with the family restaurant. He was already a very good cook, but he said that he wanted to learn about other ways of cooking, about *French* food and *French* wine. He'd get a job in one of the top restaurants and then he'd come back in a few years' time and take over the family business. That was what he told them.

And that, as you know, Ella, is how I met your father. He was working as a sous-chef. I was singing and dancing in the same club. A very nice club, a prestigious club,' she turned to David with a serious expression. 'Not tacky at all. A very nice clientele. Anyway ... We got to know one another, as young people do, and we fell in love. And we got a little bit carried away, a little bit careless. *I* was a little bit careless.'

Mamma blushed and shifted in her chair.

'And so we discovered, quite unexpectedly, but to our joy – and such a very big happiness it was – that we were expecting *you*, Ella-issima.

But what were we going to do? Enzo was a sous-chef. He earned very little money, only a bit more than the man who did the washing-up. He had a tiny, dingy room in the top of the hotel. No women allowed. And I was a dancer, living with the other girls in a *pensione*. The arrangement was part of my con-tract. As soon as I had to stop working, I'd have nowhere to live. So we had to do something quickly.

A friend of your father's told him about a hotel on the south coast of England where he'd worked the summer season. You could earn good money, he said. There was plenty of work, and it was cheap to live there. Your father arranged it all the very next day.

He didn't want to go back to Italy and his family, you see. Not then. Not until he felt he'd made something of himself. Because then his father would not be able to say, "I told you so." We got married that weekend, spent a few weeks sorting out my visa and then we took the ferry across the English Channel, hanging over the rail, laughing and shouting into the waves for the entire crossing. Everything we owned, we carried with us in two small duffel bags.

It was hard at first. It wasn't what we expected. The hotel was old and shabby but it did a good, steady trade in coach loads of pensioners. I could have got a job cleaning rooms but your father wouldn't hear of it. He wouldn't let me lift a finger. So I put all my energy into making a home. We found a flat, quite a nice basement flat, not far from the sea with a tiny courtyard, I fixed it all up and we were happy. We were so excited about you, Ella. We used to lie awake at night and your father would put his mouth to my belly and talk to you. He used to tell you all his favourite stories.

Anyway, let's say that inside the flat I felt safe and happy, nothing could spoil it for us. But outside, in the town, it was a different matter. There was trouble. Not a lot of money to go around. Businesses failing, shops boarded-up. There were a lot of people coming in, on boats and trains. People from Congo. People like me from Iran. People from Syria, Sierra Leone. Some of them had hidden in shipping containers to get to England or clung to the bottoms of lorries. They were desperate. They all wanted a better life, I suppose. The camps in Calais were terrible. We saw one of them as we came through. Holding centres, they call them, fenced round with barbed wire. People living like animals. No wonder they wanted to leave.

And so there were problems in the town. The local people didn't like all these foreigners coming in. They said they were taking their jobs. It didn't matter that Enzo and I were not illegals. We had proper passports and papers. All we wanted was to work hard, keep ourselves to ourselves. What the people in the town saw was that we were not like them. Or rather, that *I* was not like them. Enzo, you see, didn't look much different. He spoke beautiful English, almost perfect. But I had this dark skin and black hair and I spoke with a funny accent – even funnier back then – and I would mix up my English with the French words I'd learned.

"Dirty Arab. Go home," they would shout, hanging out of their cars as I walked down the street with my bags of shopping. Sometimes they would proposition me, ask me for sex as if I was a prostitute and then spit at my feet when I refused, saying I was stuck-up, ideas above myself, that I thought I was too good for them.

I made one friend, a woman from the upstairs flat. She was very kind to me. She told me not to pay any attention. She said they didn't know any better. That the shipyards, the steel industry had closed down and they weren't qualified to work in the new kinds of jobs – call centres, offices, that kind of thing. So they got bored and went down the pub where their heads were being filled with nonsense: National Front, BNP . . .

I felt differently after that. I began to feel a bit sorry. I realised that perhaps I was the lucky one. I had an education. I had at least a chance of something better. But then one day . . .'

Mamma stopped. She looked down at her hand in David's. She spread her other hand on the table and then closed it into a fist.

'You don't have to –' David began.

'Oh, I do, I do,' she said. 'I'm nearly at the end now. And then it is done. *Done.*'

She took a deep breath.

'So, one day, I was walking through the shopping centre. I was on my way to meet Enzo at the end of his shift. We liked to walk down by the sea together before dinner.'

Mamma smiled, remembering something.

'Yes, we loved to do that. It was so nice down there. The air was so fresh that it washed you clean. You could forget everything. And that evening, I remember, I'd made a special effort to look nice. I can remember exactly what I was wearing. I was six months' pregnant by then and I was very proud of how I looked. I put on a sundress, white and covered with big yellow sunflowers. I took a pink rose from the vase on the kitchen table and put it in my hair.

There was a short-cut I could take to the hotel where Enzo worked. You had to pass through a shopping centre. Well, I didn't like to go in that shopping centre. It always gave me a bad feeling. But it was quicker to walk that way. It took much longer to go all the way around. Over and over again, I have asked myself why I didn't just walk round. But it was five o'clock in the evening so most of the shops in there were just closing and the exit was right next door to Enzo's hotel.

They appeared from nowhere. I still couldn't tell you where they came from. I was alone, walking through the shopping centre and then suddenly they were all around me, five or six of them in a circle, just a little way inside the entrance.

"Well, what have we here, then?" one of them said. "Pretty lady . . ."

I saw that he had a long scar right across his cheek. In that moment, I knew I was in real trouble. I had never felt more afraid. They pressed in closer around me. One of them reached out and touched my hair. Another put his face right up to mine. I could smell the alcohol on his breath and he –'

Mamma glanced across at me.

I kept my face very still.

'You see, Ella. This is what I was trying to say before. This man, he . . .' She pressed her lips together. 'This is very hard to say to my own daughter. But Ella, you need to know.'

Mamma's eyes flashed. I heard her breath snag in her throat. Underneath the kitchen table, I dug my nails into my palms. I moved my head, very slightly, in a kind of nod.

'He took my breast in his hand,' Mamma said, 'and squeezed it so hard that tears came to my eyes and I couldn't see clearly anymore. All I could think about was the baby inside me.

"Yeah, you like that, don't you?" he was saying and I shook my head as hard as I could. He put his finger under my chin and tilted my head so that I had to look at him.

"Oi. Did you hear that?" he said to the rest of them. "Our little foreign lady here doesn't like me? Boo hoo. Thinks I'm not good enough for her, eh? Maybe she'll like one of you better."

One of the others came up to me then and tried to kiss me. His lips brushed the edge of my mouth. I pushed him away. He grabbed my arm and twisted it hard behind my back while another put his hands between my legs.

I found my voice then. I started to scream and scream.

And that's when it all went wrong.

A figure came running into the shopping centre and I saw instantly that it was Enzo. He must have heard me screaming. Whether he knew it was me, or just heard a woman who needed help, I'll never know.

He stopped when he saw me.

"Farah!" he said, because that was my name back then. David, you should know, that is my real name: Farah.'

David nodded. He didn't seem very surprised.

Mamma continued. 'When they saw Enzo and heard him say my name, the men took a few steps back from me.

"Is this your girlfriend, mate? *This* one?"

"She's my wife," Enzo said, quietly. All the time, he was looking at me. He never took his eyes off me. He gestured for me to come towards him.

I have wondered many times why they didn't just run away. Perhaps they panicked. Perhaps they had not yet had their fun. Perhaps they were just too full of drink to think about what they were doing. I don't know.

"You should be ashamed of yourself," the one with the scar said. "Fucking a dirty Arab. Planting one in her an' all. There's too many of 'em as it is. They're at it like rabbits."

Still Enzo refused to respond. Even from where I was standing, I could see the muscle working in his cheek with the effort he was making to control himself.

"Yeah," said another. "You're letting the side down, mate," and he laughed, just a very ordinary laugh and then the man with the scar on his face slipped a knife out of his pocket and, quick as a flash, slipped it into Enzo's stomach.

It sounds strange to say it, but it wasn't even violently done. So quickly, so casually, as if he did that kind of thing every day.

Enzo looked at him in disbelief. He watched as the man pulled the knife out. He watched as the blood began to spread across his stomach, flowering red across his shirt.'

Mamma's face was wet with tears. She pulled herself up a bit higher in the chair as if steeling herself to go on.

'Enzo fell to the floor unconscious,' she said, 'and I never spoke to him again. I ripped the straps off my sundress and tried to stop the blood. I kept pressing the cotton against his shirt. Harder, harder. But it was no use. A man walking his dog ran to help us. He called an ambulance. But by the time it came, he had lost so much blood. He died in the operating theatre. The knife had severed a major artery.'

Mamma looked at David.

'So you see?' she said. 'It was my fault. He died because he loved me. This is what happens if you fall in love with me. This is what happens when you love a dirty Arab woman. Nothing good can ever come of it.'

'No,' David said. 'No, Fabia, I won't let you say that.' He took her firmly by the shoulders. 'Look at me, Fabia. Listen. Please. This is just not true.'

I swiped at my tears with the corner of my sleeve. The air above the kitchen table crackled with static and, in the corners of the room, I could hear the Signals stirring. Jagged edges of red and yellow.

'Mamma,' I tried to say but my mouth made no sound.

I couldn't believe that she'd managed to keep this from me for so long. What must it have cost her? I thought back over all of her fears for me – all of the mixed messages, the lipsticked smiles, the secrets and silences, the pleas to be careful, to be quiet, to fit in, to make friends. In that moment, they all made perfect sense. One by one, I saw them flutter and settle on the kitchen floor, like brightly coloured remnants, as if Mamma had taken her scrap bag and shaken it out all over us.

Perhaps we sat like that for a long time. Perhaps it was just seconds, but then I heard a pigeon scrabbling on the roof and, right on cue, the Minster bells began to chime. I let myself follow the sound out through the kitchen window, across the jumble of rooftops, out into that familiar stretch of sky. It's a strange thing to say but I felt lighter somehow and free, as if I could just launch myself out of the window, let the wind lift me, soar higher and higher.

'Ella-issima? *Tesora*?' Her voice was small, uncertain, calling me back. She sat slumped against David. She could barely look me in the eye.

That was when I realised. She thought I was going to stamp my feet, rage at her like a child, demand to know why she'd never told me, tell her that everything was her fault.

I pushed back my chair, stood up.

'Mamma,' I said and this time my voice came out clear and strong.

She smiled then, a small, sad smile and reached her hand across the table. I threw my arms around her, and I held on tight.

Epilogue

A letter arrived this morning, addressed to me in familiar copperplate handwriting. As I unfolded the pink paper at the kitchen table, two photographs fell onto my plate.

One is a picture of Mamma and me. The other is older, faded black and white. A little girl in a white dress, standing in a garden. A statuesque woman in high-waisted trousers and a man's cotton shirt is holding the little girl's hand. She looks squarely into the camera. A smile plays at the corner of her mouth.

I flip it over. On the back someone whose writing I don't recognise has scrawled 'Farah, aged 2' in pencil.

I prop the photos against my coffee cup and smooth out the letter.

> *Ella-issima,*
>
> *I wanted to send you these photos. David says I could scan them in and email them to you, but you know me. I'd rather do it this way.*
>
> *One photo is, of course, of you and me from your last trip. Wasn't it fun, tesora? And don't we look good?!!*
>
> *It was so, so lovely to see you all. I couldn't believe how much Grace had grown. And she just looks so much like you!!! I've been boring everyone here with all the photos we took and David still insists on calling me Granny Fab.*
>
> *The other photo is of me and my beloved grandmother. It arrived in the post from Madaar-Bozorg this morning and I absolutely wanted you to have it. Because I would have been almost the same age in this picture as Grace is now. Can you believe that?*

Madaar-Bozorg is 97 – and, as she says in her last letter, still with all parts working.

Yes, tesora, I wanted you to see for yourself that you and Grace come from a long line of very strong women.

David's job is going really well. He loves it here – and so do I. But he's still working out how to grow his roses in the California sunshine.

I think about you all the time, tesora. I still wish you'd consider moving out here. I miss you so much. But, as you say, England is your home in a way that it really never was mine. As long as you're happy, carina.

One more thing and then I must go and open up. The new shop is so busy these days. People here are mad about vintage. I can't keep up with these ladies.

I saw Katrina yesterday in Luccia's, having breakfast! Well, brunch as they call it here. Can you imagine? It was such a coincidence. I almost couldn't believe it was her.

She's living in LA with her new film star husband. He's terribly glamorous – and so is she. Her next film is a drama about pirates. Katrina plays the pirate queen. She'll be filming in New Zealand, apparently. But she especially asked me to send you her love.

So tesora, call me when you get this.

All our love to Billy, Grace and you.

Baci,
Mamma

I look up from the letter and over at baby Grace, who's already getting impatient with me. She's wriggling her legs and holding out her fat little arms.

'Mamma,' she says. 'Mamma.'

I smile and pick her up and balance her on my hip. She wrinkles her nose and pushes her face into the crook of my neck. She smells of baby and toast and Marseilles soap and something I can't quite place, a fragrance that's distinctively hers.

I pick up the photo of Mamma and me again, holding it safely out of Grace's reach.

We're standing together, leaning on a white fence. Beyond us is the Californian ocean. Mamma is laughing into the camera. She's wearing red lipstick and giant sunglasses. Her black hair is blowing out behind her in the wind.

My face looks better than it usually does in photographs, probably because I too am wearing oversized shades. And for once, I'm smiling. Mamma's arm is draped around my shoulders and I look surprisingly relaxed.

I'm wearing the blue 1950s swimming costume that Mamma found for me, double-layered and meticulously lined, with ruched sides and a halter neck.

'It was made for the hourglass figure,' she said, 'For real women, not today's stick insects.' Even I can see that I look good in it.

I take both photographs and tuck them into the top corner of my dressing-table mirror. With my one free hand, I attempt to tidy my hair.

'Mamma,' Grace says again, her face dimpling. 'Mamma.'

I wonder if she's laughing at me?

I go back to the kitchen, pick up my steaming coffee cup and drain it in one gulp. Now I'm ready. I carry Grace carefully down the stairs to the shop.

Five years ago, when Billy and I announced that we were moving in together, some people were very worried for us. Billy was only just starting his degree. I was working as a waitress, helping Mamma in the shop, scribbling stories in my spare time. Everyone told us we were too young, that later we'd make different choices.

Everyone except Mamma.

'Love is love is love,' she said, kissing us each on both cheeks.

David, whose been like a dad to me these past five years – the only one I've ever really known – nodded too.

'He's OK, Billy,' is all he said.

Later, when David got the big, new job, the one he really couldn't refuse – consultant paediatrician in sunny San Diego – Mamma offered me the lease to the shop.

In our first year, we did so well that I was able to take over the café next door, which has given us a little more space. Poor old Ida had soldiered on for a few years but she was more than ready to sell her lease to me.

'Your mum must be so proud of you, luvvie,' she said. 'When I think of how you started out. You had nothing, you and your mum, did you? And you've turned it into really quite something.'

These days, Happily Ever After isn't just a bookshop, but a thriving community café where people can browse through our stock and enjoy a snack or a glass of wine and, of course, our coffee is the best in town.

Today, I'm planning our next book group and writing workshops, which are proving extremely popular.

Lots of Billy's students like to hang around in the shop. We put on seminars and hold reading groups in politics and history, which are Billy's great passions, of course, and then talks and signings by foreign writers. We're getting quite a following.

It's a year since Mamma and David left. I miss them every day. Mamma found it very hard to leave. Right up until the last moment, I'm not sure David was convinced that she'd go with him. But I told her to give it a try.

'Sink or swim,' I said. 'Remember?'

She's always had a thing about America. She loves it there – the sunshine, the ocean – and we'll visit one another often, especially now that Grace has arrived.

Billy, Grace and I live over the café now. It's a bigger flat, with three large bedrooms, so I can use the old flat – the little living room and kitchen and the bedroom that Mamma and I used to share – as a storeroom and a rather luxurious office.

Tonight, when Billy gets home and we've put Grace to bed, I'll slip over there and dial Mamma's number. We'll chat a little, about this and that. Then I'll settle down to an hour or so of writing.

My first novel was a quiet word-of-mouth success. What we call, in the trade, a slow-burner. But there's a new story that I've been carrying around in my head lately.

I know how it begins, the shape of it, the feel of it, how the words sound in my mouth when I say them out loud, how all the different pieces might fit together.

And now I think I know how it ends.

But this old photograph of Mamma and Madaar-Bozorg has sparked off new connections. My mind won't stay still.

I'm trying to make sense of it, trying to relax my mind to that single, still point, let my breathing go quiet, let the raw edges find their own pattern and the rougher seams smooth themselves.

What would Mamma do?

I can feel her now, all around me, even though she's thousands of miles away. A faint crackle under my fingers, a squiggle of blue, a flicker of yellow.

'*Shhhh.*' The Signals whisper. '*Shhhh . . . Listen . . .*'

I can hear her now on the other side of the ocean, her voice with its slow rich vowels as she stirs the sugar in her cup of coffee, seven times and always anti-clockwise.

'What do you feel, *carina*?' she says, 'What do you feel, deep inside you? What does this fabric already know? What does it want to be?'

Grace sits in the middle of the shop floor and looks at me with her calm, clear eyes. I smile at her and scribble quickly in my notebook:

'An overcoat, a pair of leopard-print shoes, a plume of emerald green feathers . . .'

Our story, it seems – Mamma's and mine – is never finished. I can't wait to get started.

Author's Note

I am grateful to Clarissa Pinkola Estés for her telling of the stories of the soulskin and La Llorona (The Weeping Woman) in *Women Who Run with the Wolves: Contacting the Power of the Wild Woman*, 1992, Rider, which inspired some of Fabia's storytelling; and to Mark Strand for his beautiful poem, 'The Dress' in *Darker: Poems*, 1970, Atheneum.

Acknowledgements

So many people over the years have supported me in my writing but I would particularly like to thank the following:

For their enthusiasm, detailed feedback, unstinting support and all-round brilliance, the wonderful Zoe King, Elizabeth Bonsor, Jessica Maslen, Ellen Marsh and Josephine Hayes at The Blair Partnership.

For his invaluable editorial eye, the fabulous Joel Richardson at Twenty7 Books.

For all their support of my writing – and of me – since the early days: Celia Hunt, Dan Lehain, Sonja Linden, Tracy Macario, Walter Mérida, Lydia Noor, Rebecca O'Rourke, Dean Parkin, Aimee Phillips, Christopher Reid, Lizzie Talbot, Angelika Wienrich, Steve Willcox.

For their generous feedback on the early manuscript, Debora Geary, Helen Harrop, Anne Nicholls and Verity Nicholls.

I would also like to thank all the colleagues and students I've worked with over the years as a teacher of writing at the universities of Sussex, Leeds, York and Teesside and through many courses and workshops. I have learned so much from all of you.

A special thank you to Roger Nicholls for issuing me with a challenge and to Anne Nicholls, Verity Nicholls and Tom Smith for their love, encouragement and, above all, their practical support in helping me to get the writing done.

Finally, I want to thank my own *tesora*, Violetta Belle, born on a full moon night and already a teller of her own stories.

Violetta, although I began this book a year before you were born, I must have known somehow that you were about to enter my story. Thank you for teaching me the true meaning of everyday magic.

Enjoyed *The Dress*?

Read on for reading group questions, an exclusive Q&A with Sophie Nicholls and a special invitation from Fabia herself . . .

Reading Group Questions

- Fabia won't teach Ella the 'old language' from Iran as she thinks it can only bring bad luck. Why do you think this is, and does it tie into her feelings of being an outsider?

- Fabia doesn't like to follow a pattern when she sews. How might this be a metaphor for how she approaches life?

- How important do you think the stories and history behind vintage clothes are? Can these garments ever be more than just items of clothing?

- Fabia tells Ella that they'll be happy in a city as 'in a bigger place, no one is interested in other people's business'. To what extent do you think this is true?

- Fabia is very brave to move to a new city and a new country. From where do you think she draws this courage?

- In what ways do you think her lack of a father figure has affected Ella?

- Do you believe in 'everyday magic'?

Want to join the conversation? Let us know what you thought of the book on Twitter @BonnierZaffre @wordsauce

An Interview with Sophie Nicholls

The Dress is the first book in your series. How did you get the idea for the books?

Like everything I write, _The Dress_ began with a voice in my head. I heard Ella telling what is now the frame story in the Prologue. I didn't know who she was or why she was talking to me. I carried her around in my head for a few days – and she didn't go away. So I decided that I had to give her a chance to tell me more.

And as I began to write, Ella's voice and who she was came together with a setting – the shop – which is a real vintage dress shop called Priestley's in York, in a real courtyard, just off Grape Lane. It's a wonderful shop, somewhere that I'd visited many, many times and it had always struck me as a place where a story could happen.

After that, Fabia entered the story very quickly. I knew exactly what she looked like, what she sounded like from that point on. And then the vaguest idea began to unfold: what if Fabia had some kind of secret, something she wanted to hide? And what if this meant that she was somehow vulnerable to other people's less honourable intentions? What if she put a dress in the shop window and it turned out that, unbeknown to her, the dress had been stolen from someone else? What then? I didn't know how the story would unfold but I just decided to have fun with it and let Fabia and Ella lead me.

The descriptions of the amazing clothes and accessories that Fabia makes and sells are such a joy. How important is fashion (and particularly vintage fashion) to you? Are you more of a Fabia or an Ella?

I think that I'm a little bit of both – or rather, there's a little of me in both Fabia and Ella. I love clothes and I love vintage clothes. I love the idea of a garment having a history – and even perhaps being imbued with some of the life of the person who once wore it. But I think I love clothes much more than I love fashion.

I'm certainly nowhere near as flamboyant as Fabia. One of the wonderful things about being a writer is that you get to try on other personas and play in other people's wardrobes for a while. In real-life, I love classic pieces in black, grey and navy. I can get obsessed about the particular cut of a jacket or the fabric of a blouse or the shape of a shoe. I'm also rather partial to red lipstick and leopard print shoes. But I'm very fussy. I'm on a lifelong search for the perfect white shirt and the perfect little black dress. It's the fabric and the finish and the fit of something that really gives me the greatest pleasure. And in the end, I believe that we should all wear whatever we want to wear – and really not waste any time caring about what anyone else might think.

The mother/daughter relationship between Fabia and Ella is lovely. Did you draw on personal experience for this?

My own mother has been an enormous influence on my life. She is also a brilliant grandmother. I come from a line of very strong women. I was lucky enough to spend a lot of time with my paternal grandmother when I was very small; and my own daughter is named after my maternal grandmother. I really think that being a mum is the most difficult job I've ever done; and I believe very much in the need for women to gather a circle of other women around us to support us – whether these are actual family members or our chosen family. This is why the relationship between Fabia and Madaar-Bozorg is also so central to the trilogy. Being a woman in what is still very much a world made for men can be tough – and we need to support one another. That's what feminism is all about for me.

Everyday magic is an important theme within *The Dress*. Do you believe in magic?

Without a doubt! Like Fabia, I believe that magic is everywhere, when you know how to look. Slowing down and really noticing, really looking at the world around us, is difficult when we're always rushing around from place to place. But this is what a story can do. This is what reading can do. Putting words in a certain order or shape on the page, finding or losing yourself between the pages of a book, just standing and seeing – really seeing – that piece of sky outside your window is a kind of magic. So many things are transformed by the simple act of looking.

I also believe in the power of instinct. The Signals in the book are also, to an extent, a very real kind of 'magic' for me. I think that we probably use a tiny percentage of our minds and bodies in our everyday way of being in the world. Whenever I make a bad decision, whenever something goes wrong, I can usually trace it back to a feeling that I had and talked myself out of with my logical brain.

Finally, I think that the stories we tell ourselves inside ou own minds have enormous power. They can hold us back o open us up to new possibilities. The words we carry with us whether literally stitched into the hem of our dress or simpl going round and round in our heads – are incantations. The are little spells. If the words you're carrying around with you are unhelpful – if you're being unkind or harsh to yourself i some way – perhaps it's time to find new words, new magic?

Billy and Ella have a strong bond from their first meeting Did you enjoy writing their characters?

I loved writing Billy and Ella – and, in fact, I felt a huge sense o loss when I came to the end of book three and had to let then go. Writers spend so much time immersed in the worlds and characters that we've created. It is one of the huge pleasures o writing novels. But it makes it difficult to say goodbye. I like to think that there's a parallel universe somewhere, in which Billy and Ella and Grace – and Fabia and David and all my othe characters – are continuing to live out their stories. Sometime I even catch myself walking around York – I live close by – and wondering what they're doing now . . .

Where does book two in the series see Fabia and Ella?

I don't want to spoil the story for anyone but what I can say is that, in book two, we see Ella very much stepping into her own life. She is now running the shop in the courtyard – in her own way, a very different way from Fabia's, as you'll discover. A first, we see her struggle with that, with being so far away from Fabia – who is living in the States – and with being a mother herself. But I think – I hope – that we see her really grow as a character. We also meet Bryony, who is absolutely one of my favourite characters in the series.

Fabia invites you to find
your own word – a word that
you can carry in your pocket
or perhaps even slip inside
the seam of a sleeve or stitch
into the hem of a dress.

Find out more
and download Ella's map of York

www.sophienicholls.com